MW00627587

The High Fiving Awesomers

A Vendetta Against High Fives and Awesome

By Matthew P. Barkevich

Copyright © Matthew P. Barkevich 2021

To my sister Darlene, I miss you

Praise for *The High Fiving Awesomers*

*"I thoroughly enjoyed your story, while also being quite perplexed, shocked, saddened, and laughing outrageously at it. More on this later, but these are good responses to have as it shows your work generates an emotional reaction. The characters are complex and multi-faceted, as is the plot, and there's good use of narrative, action, dialogue, and inner thought."*

*"It definitely felt like the reader was taken along for the ride with this wonderful, eclectic, and rich collection of characters, scenes, and events that do much to color the backdrop of the story and paint the landscape of R. W.'s life."*

-Joanne from First Editing

*"The High Fiving Awesomers sounds disturbing, but satirically, it succeeds in delivering its message. It doesn't project a crusading image of opposing any system, but what it does is celebrate the strangeness that we all have. I don't know quite how I would deal with a person like McGurski, but I do see a part of myself in him. Matthew Barkevich understands the nature of multiple disorders. When he presents his protagonist, he makes you identify with the antisocial leanings associated with those suffering from mental instability. The use of the first-person narrative further amplifies it. It's not a feel-good story, but one that you should read to help you get out of your shell—and make you reach out in the process."*

-Vincent Dublado for Readers' Favorite

The High Fiving Awesomers

A Vendetta Against High Fives and Awesome

Copyright © Matthew P. Barkevich 2021

All rights reserved. Printed in the United States of America. No part of this book may be used or reproduced in any manner whatsoever without written permission except in the case of brief quotations embodied in critical articles and reviews.

This book is a work of fiction. Names, characters, businesses, organizations, places, events and incidents either are the product of the author's imagination or are used fictitiously. Any resemblance to actual persons, living or dead, events or locales is entirely coincidental.

Published by:

Mental Mind Force

For information contact

www.mentalmindforce.com


Cover design by Kayla Schweisberger

https://www.kazitazartworks.com/


ISBN: 978-1-7378016-0-3 (paperback)

First Edition 2021

10 9 8 7 6 5 4 3 2 1

## Foreword

The purpose of this satirical piece is to expose and poke fun of normal behavior. According to worldbank.org, "One billion people, or 15% of the world's population, experience some form of disability." As these numbers rise, variations in the way their stories are told should be considered. I chose the first person narrative point of view to allow the reader a glimpse into the mind of a person with multiple disorders.

This is not a feel good story of a person with disabilities overcoming challenges and winning the day. The tale of R. W. McGurski is gritty, crude, and humorous because he is self-aware of the general population's obsession with normalcy. Obstacles in his life transform him into an antihero that retaliates against humankind.

If you feel slighted or misrepresented, remember this is fiction, bozo. The intent is to extend your boundaries of socialization and to forge a bulletproof attitude. Try volunteering at places with people with disabilities and you'll feel fulfilled. I know I have. You are not alone.

## Prologue

"The company is legit, but probably a cult. If you look close enough, everything is a contradiction."

Mazetti tilts her head, scrunches her nose, and squints her eyes in response to my rehearsed statement. For months I've endured their pretentious law books, framed diplomas, and the barely audible hum of fluorescent lighting in their stuffy wood-trimmed office. I hand her my report, which undoubtedly will be our last handoff. My escape is near. To live outside of society is my immediate goal.

"The title of your report is, *The High Fiving Awesomers*?" She continues reading. "The gates of life closed on them with no recourse but foolishness. Narrating this mess is my service to you. You'll see, it's in my report." She skims and reads from another section. "I will throw you through three sheets of drywall."

I defend my prose. "That's my new catch phrase."

She reads another excerpt. "The half-pint sales manager wears five finger running shoes, tan slacks, and a blue shirt aggressively tucked in. His haphazard, overuse of the word "awesome" tests the limits of my sanity. He could awesome a speck!" Her lips squeeze together, eyes widen, and jaw tightens. She hurls the three pages like a Frisbee at me. It's obvious she is not fond of my discovery. The volume of her voice increases as she demands answers. "What is this, a personal narrative? Is this a joke?"

My eyes dart back and forth from the bulging veins on her temple to the throbbing vein on the side of her throat. She steps in closer to my face. This is troublesome; at this proximity, I can no longer track her engorged veins. Wow, can she radiate heat.

"Do you know how much time and money you wasted on this investigation? You got squat thrusts. I can't bill the client for this."

I correct her and say, "You mean I got squat. As in little or nothing. Squat thrusts are an exercise. Great cardio."

She barks at me in an impolite manner to leave permanently. Before my departure, I whip out a notepad and scribble, "Do not correct your boss if she says 'Squat thrusts instead of squat.'" I flip a page and write, "Do not add the Law Offices of Schooster and Mazetti as references." This is my takeaway.

***

Three years later …

In the aftermath of my dismissal as an investigator for the Santa Barbara Law Office of Schooster and Mazetti and a few trips to Chumash Casino, I had no money for rent. Out of necessity, my tan van became my headquarters. I ripped out the bench seating and installed my sole piece of furniture, a full-size bed.

Without a job, I became a library guy. Me and an assortment of people suffering from mental illness and veterans without homes comprise the bulk of library patrons. Our conversations revolve around various schemes, tragedy, and boasts of past accomplishments. However, a particular discussion I overheard stood out. An old-timer with skid marks on his pants imparted the solid advice, "Never trust anyone wearing two watches. They are time travelers. One watch for the future and one for the past." I suppose the present is too fleeting to warrant a time piece. A librarian escorted the old-timer outside due to hygiene issues before part two of his rant could be entertained.

I rarely talk to anyone. Greeting the library staff by name and saying "good afternoon" is enough to keep my hinges tight. As a result, the librarians/de facto social workers never considered me unhinged. I applaud their patience and differentiated approach to explaining we can't bathe in their public restrooms.

My preference would be to sign the books out and read in the wilderness, but since I do not have an address, I'm forced to read within the confines of the library. I read books on mysticism for three to six hours a day and devoured a series from the Yogi Publication Society. Their titles ranged from *Mind-Power the Secrets of Mental Magic* to *Thought Vibration and The Art and Science of Personal Magnetism.* These books are my therapy.

I'm not a full-time library guy. In the morning, I'm a freelance recycler, and I scratch enough money together each day to purchase sardines, bananas, and gas for the van. Part of my day I swim laps in the Pacific Ocean, bust out pushups and pull-ups on tree limbs, and loiter outside martial arts studios. I peer through their oversized windows and duplicate their motions until someone wearing pajamas inevitably persuades me to leave. At night, I drive to the suburbs and park on the street. Between 11 p.m. and 6 a.m. I sleep inside the van without the threat of tow trucks, harassment by homeowners, or the police. By 6 a.m. I clear out and head towards the ocean. The community parks open at 6 a.m. and allows you to park for free at three hours a clip.

In one of the most affluent places in the world, I survive on less than $20 a day. For a brief period, I cracked the code to freedom, but expensive van repairs and building relationships exposed this lifestyle. How do I explain to potential dates I live in a van? My current existence offers unlimited freedom, but ironically, the paradox is my lifestyle does not provide the money to explore and appreciate free time. At thirty-six-years-old, my situation forced me to revise my goals to include steady employment, a house with a warm shower, and courtship. It is crucial for me to achieve these goals without becoming dull or sacrificing style.

Occasionally at the library, social workers come in and ask the "regulars" questions and in return, they give us a hot meal. This afternoon, a gentleman holding a clipboard, but without a name tag, asked me random questions. The typical questions were "how long have you been homeless?" or "when was your last medical check-up?" He inquired if I spoke foreign languages. "Does Esperanto count?" I asked. His eyes widened as he hastily wrote, "Fluent in Esperanto!" After his second question, I was unsure if he was a social worker, or CIA. He asked, "Is it possible to punch through a brick wall?" My reply, "Certainly."

This marked the beginning. This is my saga. In the movie version, the credits will read, *Meta-Fistical, Beyond the Fist* featuring R. W. McGurski. Something big is going to happen.

## Chapter 1 Alexandra, The Overlord

Sometime in 2017 …

At 5:33 a.m., I'm awake but not because I want to be. The distinctive metallic brake noise from the garbage truck vexes me. "Oh, cripes!" I must spring out of bed to the driver's seat and scram before the trash guys pass with their surplus of foul smells. The unusual frost on my windshield and impending odor are not the only things troubling me this morning. There is an ominous envelope looming underneath the windshield wiper. If I'm fast enough, I can open the door and grab the envelope in three seconds before the freezing air invades the confines of my seventy-square-foot mobile headquarters. Probabilities lean towards either a parking ticket or a community violation ordinance. The first outcome will require extra recycling to pay for the ticket, while the second entails searching for a new parking spot. An expected chill accompanies the fetched letter, but is nothing a burst of pushups can't fix. The pushups can wait; reading the letter is the priority. Sliding the letter out of the envelope, my hands automatically calibrate the density of the parchment. This is no parking citation. Rubbing the paper in-between my index finger and thumb, I determine it to be high-grade resume paper. In the past, I sorted millions of letters in the post office, but this one is special. The fine penmanship, old world charm, and inscriptions delicately written in Esperanto are spellbinding. It's a recruitment letter from a group called The Foundation. If I accept, my role will be to inscribe and deliver letters.

Writing and delivering letters is a clear upgrade from recycling. The toll of merry-go-round lousy jobs and unemployment has me entertaining the idea of reenlisting. A common thread amongst the veterans at the library is the desire to be involved in prestigious endeavors at a level of responsibility comparative to active duty. I was not exempt from these ambitions either.

The lure of The Foundation is financial independence and the unknown. Mentally, I agree to their terms. It's a fresh beginning for my brand of turmoil. If a mysterious outfit will pay me handsomely to write notes in Esperanto, I'm ready. I reread the letter three times and reminisce about speaking Esperanto with my father.

The flipped over trash cans the length of the street is the first clue the garbage truck has hauled away the trash and the second is the stench of rotten banana peels. The potentially life-changing contents of the letter had me mesmerized, unaware of the sound and smell of the truck until it passed. In the letter, The Foundation asked to meet at a seafood restaurant on East Cabrillo Blvd for outside dining at noon. My contact is a female who uses the preposterous code name "Overlord." The campy code name makes me wonder if this a prank by the University of California Santa Barbara (UCSB) students. I doubt it as the expensive resume paper, and fine penmanship are too elaborate for a college prank. Regardless, it's an adventure and with ample time to prep, I'll boogie over to Leadbetter Beach for a prime parking space near the outdoor showers.

My morning rituals begin by clearing a narrow passage between the two front seats—enough space to generate heat. Eighty-seven pushups is the exact number required to defeat the chill. With my body radiating heat, I start the van. The van requires more time than me to warm up.

***

"What the …?" an F 150 truck pulls out in front of me. My lumbering van is slow to move and slower to brake. I lay on the brakes and horn, barely missing him. He flips me the bird. I don't return his one-finger salute, I don't tailgate, or high beam him. At the next light, I pull alongside him. He has a lot to say to me. None of it is nice. I smile, enraging him further. My indifference has pushed him too far. I think he needs validation. Getting out of his truck and waving his arms in a menacing fashion is a social cue I comprehend and I'm ready for. It's unusual for me to have things to do and places to be and now this rascal is in my way. I'm going to starch him. My motto is, "I don't get into battles, I end threats." I'm a hypocrite though because I fight battles quite often. We meet in front of our vehicles and I can tell he doesn't want to throw down because he whipped out a can of pepper spray. This jerk-store is pepper spraying me. I'm able to turn my head and shield my eyes with my arms to avoid the full brunt, but the mist from 3,000,000 Scoville heat units activates my tear ducts at maximum capacity. My eyes seal shut. My nose spasms with snot, and I can't stop coughing. With no food in my stomach, I bend over and dry heave. I try to blink and flush the searing heat from my eyes. It feels like my eyelids ingested a dozen jalapenos.

Did he punch me too? There it is again, another shot to my nose. The burning and excruciating pain from the mace overshadow his puny physical assault. I can't wait for his next punch, as I've got a surprise for him. "Are you punching or tickling me?" I shout. That should stir him up. Predictably, he punches again, so I turn my head to roll with the punch and grab his arm before he can retract. With his arm trapped, his limb guides me to the collar of his shirt. Instinctively, I pull his shirt over his head, trapping his arms with his own garment, hockey style. I hold him in check with my left hand

and connect with a flurry of right hooks to his beefy flanks. Tenderizing him like a ribeye steak, I season and pepper him with my five-sided fist-agons. "Ahhhh," is the accompanying sound with each connection. There is little resistance. The sensation of hitting ribs and then bone collapsing into broken mush signals the threat is over. My kind of pepper doesn't come from a can, it comes from my hands, man. My adrenaline rush and rapid blinking allows me to endure the stinging pain and barely open one eye. Mr. Pepper spray has regressed to the fetal position on the road. The shred of morals I have are enough to prevent me from leaving him in the street. He moans as I drag him by one arm to the sidewalk. Before fleeing the crime scene, I remind him, "You started it."

***

I've got to make tracks because being convicted of felony battery is not on my to do list. Fortunately, at 5:37 a.m. nobody is on the road. That's great because my eyes are on fire. The rims and passenger side of my van make different sounds as I bang into objects. Each swerve into a sidewalk emits a low decibel grinding noise and cool sparks. Going over a bridge is an extra charge of adrenaline. The high-pitched sound of metal on metal results from the passenger side bouncing off a guardrail. When driving nearly blind, sidewalks and guard rails provide wonderful feedback. While it is a thrill, my poor tan van is getting chewed up.

I pronounce myself the champion of the one man crash up derby as I arrive at my destination. Beware citizens of the Convenient Mark parking lot, the champ is here. I prop one eye open with my fingers and stumble towards the door of the shop. Before entering, I plug one nostril and blow a snot rocket of blood and mucus onto the blacktop. It congeals into the shape of the letter S. With blurred vision, I admire my newly christened street art and internally title the exhibit "Organic Freestyle." I wipe the remaining gooey danglers from my nose off on my arm. "Oh, Nelly! Ahhhh!" Return of the burn part two. There must have been residual pepper spray on my sleeve. Spinning in circles and jumping on one leg does nothing to ease the fire in my nasal passages. The dragon's breath has struck me twice. A surfer props his board against the wall, gives me a nod, and goes inside. His approval rating of my status is noted.

I gather myself, summoning enough chi energy force to enter the Convenient Mark and buy milk to neutralize the pepper. Are you kidding me? Are my watery eyes deceiving me or does milk cost $7 a gallon? How is milk twice the price of gas? Funds are tight, but my eyes are screaming for salvation.

Passing the rack of cheap sunglasses offers me a compulsory mirror to witness my metamorphosis. "Hey good looking," I say out loud to myself. The waterfall of tears from my blood-shot eyes and swollen nose will be an interesting conversation piece at my interview later today. Each breath creates a blood and mucus snot bubble. I've learned that to breathe through my mouth lessens the burn in my nose. The pain in my eyes hurts more than handing over a substantial portion of my rainy day funds to buy overpriced skim milk I won't get to drink. The worst pain has yet to come. Worse than pepper spray, and worse than blowing my last remaining bucks on milk is the misguided misery of hearing the clerk ask, "What happened to you?" Those inane, pointless words are what I fear and dread. I close my eyes; if I don't see him, maybe he won't see me. I hand him one hours' worth of recycling money.

Relief comes in many forms, and the exchange of currency for dairy does not include dialogue. During the whole transaction, I guess the clerk never looked at me until he hands me the change. I open my one eye, and for whatever reason, this young fellow makes eye contact. "If the milk is for pepper spray, whole milk works better," he says in a monotone voice.

Sage wisdom from the Convenient Mark clerk. The early shift undoubtedly has their share of delinquents. I sprint to switch out the skim for whole and within three steps out the door, tilt my head back, and pour milk into my eyes. The milk goes up my nose; I accidentally waterboarded myself with milk. This is not a dairy high, and milk is clearly not meant to be snorted. Back to coughing again. Regaining a little composure, I plug my nose and pour the rest of the milk in my eye sockets. It soothes the sting down to the orbital bones. Drats, my artwork on the blacktop has been white-washed with milk. A self portrait of myself in this state would be titled, "Plop of meat sulking in pool of milk while sitting on a curb." I tune out the world with my eyes closed until a squeaky woman's voice asks, "Sir, are you okay?"

I mutter, "Buzz off."

"What?"

"I said buzz off; can't you see I'm irritable?"

Even an optimist can mope.

The interaction is my cue to amscray.

***

I can see again and cringe at the side of my dented tan van. I'm humored by the thought of a *Fast Times at Ridgemont High* quote from the character Jeff Spicolli, "My old man, he's a television repairman, he's got this ultimate set of tools, I can fix it." It's a good laugh, but induces more coughing. Freaking pepper spray. Onward to Shoreline Park. It's 5:59 a.m. and the gates remain closed to the parking lot. Outside the gate, I'm glamorously loitering in an idling van with the heat pumping. An attendant arrives in a golf cart, driving with his left hand on the wheel and his right hand snug in his coat pocket. He tries to unlock the gate and fumbles with the key. The brisk sea breeze compromises his dexterity. I'm in no rush; in an hour the sun will rise and melt the frost off the grass.

A few hours later, I clear out my lungs with sprints up the steep mesa and multiple sets of twenty-five pushups to elevate my core body temperature. With a light sweat, and regular intervals of coughing pepper spray induced phlegm achieved, I test my willpower in the fifty-degree Fahrenheit outdoor shower. The water temperature challenges my constitution. After enduring a minute of ice water, an exhilarating adrenaline rush mitigates the chill. The benefit of showering with my clothes on is I can concurrently clean myself and my clothes. Through trial and error, I've learned the most effective way trick to dry clothes:

Step 1 Wring them out.

Step 2 Roll clothes inside a towel.

Step 3 Apply pressure to blot the dampness.

Step 4 Patiently hold below a bathroom hand dryer.

Step 5 Run to the van and crank the heater.

My ensemble for the interview is pieced together via thrift stores. Jeans, a solid black merino wool t-shirt, and a dark brown velvet blazer round out my professional attire. It is presentable, but not as formal as the traditional interview black jacket, white-collared shirt, and slacks. The mirrors in the bathroom at Shoreline Park are clean of graffiti and provide an opportunity for me to check my appearance. It is an improvement from three hours ago. My nose is swollen and my eyes are bloodshot, but we're meeting outside on a sunny day, which is a righteous excuse to wear dollar store sunglasses to conceal the consequences from my early morning escapades. I kind of look like a henchman from a 1970s exploitation film with my outfit, collar-length hair, and goatee. I'm hip to the jive.

In the mirror, I rehearse my greeting mantra: eye contact, shake hands, smile, and introduce myself. What comes natural to most is an effort for me. It's worth it. This interview will change everything.

I play the game and reposition the van into a different parking spot. Hopefully, code enforcement aren't sticklers and grant me three more hours of free parking. The restaurant is across from Stearns Wharf, and I can't afford the meter parking there. From Shoreline Park, it's a mile and half stroll past the Santa Barbara Yacht Club, fish market, and Santa Barbara City College athletic field. One of my traditions is guessing how many athletes will be running the bleachers. Occasionally, I back my guess up with a friendly wager. For gamblers, it's easy to find action.

***

I've passed this restaurant hundreds of times without noticing the aged brick, the brass door fixtures in the shape of a butterfly, or the triangle of wood beams over the entrance. The faint smell of fish from outside intensifies as I climb the stairs.

11:50 a.m. I peruse the elevated patio in search of an Overlord. I don't know who or what I'm looking for. Pacing draws the attention of a waitress.

"Are you meeting someone?" she asks.

How do I answer? I can't say I'm supposed to meet an Overlord. She'll just say, "What's an Overlord?" I'll respond with a stupid remark, "Oh, a ruler or person of great power." And she will innocently say, "Do you need to speak to my manager?"

Back to reality.

"Yes, I'm waiting for someone, but I've never met her—"

Before I complete the sentence, she interrupts, "Are you here on a blind date?"

She believes she's cracked the puzzle. Considering my reluctance to finish my sentence, it's a good guess. I play along. "Yes."

The charade ends with a lady in her late seventies abbreviating my torment with a greeting. "You must be R. W."

Thank God she's a hugger, and I don't have to subject her to my sweaty hands. She chases her hug with two alternating pecks on my cheeks. How Euro of her. I hope there's no residual pepper spray on my cheeks. Meanwhile, the waitress hovers nearby as if eavesdropping.

"Yes, I'm R. W., which makes you the Overlord." I resist the temptation to mock the ludicrous title.

She smiles. "Please call me Alexandra."

I open both of my palms at waist level, shrug my shoulders, and mouth the word "what" to the waitress. The waitress raises her eyebrows and slinks away without a word.

Alexandra's face is familiar. I've seen her at various festivals throughout the years. She hires a personal photography team to ensure evidence of her presence appears in the local magazines. She's a fancy lady with dresses galore and delusions of grandeur to match a hefty scoop of vanity. Who else would pose the exact same way in every photo? I've memorized the pose. She leads with her left shoulder forward, head turned to the left, and both hands gallantly on her hips. Her sporty bob cut hairdo detracts from her formality and suggests she's the fun aunt.

Her frail arms quiver as if it's taxing to move the black wrought-iron chair. The dragging sound of metal on brick pavers is unnerving. Fortunately, there are fluffy cushions to soften the cold hard iron. I'd like to lend a hand, but my gut says to ease back on the chivalry.

I lay on the charm instead. "Nice to meet you. I detect a slight Portuguese accent, so I'm guessing you're from Porto."

"Impressive; I'm from Vila Nova de Gaia, on the south side of the Douro River, but technically it is a district of Porto.

My file said you have experience as an investigator, but there's no way you could have known where I was from before our meeting."

"It was an educated guess. You look really familiar to me; aren't you the Santa Barbara homecoming queen? Your picture is always in the local magazines and I've seen you at all the festivals."

"Homecoming queen? That's hilarious. I'll have to tell my friends that. But seriously, I don't go to all the festivals."

I get a bit cheeky and show off. "Which ones do you skip? The Jazz Festival, French Festival, Greek Festival, Italian Festival, Old Spanish Days Fiesta, Tequila Harvest Festival, Harbor and Seafood Festival, Dog Parade, Women's Festival, Starry Nites Festival, Earth Day Festival, Lucidity Festival, Santa Barbara Fair and Expo, Matador Music Festival, Gem Fair, I Madonnari Street Painting Festival, Fork and Cork Classic, Ocean Festival, Summer Solstice parade, Home and Garden Expo, Skaters Point Music Festival, Ocean Awareness Festival, Live Oak Music Festival, National Woodies Club Woodies at the Beach Festival," (I pause for a deep inhalation and continue), California Wine Festival, Anchors and Ales: A Beer Tasting Experience, Sea Glass and Ocean Arts Festival, Celebration of Harvest Festival, Antiques Show, Lemon Festival, and Avocado Festival round out the list. There are thirty-one annual festivals each year in Santa Barbara You attend all of them, don't you?"

Her face turns red. Is she menopausal? Embarrassed? I'm oblivious to reading emotions.

She raises her right hand and says, "Guilty as charged. My word, you have an incredible memory."

We pause our dialogue as the waitress delivers a Bloody Mary to Alexandra and a Stella Artois to me.

"I took the liberty of ordering drinks, but please order anything you like. The Foundation has it covered." She waves the symbol of affluence, a black credit card, to punctuate her point.

What a treat! I haven't been to a restaurant in years. I hope my manners pass muster. Sifting through the menu, the reassuring smell of fresh seafood far more aromatic than sardines influences my order of macadamia nut crusted sea bass with mashed potatoes and asparagus. She orders a dainty shrimp cocktail and sits with her back to the spectacular view of sixty-foot palm trees, the iconic Dolphin Fountain, Stearns Wharf, East Beach, and the Pacific Ocean. My focus is on her, but when she nibbles on her shrimp, I sneak a peek at the surrounding glorious landscape and landmarks. An elevated point of view (POV) can change your perception of a familiar place. Did she offer me the seat with the grand views out of consideration, or is this an intentional test of my Attention Deficit Disorder (ADD)?

"Seriously, how did you guess I'm from Porto?" she inquires.

"In the Air Force, a few times a year, I delivered documents to the base in Azores and the U.S. Embassy in Lisbon. After completing those assignments, I'd refresh with a week of leave in Porto."

"The secret is out on Porto; in the past fifteen years it's exploded and become a European hotspot."

"A city on the beach with old world charm is tough to beat."

"Kind of like Santa Barbara."

I raise my bottle to her glass and say, "*Saúde* (Portuguese for cheers) to Portugal and your generosity."

"*Saúde.*" To take a drink, she has to maneuver around the Bloody Mary obstacle course. Standing in the way of her libation is a tooth pick of olives, celery stalk, and a giant slice of bacon. With deftness she negotiates past them all for a sip. "You are probably wondering why you're here."

I nod.

"I represent a collective organization of exceptional individuals with access to generational knowledge. Your role is sharing and safeguarding this wisdom. We'll pay you to translate English to Esperanto and inscribe it into letter format. We'll pay you more if you deliver these letters to members and potential new recruits."

"I can do that." I am grateful, but unemotional. This meeting has exceeded my expectations and is a huge opportunity, but showing emotions is not in my nature.

"Our scouts believe you are the ideal candidate for this position. Your military background and fluency in Esperanto sealed the deal."

She explains the six categories of letters I'll be inscribing are derived from a book called *The Stockpile*. The highlights of *The Stockpile* include Edward Leedskalnin's formula to build the coral castle in Miami, Florida, and the Tibetan Arjopas' ability to run for hours at great speeds. Other parts of the book include fighting techniques, special healing modalities, and deep breathing skills. I'm riveted by these mysteries and press for more on the Tibetan Arjopas. The particulars are shared in hushed tones as if she is briefing me for a top secret case. She said the Tibetan Arjopas meditate themselves into a breathing trance which allows them to nearly float across the land, and if I joined The Foundation, I'd learn the secret to float running too.

She expresses how people with these supernatural abilities share a similar connection. For example, Edward Leedskalnin toiled at night, leery of curious humans. Through use of magnetic frequencies at demarcated angles, he manipulated the weight of objects and allegedly levitated tons of coral rock in the air. The Tibetan Arjopas, as well as The Foundation, are secretive by nature and share a distrust of the general population.

I'm entranced by these fantastic stories reminiscent of my favorite TV show *In Search Of* narrated by Leonard Nimoy, but I am also skeptical. How can the mysteries of the world somehow be entrusted in a how to manual belonging to members of The Foundation? She must have sensed my disbelief.

She counters with a logical scenario. "If a natural catastrophe wiped out the energy grid and obliterated much of society, how many of the surviving members could build a TV, microwave, or computer? These things exist and seem almost magical, but few people could develop significant technology from scratch. The Foundation safeguards this lost generational wisdom and doles out trickles of it to people with potential."

Their rationale is too much data can lead to disinformation. They believe few can balance the demands, responsibility, and insight of generational wisdom. She cautions, with an example from a member of The Foundation who fell into self-imposed seclusion and madness, from trying to read too much knowledge.

Gorging on information shows a lack of discipline and although I welcome chaos, discipline is a nonnegotiable asset. My stance conflicts with their ideology. If I was in charge, I'd choose to release the wisdom to the masses to eradicate staleness in humans. For now, my inclinations remain private. Don't mess this up, I tell myself. Keep your mouth shut and listen. This might be my last chance at a real job.

I distract my urges and stab at the sea bass drizzled in butter. It flakes apart, tender to the touch to the point where I have to reposition my miniature trident to scoop it up. My mouth receives the aquatic offering and I unintentionally close my eyes to enhance the flavor. I barely need to chew. Compliments to the fisherman, bass, and chef.

"You might think we are hoarding this wisdom, but we're not. We've been waiting for the right time to recruit more people to The Foundation."

Did she read my mind or did I accidentally project my ambitions to her?

She adds, "Before initiating additional recruits, people need to show their worthiness."

Her disdain for the public surpasses mine. She has proclaimed if the hordes had this kind of power, it would become common, and only rare things can be priceless. Internally, again I disagreed, because I know there are two gifts everyone receives in this world that are priceless. In fact, these two miraculous gifts are bestowed on every creature, from humans to a single cell amoeba. Time and energy are our two gifts. An aging billionaire cannot buy the energy of a youth or their potential longevity. It is how we direct our time and energy that renders them into priceless memories. I resist my urge to argue by staying quiet as I prepare to hop aboard The Foundation gravy train.

She's in tune with the fluctuations of my attention span and concludes with a summary of her three passions: The Foundation, her psychiatry practice, and attending the slew of festivals in Santa Barbara County.

She stands, embraces me with a warm hug and says, "I believe you'll make an excellent addition to The Foundation. However, there is one more person you'll need to speak with to gain acceptance. He should be arriving soon."

## Chapter 2 Claude, The Minister

Alexandra mentioned there would be one more person to interview me. I try not to squirm around in my seat too much as we wait. My attention is diverted to a table near us littered with balloons. An old couple is celebrating their thirtieth wedding anniversary with their adult children and are getting louder. They are making a mockery of fine dining. I believe it is in my best interest to reframe from shouting at them to shut up. Finally, he arrives.

"I'd like to introduce you to The Minister," says Alexandra, introducing me to another member of The Foundation.

I stand to greet him and look up at this athletically lean baby boomer. He'd make a great casino pit boss. Dressed in a blue three-piece suit with a red tie, he resembles what the singer Seal will look like when he's seventy. I try not to stare at his misaligned jaw, but after each glance away, I'm drawn back to eyeball his mashed up mandible. He's like a vintage Ferrari with a crunched front fender. I appreciate the caliber of the car, but it's almost impossible not to fixate on the one flaw. I rededicate myself to make eye contact.

With my first interview cleared, I can't afford to coast through the second. My dreams of cashing paychecks again rest in the hands of this man. The unreasonable alternative is recycling.

"Don't call me The Minister. Please call me Claude."

"I'm R. W. McGurski."

His grip is strong, and the suit is not fooling me. He's not a pencil pusher. Although his hands are smooth, it's obvious the strength in his hands is a crucial part of his trade. There is no comment about my sweaty hands and he doesn't wipe the sweat off on his pants. If I concentrate, I can manage most of my nuances in spurts, but the sweat is uncontrollable.

Alexandra slips away and stiffs me with the bill. Is this a con job? A hoax to capture my imagination with a fantasy world and leave me to pay the bill? $111.33? Are you kidding me? On a side note, those are attractive numbers. Some might say I have a weird appreciation for numbers divisible by three. I stare at the edge of the table where the bill rests, and intermittingly gaze at her three deserted shrimp curled over the edge of what looks like an ice cream sundae glass container, then back to the bill. If the restaurant doesn't accept an I.O.U., I'll be washing dishes. Fortunately, she comes back and says, "Oh, I almost forgot about the check."

I resist the temptation to ask her if I can finish her remaining shrimp. It's a once in a life-time job offer and I'm fixated on Claude's broken jaw, the check, and three uneaten crustaceans. I cut myself some slack, considering this is my first normal conversation in weeks. Recent conversations with my library brethren have included a fascinating deliberation on what makes a better pillow, magazines or newspapers? The unanimous verdict was newspapers are softer, but leave ink stains on your face. My thought process is now divided between Claude, makeshift newspaper pillows, and pondering if psychiatrists are ever completely off duty. Did Alexandra deliberately leave the check to gauge my response? I imagine she'll mark in her planner: McGurski has trust issues. I'm in my head again, Claude's staring at me, perhaps studying me, trying to decipher where is my attention. I vacillate between charm and being an imbecile. Is it balance or an imbalance? Before speaking again, he patiently waits for me to come back to earth.

"Alexandra weaves an almost unbelievable story. I assure you it's real."

I nod.

The waitress returns and sees my second interviewer. "Another Stella?" she asks, then bends towards me to whisper, "Another blind date?"

"Sure," I say.

"And for you, sir?" She turns to Claude.

"A Perrier and a straw please."

She nudges me before walking off, quietly laughing.

Claude's French accent is thick, but misleading as he's Haitian. I don't comment on his accent because I have never been to Haiti and know very little about it. Eventually, when the topic of Haiti organically manifests, then I'll learn more about the island country.

"Allow me to fill in the gaps about The Foundation."

His first outlandish proclamation is The Foundation's origins date back to 2500 BC from the teachings of Hermes Trismegistus (Trismegistus meaning thrice great). The same Hermes is responsible for one of my favorite quotes, "As above, so below, as within, so without, as the universe, so the soul ..." Although The Foundation declare their exaggerated origins can be traced back to Hermes, he states they are not part of the Hermetic Order. My response to this is a subdued disbelief.

Besides Hermes, The Foundation adds to their collection of wisdom from obscure literature and people of exceptional nature. They gather what they deem as valuable and discard the rest.

Claude hinted the chapters in *The Stockpile* on combat inspired Bruce Lee to develop Jeet Kune Do (JKD), which means, way of the intercepting fist. I could talk all day about martial arts, and I think Claude is a kindred spirit.

"Martial art styles typically contain a few key moves forming a greater sequence of moves. The rest is clutter. Our chapters on combat are similar to the philosophy of JKD. Do you think this is by coincidence?"

He claims the chapters on combat represent the efficient aspects of pressure points, striking from boxing, the elbows and knees from Muay Thai, judo throws, Greco Roman takedowns, submissions of Jiu-Jitsu, the berserker mentality of the Vikings, the toughness of a Spartan, and the superior training methods of Delta Force. Somehow, Claude knows I'm a martial arts enthusiast, which makes me suspicious he's exploiting my interests.

He continues, "These combined core moves from each martial art are presently called Mixed Martial Arts."

"Did you know Jeff Blatnick coined the term Mixed Martial Arts?" I assert.

"No, never heard of him."

"Jeff won the super heavyweight wrestling gold medal for the U.S. in the 84 Olympics and was the first analyst for the Ultimate Fighting Championship (UFC)."

"Oh."

"That's the problem. Everyone is familiar with Bruce Lee, but only a few know Jeff Blatnick. After beating Hodgkin's Lymphoma, two years later he won an Olympic gold medal in Greco-Roman wrestling. A person dedicated to a craft combined with irresistible willpower is an unstoppable combination."

"Okay, but Bruce was an icon. His movies got millions of people involved in martial arts," Claude declares.

"True, but wrestling is the first martial art form, and Jeff competed at the highest level. Not once did Blatnick get a cover spread on a martial arts magazine. Instead, they trot out Bruce Lee's picture at least twice a year to promote their agenda."

"You sound like his personal agent."

"If Bruce and Jeff were alive. I'd book that match."

"Are you saying Jeff Blatnick would beat Bruce Lee in a fight?"

"When they were both alive, in their prime, I'd bet my van on Jeff Blatnick."

Claude's eyes loom wider and his pitch changes. "There's no way. Bruce was the man."

"In his prime, Jeff was 6'2" and weighed 248 pounds. Bruce Lee was 5'7" and 135 pounds. It'd be a massacre."

"Speaking from experience, the bigger man doesn't always win," Claude relates as he rubs his misaligned jaw.

"True, but Blatnick's willpower, patience, and grinding were legendary."

"Bruce was the Fist of Fury; his speed would outclass anyone."

"In a real fracas, Blatnick would catch Bruce and squash him."

"No way."

We are two grown men who have regressed to six-year-olds boasting that my dad could beat up your dad.

I continue, "Blatnick won NCAA Division II Freestyle Heavy Weight championships in 78 and 79, AAU super heavyweight in 80 and 81, and the Olympics in 84. Bruce never competed. He was a celebrity and besides *Enter the Dragon*, Bruce Lee's film catalog did not match his talent. How did Bruce become popular without professionally competing in the martial arts and only starring in one decent film?"

"Blasphemy. Bruce was a philosopher too. Remember he said, 'Be like water, my friend.'"

I'll take his advice to be like water and let this debate flow over. In Niskayuna, New York, Blatnick was our hometown hero and I always felt he was overshadowed by other combat athletes like Mike Tyson and Bruce Lee. Besides being a wrestling champion, I knew Blatnick as a dedicated volunteer at the Special Olympics and a pioneering analyst for the Ultimate Fighting Championship.

Could Claude have known Bruce? Maybe he was a junior member of The Foundation and stole the wisdom to seek fame. The suspicious circumstances of Bruce's death have always been puzzling.

Claude and I settle our differences with a toast to Bruce Lee and a toast to Jeff Blatnick. We agree to disagree though; I believe my arguments have more merit and his are solely based on emotion. Regardless, arguing with an interviewer is not a sound tactic.

Claude explains the second chapter on combat addresses the mental side of fighting. These attacks range from advanced thought projectiles to the simplest of verbal assaults. Your eyes can convey a threat and temporarily paralyze your opponent with a chi-filled intense stare. This magnetic stare seems supernatural, but it exists in nature. Cats and snakes can freeze their prey with a magnetic stare.

"Did you know, a concentrated thought wave can be delivered on an invisible current into the mind of your target?

Focus and persistence are the tools to find the right currents to enter a person's consciousness. The mind sends and receives messages on an electrical platform every second, so once you perceive the current leading to your opponent's mental platform, send your message directly into their mind," says Claude.

"If I want to persuade someone to my cause, I can send a direct mental command to them?" I ask.

"Yes, but ethical implications are to be considered with these techniques. If you have good intentions, the correct path is close," says Claude.

I'm familiar with these mental techniques from my research in the library. Humans are easily influenced because most humans don't protect themselves from even their own negative thoughts, let alone someone else's. In most situations, I avoid harsh techniques and prefer mind clouding. It is not as intrusive and merely confuses the subject.

The third part of combat is battle strategy. Claude speculates General Patton had access to these ancient battle strategies.

Patton is another successful, charismatic, outspoken figure who died under suspicious circumstances. Is it possible assassins killed Patton and Bruce Lee for stepping out of the shadows and showcasing the power derived from *The Stockpile*?

As if he knew what I was thinking, Claude says, "The public is offered glimpses, but should never get extended views of excellence." In a similar manner that Alexandra ripped into the public, he shows his animosity towards them too. He massages his jaw and sips his Perrier before continuing.

Claude's sale pitch on the next chapter of *The Stockpile* lures me in further. He insists breathing is the root of the entire system and explains that when each person is born, breathing is the first significant action. The complexity of breathing fluctuates due to excitement, depression, curiosity, anger, and love. The link between breathing and emotions is physical and mental. Master your breathing and you master your emotions.

Utilizing acute breathing, projecting appropriate mental vibrations and pressure points, Claude assured me injuries could be healed almost instantly. But if this is true, why hasn't he healed his jaw?

He says there are numerous chapters illustrating how to strengthen the link between breath-work, meditation, and exercise. Yoga is one example of these breath-work exercises The Foundation has graciously imparted to the masses. Or is this another wild claim?

He states, "Few would doubt the positive effect yoga has had on people's lives. Devotees can spend their entire life practicing the contents of one aspect of yoga. Unfortunately, profiteers and tricksters have misrepresented the intent of these gifts to the public. The result is often a misinterpreted interpretation of yoga."

The two-pronged approach from Alexandra and Claude is wearing down my skepticism. Maybe this isn't mumbo jumbo. If The Foundation's rhetoric is based on a sham, I'll be okay. From what I've seen in life, it's hard for me to trust anyone. I'll set aside my ego and embrace the possibility of this fantasy world.

Much like Alexandra, Claude senses when I need assurance. He says conspiracy theorists labeled The Foundation the one percent crowd, but their theory is wrong. The Foundation is not a cult and not every member is rich. To say they dabble in the occult would be misleading, too.

They present themselves to me as one faction of a thousand worldwide wisdom seekers. The size of the organization comes across as overreaching, perhaps in the future I'll endeavor to discover their real numbers. In terms of financials, his generous salary offer effectively ends my days of scrounging for recyclables and paves the way to home ownership.

In identical fashion to Alexandra, he concludes with a summary of his three passions: The Foundation, his physical therapy practice, and order. I resist the urge to ask him for advice on a sore shoulder. I know the answer: rest, ice, compression, elevation (RICE), and back off the pull-ups and laps in the ocean. I get the impression Claude is a classy gentleman. We balance each other out.

Claude motions to the waitress for the check; this is my signal the interview is winding down and my last chance to rescue the three remaining shrimp. While he is busy with her, I pounce on the crustaceans. None shall go to waste on my watch.

He catches me in the act. "Man, you let nothing go to waste, do you?"

I want to answer him, but my mouth is stuffed with shrimp. I shake my head back and forth. Cripes, did I blow this interview because I ate Alexandra's leftover shrimp? Or maybe my insistence on Jeff Blatnick beating Bruce Lee in a fight? Perhaps my sweaty hands disgusted him?

His crooked attempt at a smile with his mangled jaw reassures me. At the conclusion of the interview, we stand, and he avoids the wet handshake by embracing me with a hug. He informs me, "You're in."

## Chapter 3 Brown Town

I depart Claude's company and feel a light buzz from the two beers. "*ERRRareeosquibila*," emanates from my stomach. It's a clear message my digestive system is not ready for savory delicacies. Descending the stairs, I clench my butt cheeks to hold the bass at bay. I'm going to wreck the downstairs bathroom. To my deepest dismay, the door is locked.

I knock and frantically ask, "You almost done in there?"

"Nope, going to be here awhile," says the unconcerned voice.

Did he have the bass too? Reactionary Lamaze breathing kicks in, and a new plan of bathroom elimination is the top priority. I can relate to the wolf in the three little pigs. I'd like to huff, puff, and blow the door of the bathroom down. My stomach and intestines are festering a low grade fever throughout my body. I'm the equivalent of a crock pot bubbling over. I survey my options. East Beach has a public restroom 600 yards away. I estimate I can sprint there in one minute and twenty seconds, but there is a high probability it's occupied by dirt surfers. My other option is a thirty-second dash into the Pacific Ocean, which I take.

I can't wait for the crosswalk light, so I zig zag across E. Cabrillo Blvd, dodging cars frogger style and kick my shoes off, toss my velvet jacket to the sand, and peel off my shirt. A yard sale of discarded clothes is left in my wake. I calculate removal of my pants will take too long and could induce labor. In a jiff, I'm in waist-deep water and urgently yank down my pants to unleash a scatter bomb. I deliberately position myself facing the incoming waves to direct the brown-infused water away from me. Pressure releases as my butt cannon blasts another round of brown chum. I laugh at myself and am comforted by my mother's mantra, "Accidents happen." I doubt her advice was intended for me in my mid-thirties. This ordeal begs the question: was the bass more satisfying going in or out? Evidently, my butt has a catch and release policy on expensive fish. Returning the bass back to the ocean is my fish story. The moral of this story is, do not eat oysters during red tide or a McGurski-manufactured brown tide. The fish you eat today may have McGurski DNA. "We are all one," is written on the label of my Bronner's soap container. I finally understand Dr. Bronner's message.

I feel like I'm being watched. I listen to my sixth sense and notice the tourists on the beach are pointing fingers and laughing. Some are clapping and others turn away, and my educated guess is my antics disgust them. Oh well, show's over. I swim parallel to shore for thirty yards to avoid friendly brown fire and retrieve my apparel.

My cronies at the library would be proud of my first aqua-dump. That's correct, there is a name for it. The benefit of the aqua-dump is the ocean is one huge bidet. There's no wiping required.

In the ocean I was oblivious to the cold water, but as I collect my clothes, I rub the goosebumps and warm myself the old-fashioned way. It's a mile and a half back to the van and by the position of the sun, it has to be at least 4 p.m. My pace increases to a fast run to fight the chill, but mostly trying to avoid a potential parking ticket. A bicyclist zooms past me and says, "On your left," in an incredibly annoying voice.

The last stretch to Shoreline Park is up a steep hill, and in short order, I gain ground on the bicyclist. Before I pass the spandex clad cycler, I say, "I'm passing you, slowpoke." My antagonism has no limits.

At the top of the hill, I enter the parking lot of Shoreline Park and close in on the van. I slow my pace to build the anticipation. Will I let a five-by-seven-inch piece of paper control my mood? Until I get a taste of The Foundation payroll, a parking ticket is a big deal. I creep to the front of the van and there is nothing on the windshield. Hooray, no ticket.

My celebration consists of changing my wet pants and fanning the interior of the van with a piece of cardboard. I think it's a good idea to remove the possibility of residual pepper spray with an artificial breeze. *Achew, achew, achew.* Clusters of three are the way I sneeze. Here is comes again, *Achew, achew, achew.* This is great. The sneeze is my barometer and when I stop sneezing, I'll know the remaining particles of pepper spray have been eradicated.

\*\*\*

The last business of the night is to log an entry into my war journal. This is where I express my gratitude and catalog the day's events. The road rage was fun, and I have often wondered how I would react to pepper spray. Now I know. I rate the experience in my thrill-seeking achievement charts as below average and recommend it only to the gnarliest of adventure seekers. I'm stoked about my new career, not crapping my pants, broadcasting my first aqua-dump to an audience, and resisting the urge to gamble. I realize I'm making the necessary changes in my lifestyle, and overall I rate today A plus. My scalp itches; hopefully, it's from the salt water and not lice. Tonight I'm going to indulge and scratch instead of patting my head.

Is this what my days will be like working for The Foundation?

## Chapter 4 Three Years Later

Working for The Foundation has kept me busy. Alexandra's orders are to wait inside an office supply store off East Gutierrez Street in downtown Santa Barbara. She probably chose this location because of the lack of people. I indulge in the comforts of an ergonomic business chair and sidle over to a slanted writing table. I prop my feet on the writing table, fold my arms behind my head in a carefree pose. This writing station has the makings of a suitable headquarters. I could ply my craft in these conditions.

While waiting for my contact, I contemplate the last three years I've scribed and delivered letters for The Foundation. Financially, I've done well and bought a two-bedroom, one-bath ranch and, with the help of a specialist, I learned to control my disorders. Things are swell, but there remains an indescribable void in my life I can't fill with work, money or possessions.

My contact interrupts my introspection. It's no-nonsense Darcy, a member of The Foundation's security team. Her long black hair neatly tied in a top bun reminds me of the librarians.

"May I help you?" I jokingly ask.

"Shut up, McGurski. This serious."

She's normally brusque and routinely leaves out the verb is.

"One of The Foundation members has recently passed away."

"Who died?" I ask.

"Oscar."

"Who's Oscar?"

"The head researcher for The Foundation."

"How come I've never heard of him?"

"Oscar preferred solitude."

She explains Oscar's role was gathering books, research, and occasional recruitment. An audit of his inventory revealed the Movement Letter was missing from his collection. "We think the missing letter (is) inside Oscar's desk, and the company dealing with the estate accidentally sold the desk to an antique store. Varla searched the antique store—"

"Who's Varla?"

"She (is) our new investigator."

"They must deliberately keep these people away from me."

"Varla verified a Johnny Santos bought the desk. Turns out, he (is) a journalist."

My reply is succinct. "Time for action."

She counters, "When I visited Santos' house, nobody answered the door. I think Santos found (the) letter."

"You mean found *the* letter." Occasionally, I correct her English, but resist correcting every mistake because I don't want to give her a complex.

"Oh, thank you for the correction."

This caper has legs. To an outsider, the appearance of the letter would manifest an irresistible curiosity similar to the untranslatable, mysterious Voynich manuscript, a medieval book written in the 15th century. Its unknown language and unusual drawings continue to fascinate and stump scholars. How could Santos resist the detailed penmanship, the fine parchment, and obscure language? The letter has a hypnotic quality which would compel Santos to seek answers. If he revealed the contents to the public, as journalists are inclined to do, The Foundation would be displeased. They do not tolerate interlopers or breaches of their privacy.

She breaks my daydream. "Write a Letter of Action. Santos' address (is) 108 Veronica Springs Court."

"It'll be ready in two days."

"Negative, Alexandra wants it by tomorrow."

Alexandra is heavily connected. In this region, she is the equivalent of the orchestra *maestra*; she moves the wand and music is made.

"Or what?" I'm deliberately testing boundaries.

"You will not like the answer."

"Do you hear that?" I change the subject to mess with her.

"What?"

"The piped in music over the loudspeaker; does it sound like the band Simply Red but turned into elevator music?"

"You're impossible; just inscribe the letter, you idiot."

"It'll be ready tomorrow before sunrise." Rats, this calls for extreme focus and maybe a headache.

"Perfect." She turns around, nimbly negotiating a myriad of unsold overpriced office furniture and liberates her hair from the bun. This must be her last mission for the day.

It occurs to me I didn't offer her a seat. Our entire discussion happened with me sitting and her standing a few feet away. Or maybe she was standing to be in a position of control. "Darcy, next time bring rope wraps and we'll do some light sparring."

She turns back and says, "You want your scars to look as bad as mine?" as she points to the scars around her eyebrows.

The scar tissue above her eyebrows rivals my own. It's a lifestyle hazard.

\*\*\*

How could a letter go missing? There are rigid and ridiculously campy protocols with the handling of letters. We deliver letters at sunrise, and they must be read immediately, outside, facing the sun. The Foundation letter-reading ceremony echoes their mission statement, "A new day. A new way." After the reading ceremony, the letter is promptly secured, and a witness verifies it.

I decide to speculate later, as I need to prepare to inscribe a Letter of Action. While I'm in the office supply store, I'll make the most of my surroundings and gather a pack of high quality resume paper, a deluxe fountain pen, and setup shop in my temporary office.

If this letter is inscribed incorrectly, my silhouette will haunt me. My shadow is my sole dependent, while my silhouette is distant and abstract. These weird sentences invade my mind space and are an indication I'm sensing the pressure of a deadline. To enhance my concentration, I choose breathing technique number forty-one from the breathing chapter of *The Stockpile*. I raise my hands above my head and breathe in deeply, bend forward dangling my arms near the floor, and hold my breath for ten seconds while allowing the sensation of my skull cavity to be cleansed with fresh blood and oxygen. I return to the standing position with my arms over my head, while holding my breath for a five count. Then I bend forward and exhale. Three cycles of this and I'm radiating chi. I channel this surplus chi to flow through my writing hand. Summoning chi to your hands is the easiest. The amount of nerves connecting your hands to your brain outnumbers any part of your body. This is why we are capable of complex tasks with our five digit friends. The dexterity of a nimble hand can boast numerous pleasing achievements.

I complete my routine and with the exuberance of a freshman cheerleader who made the squad, I belt out, "I'm ready to write!"

A store clerk in his early twenties who watched my breathing routine, and politely waited until I finished, asks, "Sir, may I help you with anything?"

"Hold all my calls for three hours."

"Okayyyy, if you need anything, I'll be over there."

Each word inscribed on this letter has to be done in one fluid sweep. To stop before finishing a word is disruptive and jeopardizes the integrity of the message. It doesn't matter if you have to sneeze; you suppress it. If a mosquito is buzzing in your ear, accept it until you finish writing the characters. In the formation of words and symbols, you strive for excellence. I transfer heaps of chi into the letter until it radiates a hazy golden glow. With enough energy, a letter can become an organic living thing rather than a piece of parchment with ink on it.

Although the Letter of Action is pure ceremonial nonsense, I have pride in my inscriptions and regard each letter as a piece of art. The urgency is beyond me. After finishing my inscription, I'll deliver it to Alexandra tomorrow morning, she'll thank me and file the letter as documentation for The Foundation's records.

Darcy mentioned Santos' address is 108 Veronica Springs Court, and for the final touches, I'll include his address in the Letter of Action. The number 108 triggers my left hemisphere because it is ripe with symbolism.

I summon the store clerk to suggest I require immediate assistance.

His full trot shows he is desperate to provide service. "Yes, are you interested in this workstation?" he asks.

Without acknowledging his question, I dive into a sermon. "Did you know Buddhists proclaim there are one hundred and eight feelings? Sounds like a lot, doesn't it? I mean, how many can you name?"

"Uh, happy, sad, mad, excited, jealous, uh … I know there's more, but there's no way there are one hundred and eight."

"Check this out, it'll blow your mind. I can prove there are one hundred and eight with math. Pretend there are six senses (actually there are seven): smell, touch, taste, hearing, sight, and consciousness. Each of the six senses can experience three types of feelings: pain, pleasure, or neutral. These feelings can be produced in two ways: internally or externally and are affected by three zones: past, present and future, which equals one hundred and eight feelings. Six senses × three pain/pleasure/neutral × two internally or externally produced × three past/future/present = one hundred and eight. 6x3x2x3=108."

"Wow, that's pretty cool, mister. You should have bet me on it."

He's right; I was so pumped about the numbers, I missed the opportunity to gamble. I can't tell if that's a good thing or a bad thing. The Specialist warned me about controlling my urges and freaking people out with numbers, but a little more won't hurt.

"There is more to the number one hundred and eight. Did you know there are also one hundred and eight pressure points on the human body?"

"Didn't know that. Anything else about one hundred and eight?" he eagerly asks.

I can't believe he's asking for more. This kid has got promise.

"These pressure points can be applied for healing, neutralizing, or destruction. The internal temperature of one hundred and eight Fahrenheit is when the human body's vital organs fail." I breathe deeply and purge myself, otherwise I will continue to chase numbers.

"Sir, did you take the day off from school today?"

"No, why?"

"I assume you are a teacher."

"Why a teacher?"

"Only teachers visit office supply stores. During school hours, this place is dead. But when school gets out, they storm the store with their school credit cards and lecture us on their subjects."

"You thought I was a teacher because I was ranting about the number one hundred and eight?"

"Math teachers are in here all the time explaining how Fibonacci and the Golden ratio explain the mysteries of the universe. So yeah, you kind of fit the bill."

"This is different; you seemed interested in the number one hundred and eight."

"Are you sure you're not a teacher?"

"I'm sure."

"Here's the secret ... corporate training. Our research department discovered the one thing all teachers find irresistible and exploited it."

"What is it?"

"It's warped, real head games type stuff."

I'm about to shake this kid by the collar to get the answer. "You got to tell me, man."

"In order to keep the teachers coming back to our stores instead of shopping online, they train all the clerks to feign interest."

"That's it?"

"Sounds too simple, right? But think about it; teachers are passionate about their subject and their students don't care. We provide an outlet to preach their passions and actually listen to them."

"It works?"

"Yeah, but only on high school and middle school teachers. Elementary school kids accept the programming. Come back here at 2:30 p.m. for the first wave and you'll see."

"That's crazy."

"I cruised through English Lit because of them. Multiple high school English teachers proofread and rewrote my college essays because I listened to them."

"Thanks for listening, buddy. Don't expect me to do your homework for you."

"My pleasure. Stop by anytime. Remember, we're not just office supplies, we're here to listen."

The office supply store beats going to a psychologist or church confessional. Exiting the store, I'm impressed with myself. I stayed focused, inscribed the letter, and only went off task once to wax rhapsodic about the number one hundred and eight. Incredibly, it's the fastest I've inscribed a letter.

Onward to the Motorcycle Laundromat. The owner, Sarrick, is one of my few friends and is a motorcycle enthusiast, hence the name of his laundromat. He moved from India to Santa Barbara and labored in a family-run laundromat, diligently learning the craft before opening his own shop. He once explained to me the voyage to becoming your own boss begins with on-the-job training. This message resonates with me. Outside his laundromat, there is a retro style sign of an orange and white Royal Enfield Interceptor. The light bulbs around the edges of the motorcycle do not blink because that would not be classy. The interior of his shop is immaculate and without a trace of chemical odors. There is a sweetness in the air, but not overbearing. Inside, the prices are clearly written on one sign. The simplicity is perfect, and with few distractions there is room for friendly banter with Sarrick.

Before entering, I review my mental checklist. My purpose for visiting the Motorcycle Laundromat is to pick up my velvet jacket, discuss Sarrick's latest motorcycle trip, and defend the honor of my recently purchased Suzuki Intruder he'll surely besmirch. In conversation, I'm private and vague to the point of mysterious, while Sarrick is open with his dialogue. In my line of work, discreetness is appreciated.

We continue our ongoing discussion regarding scenic routes with gorgeous vista viewpoints and agree snapping pictures at the viewpoints is disrespectful to nature. Only the mind's eye can receive this type of beauty. He compares how riding motorcycles in Santa Barbara is relaxing, while riding in India is similar to playing a stressful video game.

"McGurski, what kind of person wears linens, barongs, and velvet blazers?"

Is my wardrobe grounds for suspicion? My penchant for wearing barongs (Filipino wedding shirt) with linen pants or jeans could be slightly eccentric. He is keen for details. No matter the profession, if you do it well, your awareness becomes sharp. Sarrick is one of the few non-initiated with extra sensory awareness. Wearing the same clothes for a while, you leave behind an essence in them. A shirt can become a lucky shirt because of what happened while wearing it. He is aware of this magic and perceives the stark contrast in essence left on my jacket versus the energy residue of a bowling shirt. Plus, my clothes do not have nacho cheese stains on them. The threads on my clothes are vibrating at a different level. The thrift store, dark brown, enigmatic velvet blazer, expresses a casual class and is my go to apparel for missions. I accessorize with a protective golden power amulet hanging slightly below my sternum. It shields my xiphoid process, a region known to be a Plexus of nerve force energy. This costume is the veneer of a true gentleman savage.

My clothes are congruent and in tune with my nature. I brush off his comment with a confounding laugh, as I can't afford to let him in on my trade. Finding another laundromat and friend is an unsettling predicament. I thank him for dry cleaning my clothes and check the boxes on my mental checklist.

"Hey, I almost forgot to tell you, I'm sponsoring a Little League baseball team. We call ourselves the Motorcycle Laundromat Batters. You should come check us out on Saturday mornings."

The allure of sports, numbers, and gambling is too enticing to miss. "Where and what time?"

"Nine o'clock at Elings Park off Las Positas. I knew I could count on your support."

Leaving The Motorcycle Laundromat, I take a detour to complete a covert mission at Santos' house.

## Chapter 5 Delivery and Protégé

It's been years since I've stayed out this late. The covert mission at Santos' house was almost a total bust. This is a situation where my mind power books come in handy. I'm reluctant to think about the Santos debacle, so I clear my head with a decluttering technique. When I'm mentally ready, I'll revisit the tragedy.

As per my instructions from Darcy, my objective is to deliver the Letter of Action to Alexandra before sunrise. She lives in a Mediterranean style villa with panoramic views of the Pacific Ocean in an area of Santa Barbara referred to as the American Riviera. For a non-thrill seeker, it would take twenty minutes to get to her villa. I'll ride my motorcycle and do it in seven. The series of switchbacks and narrow roads are ideal for a motorcycle, but a struggle for the tan van.

I park my bike on the street, when a middle-aged man emerges from the darkness walking his border terrier. The little scrapper tugs on his leash and is desperate to greet me. I crouch to meet the excitable rascal, but the owner responds with a yank on the leash, snapping the dog backwards. I squint in disgust and shake my head. "No way to treat a pet," I remark. The partial strangulation must have loosened the pooch's bowels because a moment later, he left a soft boiled brown egg on Alexandra's easement. I'm betting this schmuck doesn't bag it. He's part of an expanding breed of humans purposely walking their dogs early in the morning and late at night to avoid picking up poop. They believe the rules don't apply under the cover of darkness.

I'm here to help. I have a cellophane bag with a few sprigs of mint in my pocket. My intention is to munch on the remaining sprigs and offer the empty bag to this perpetrator. He's zoned in on the little baggie in my hand and the green leafy substance I shoved in my mouth. I catalog his series of expressions as being one of hopeful anticipation, confusion, and disappointment as I chew the remaining mint in my mouth.

I wave my empty baggie at him and ask, "Hey, you need a bag?"

"No, I'm good," the jerk replies.

Living in the Riviera is a sign of wealth, and this prick is not accustomed to taking orders. "I think you do," I reply.

"I'm not picking it up. Everyone up here has lawn service, so they'll pick it up," he chirps.

His indifference to the plight of the laborers triggers me to say, "If you don't pick up that crap, I will fight you six times." I realize my statement is peculiar and enforce my words with action by shoving the bag in his hands and placing my left hand on his back, forcing him to bend over. I watch him scrunching his nose and imagine the turd smells like, well, smells like crap. His defiance is neutralized and the evidence of the dog's digestive system is removed from the grass.

I don't hear Alexandra's front door open, but the light from inside her house casting a brightness onto the street alerts me.

"Oh, good morning, Alexandra," I say.

"Fletcher, is everything okay? Are you boys playing nice?" she asks.

Fletcher? What better name for a pretentious, preppy douche. I respond, "We're just rough housing."

I readjust the position of my arm to wrap it tightly around his shoulder and squeeze his bicep. Seizing control, I feed him a line to say and he does, "Everything's peaches and cream." I can't believe he says it. Fletcher has become my personal hand puppet. Under my breath, I whisper to him, "Fletcher, if you keep tugging on your dog's leash and leaving poop, there will be a reckoning." And then I release him from my clutches.

He plonks his head down and meekly shuffles away.

I'm welcomed inside with gratitude for inscribing the letter on short notice. Although there are no frescos on the ceiling, Raphael, Michelangelo, and Leonardo would feel at home inside her villa. Paintings from the Italian Renaissance adorn her walls and ornate furniture add to the visual spectacle. The antique chairs and sofa certainly weren't designed for comfort. At this early hour, Alexandra's already decked out in a pale blue dress, pearl necklace, and maybe pantyhose—with her dark skin and without pinching her legs, it's hard to tell if she's wearing them or not. Her massive wardrobe of 1960s Jackie Onassis inspired dresses somehow compliments the Italian Renaissance décor. Who knew these two eras were congruent?

I do my job and fork over the letter. She notices the glow emanating from inside the envelope and responds with one eyebrow raised. A raised eyebrow from her is sufficient praise. The three hours it took me to inscribe this foolish, but well-crafted letter, is seemingly wasted when she reads and files it in under one minute. With our transaction complete, she coaxes me to stick around for a chat.

"Typically, unless there's a ceremony or a letter being delivered, I'm not up this early," she says.

"Me neither."

"Have a seat; would you like a cup of cup of tea?"

"No thanks. Caffeine gives me the jitters."

"Suit yourself."

She smoothly drizzles the hot water over a tea bag into the teacup, adds two sugar cubes, and stirs in a back-and-forth motion. The surrounding air warms from the steam and captures the citrus smell of orange peels. This process is done with deliberate silence, order, and precision. The silence inevitably crumbles submitting to the tea party jibber jabber.

"You stir your tea differently to my father."

"He was a coffee drinker, right?"

"Absolutely, he loved his *kafo* (Esperanto for coffee)."

"I'm a tea drinker, bound by the rules of etiquette to stir in a twelve o'clock to six o'clock motion. In this fashion there is no splashing or noise."

"The silence is nice."

"Please, R. W., do not hover while I drink. Have a seat."

"I'm good." I'm not sitting to make her comfortable. What about my comfort? Even a small power play is a show of control. I'm in control and I don't feel awkward to stand while she sits.

"Well, you've made excellent progress in your training, and per tradition, it's your turn to share what you've learned. Claude and I both believe you are ready for the next chapter in your evolution."

"You're finally teaching me how to levitate?"

"No, we're not teaching you how to levitate. The Minister, I mean Claude, recommended you to mentor my son, Jacob. He's a bit hyper, so try to balance him out."

Occasionally, for whatever reason, The Foundation uses corny titles instead of their names. It's been a few years since I've heard anyone refer to Claude as The Minister. His full absurd title is The Minister of Justice, because he's obsessed with order and balance. Ironically, he's not religious.

"Who wants to be around kids? What if I don't want to mentor him?"

"You'll be exiled. Don't worry, there are always bottles and cans to be recycled."

"I changed my mind. I'll have a cup of tea." I'll sit on a three-hundred-year-old rock hard chair too. Her threat rips into my core. I'd rather collect my thoughts than collect bottles again. Although having a protégé might crimp my style, I'll be able to add mentorship to my resume. Technically, this is exile. Their scheme is to keep me too busy to practice my experimental technique, but the positive side to having a protégé is the chance to mold a developing human into a person. I know how to begin his training. With me as his mentor, he'll never be the same. If Claude recommended me, regardless of my reservations, I'll handle this assignment with class. I owe him. No complaining. I read complaining is a voluntary weakness. I will reframe this assignment in my head. Training a protégé will reinforce my base. I can revisit the fundamentals and then go beyond, otherwise I could become the worst thing of all … dull. This is all I needed to regroup.

"The tea is delightful." I'll drink the tea but stand my ground against the consumption of sugar laden confectionaries.

"Have you decided?"

"I'll take the assignment. Send the yob over tomorrow."

"Pardon me? The yob?"

"Send the brat over after school." I guess she's not hip to English slang. Yob is boy spelled backwards and means an unruly youth.

***

The next day, I hear bike brakes followed by the thud of a bike being plopped. The absence of doorbells at the McGurski ranch forces visitors to create their own noise to announce their presence. This bike riding enthusiast chooses the thick brass ring knocker. At the bottom of the knocker are two peacocks flanking a pine comb, which represents the pineal gland. It's a mystery gland that links us to remote dimensions. A developed pineal gland is a rare item. The literature that I've read theorizes most humans have calcified pineal glands, which keeps their third eye closed. The third eye senses energy in this dimension and beyond. Besides the noise of the bike and knocker, I'm aware of my guest's arrival. My pineal gland is active. There's no fluoride in my toothpaste.

This is my life in motion; one day ago I delivered a letter to Jacob's mother and today I'm his mentor. Before welcoming him, I repeat my greeting mantra: introduce myself, make eye contact, shake hands, and smile. While the previous version of myself despised handshakes, this version embraces the clutch. Claude financed the hand sweat surgery, making him responsible for the shift in my attitude towards handshakes. The procedure is called endoscopic thoracic sympathectomy surgery and boasts a 99.6% success rate. An overactive sympathetic nerve chain is the culprit. These are the nerves that send messages to the body concerning stress and impending danger. After the surgery, remarkably, I retained the threat response and lost the hand sweat. I utilized the gift of surgery and so now I can welcome Jacob with a firm dry handshake to commence his training.

"Nice to meet you, Jacob. I'm McGurski and this training is your rite of passage."

His handshake is weak. Also, he's staring at the floor instead of at me.

I immediately correct him. "A greeting requires a real handshake, a smile, and eye contact." I dangle my hand in front of him again.

"You want me to shake your hand again?" Jacob asks.

"Yes."

He complies, except for the smile.

"Add the smile."

He does but exaggerates the smile.

"Nice, teenage sarcasm. Let's do it right this time."

Full compliance. He's coachable. It's his first visit to the McGurski Ranch and his eyes are darting around. He surveys the floor lined with ninety-six potted plants of various sizes and a four-foot-by-six-foot copper pyramid. The pyramid is framed out with half-inch copper tubes and no panels on the sides, allowing one to sit inside of it.

"What's with the pyramid?"

"When you're ready, I'll show you."

He adjusts his breathing; intuitively he recognizes the purity of oxygen in the air. "You're growing weed?"

"These plants are not smoke-able. Some were abandoned, and some were runaways, so I adopted them."

"How can a plant be a runaway?"

"I was testing your listening skills. In the future, plants will replace oxygen tanks, so if you surround yourself with enough plants, you'll be saturated with the cleanest vibrant oxygen on the free market."

"Okayyyy. You may not be growing weed, but you're definitely toking."

When the word okay is stretched out, it's usually because I've said something weird. "Jacob, are you ready to begin?"

"You can call me Ladders."

"Jacob's Ladder. What would you like to learn, Ladders?" Is his nickname a biblical or movie reference? I expect he'll give a normal teenage dumbfounded presentation of, "Duh, I don't know?"

"I don't know. I want to learn crazy mystical stuff."

Teenagers are predictable creatures. I set the boundaries. "Discipline is in order. You're not learning these secrets from reading a dusty old scroll, and you're not ready for crazy mystical stuff."

"Why not?" he presses.

"Because your brain would collapse. Train to accept these gifts. You are a ladder without rungs." This is my corny attempt to play the role of the wise monk in the TV show *Kung Fu* with Ladders playing the role of the student named grasshopper. "Let's go outside."

In the backyard, we stop in front of my bamboo garden. I shimmy up the stalks with the ease of a gymnast. The calluses on my hands were meant for bearing my weight. Stopping at nine feet, my feet brace against two stalks. It's unfathomable; last year these stalks might have been five feet tall, and in a year they have shot up to thirty feet. They mature quickly and are solid. "Rungs would make things easier," I taunt. "Watch this." I pounce to a juvenile stalk, trusting it to bend without breaking and bringing me back to the ground. It flexes to a tipping point and snaps, so I drop three feet and tumble. The plant's message to me is clear; youngsters are limited in what they can handle.

Ladders is throwing pinecones at trees and looks unimpressed. I ask him to try. He wraps his hand around the bamboo stalks and inches his way to a foot off the ground.

There is an indescribable sound when a grip fails and friction is created between skin and bamboo. He loses his temporary gains as well as a filleted layer of skin from his palms.

"Ahh, man, that hurts." He shakes his hands to somehow alleviate the pain. "It looked easy when you did it."

"Radical stunts are typically appreciated after trying to duplicate it. Our minds are collective, therefore a version of yourself can perform this feat. However, your particular version requires preparation."

He concedes to lounging on the lawn chairs with his knee nervously bouncing.

"Ladders, have you found significance in your life yet?"

"I'm fifteen, so what kind of significant events have I had?"

"Is your bouncing knee significant?"

"No, it's a habit."

"A nervous habit?"

"I'm not nervous."

In a firm tone, I say, "It depletes energy and displays weakness. Eliminate it from my sight." When teaching, it is crucial to start firm, and eventually ease back if warranted. This is the teaching model I observed in the military and from effective school teachers. The fast track way to start a revolt is to be whimsical and then try to be strict.

"Hey, man, you can't talk to me that way, you work for my mother."

He's testing boundaries. I send chi energy to my eyes and visualize calming blue energy cascading over him and hold this gaze for six seconds. Simultaneously I send a simple message to an open wavelength to his mind, "Be cool." For a teenager, time moves slower and six seconds is uncomfortably long. I snap my fingers to release the mental hold and continue the conversation. This is his introduction to the mystical arts.

His attitude is typical for a teenager, but manageable. I hand him a nine-page manual written on sturdy resume paper titled Mental Mind Force.

"Ladders, read this. It will guide you closer to the crazy mystical stuff. Once you read it, you'll never be the same."

## Chapter 6 Varla

The morning marine layer rolls in, keeping the grass moist. I'm in my front yard breathing in the cool damp air while performing my ritualistic stretching. These exercises are Claude's direct influence. He taught me how to keep my muscles, fascia, and joints supple with an active stretching routine.

I stop mid-stretch as she walks towards me on the flagstone path, her feet intuitively avoiding the moss. The moss fills the gaps between the flagstones like arteries flittering around each paver. My head and upper torso raise from between my knees as my eyes strip search her from her thick thighs to her ample breasts. Her figure keeps me extra focused. What dynamic proportions. Hourglasses blush with jealously. A real firecracker with curves. These descriptions are over the top, but moments spent reflecting and appreciating the busty things in life are worthwhile. Romance and adventure entertain the masses, for me it's the bouncy things. Glimpsing her figure is like stealing a base in baseball. Read the signs; if she is distracted, steal a glance but don't leer. The game is childish, but apparently a hard-wired part of our mating rituals. She has beautiful shiny, dark shoulder length hair accenting her golden eyes and dark olive complexion. If she was famous, the tabloids would rail her features as being too much, and this adds to my infatuation. I'd estimate her to be forty-years-old, 5'5" and 190 pounds. From my point of view, her weight is distributed in all the right places. A woman like her does not bow to the will of the fashionistas, she does as she pleases. They'll be no visits to the nail salon, no plucking, tweezing, or electrolysis. Bold in several ways, she's exotic and irresistible. She initiates the conversation.

"So, you're McGurski. You're tanner than I expected."

"Here I am. What did you expect?"

"I thought you'd be a ginger."

I detect a slight French accent. If I were to pinpoint her origin, I'd guess Morocco. "I haven't had the pleasure."

"Are you sure?"

She must have caught me stealing peeks. "May I interest you in a handshake, smile, eye contact, and an exchange of names?" Did I state my greeting checklist out loud? It's a slip, but a first step in stating my desires.

"Bravo, you've figured out introductions, but you're fishing for more than my name."

She does a slight lean back with her head. It's a poker tell. I can see she is pleased with her light jab at me. Her teasing word choices are comforting. I give her a firm handshake and a smile while holding her gaze. The warmth of her hands invites my touch, this suggests she is comfortable in my presence. I lean back and sass her with a smile on my face.

"You're no fish, you're connected, so what's your role?" I ask.

"You're slick, but you're washed up," she replies.

"Harsh words."

"Dried up like a Tarpon Springs sponge." It's a Florida reference, and she delivers the line with a fake twang in a corny voice.

"A dry sponge can absorb water." My rebuttal falls flat. I regret my assortment of words; as film noir dialogue is tough on the fly.

"The Foundation has an interest in your extracurricular activities. Back off from the experimental technique."

"Are you warning or threatening me?"

"This is a courtesy visit." She turns to walk away.

"Stop by anytime." I'm smitten. Smart, feisty, brave, and curvy. The Foundation sent her to grab my attention.

She turns her head, smiles and says, "Call me Varla."

"Of course, you're the new investigator. Any leads on the Santos case?" What I said was enough for her to stop. I'm betting this is the real reason for her visit.

"I was going to ask you the same thing."

I play dumb. "I write the letters, that's it."

"How did you know I was working the case?"

"Darcy told me."

"Interesting. Maybe you and Darcy are in cahoots and stole the Movement Letter."

"Pretty wild theory," I respond.

She peruses the landscape and the ranch with a deliberately slow head turn and nods. "Pretty nice setup here. Did you do the landscaping yourself?"

"The apple and orange trees were here, but I planted the bamboo and the rest of the flowers."

"Wow, I can see the bamboo in your backyard from here. How long have you been here?"

"About three years."

"There's no way those bamboo are three years old."

"There's a saying, the first year bamboo sleeps, the second year it creeps, and the third year it leaps."

"It's pretty. It'd be a shame to lose all of this over a silly stolen letter."

"I don't know what you're talking about."

"We'll see." She walks off.

I stand tall, fixated on her wiggling butt. Thirty feet out, she does a quarter turn with her head and flips her hair to the side. She knows what she's doing.

***

Before returning to my workout, I schedule an appointment with myself to ruminate on Varla. Proper respect to the routine requires staying focused on the exercises and nothing else for the remainder of the workout. My joints are supple from stretching and primed for thirty minutes of an alternating kettlebell and jump rope fiesta. Exercising in the front yard is an opportunity to meet my neighbor's dogs and watch the world rotate. Fitness advocates claim the pump from kettlebells is total body exercise and unmatched when combined with jump ropes. I'm on autopilot jumping rope as my mind drifts to the image of Varla; this is a mind-control battle I can tolerate losing. At the completion of my workout, I cool off in the bathroom and bristle brush my skin toward my heart to remove dry cells and increase circulation. On top of the sink are the frequently used items, which include soap, toothpaste, a toothbrush, and floss. The bristle brush has not made the starting lineup of hygiene products and is back in the drawer with the less frequently used deodorant and razor. To vivify my nerve force and keep thoughts of Varla at bay, I embrace a cold shower. Old memories of the outdoor shower at Shoreline Park revisit me.

I prepare lunch and snack on blueberries and carrots, while prepping the main course: steamed asparagus, a baked potato, and trout seasoned with melted butter, lemon juice, garlic, salt, and pepper. I catch myself almost steaming the trout instead of baking it in the oven; the Varla invasion continues to distract. Another random but connected thought enters my mind; cooking for two would be as easy as cooking for one.

The meal is tasty, but pollutes the ranch with an overwhelming fishy odor. I leave the oven tray, dishes, and silverware to soak in the sink, while I brush and floss fish particles out of my back molars. During my compulsory oral hygiene routine, I question if Claude cast a voodoo love hex on me because the image of Varla encroaches into my mind again.

I've been anticipating this personal appointment with myself. For this special meeting, I sit with the plants. Their abundant oxygen assists me in meditation. To disprove people with autism supposedly have an aversion to change, I alter the position of my plants frequently. Presently, they are arranged to the first ninety-six notes of Mr. Bungle's song *Sweet Charity*. Each plant is raised or lowered a few inches to correspond to the notes of the song on the music scale. This arrangement enhances the oxygen flow emitted.

Varla has awakened my loins, and I envision her becoming an intimate part of my life. She's entered during the right stage of my life and has the gusto to keep me balanced. An unforced smile is rare for me and anytime this bombshell pops into my head, the smile comes naturally. Maybe I should prepare some dialogue for Varla's next visit, or ask Darcy where Varla likes to hang out. The need for companionship has caught up to me.

My second thought is about self-preservation and the gist of her visit. Is her message a scare tactic or test from The Foundation? She said to back off the experimental technique. The Foundation must be on to my Adrenaline Magnetic Power

(AMP) experimentation. There have been physical and mental attacks on me before, but my kind of Mental Mind Force training ends threats. A frightened subject would heed this warning, but in doing so prove unworthy of these skills. What good is the training if you don't use it when it counts?

This reminds me of a karate guy who once came outside his dojo to belittle me. He called me a loitering homeless bum and said I was stealing valor by wearing an Air Force jacket. My presence unbalanced this karate man, and for all his fancy prearranged choreographed counters, none worked against my aggression. A simple two-handed shove propelled his body through the air. The Elvis Presley song *Return to Sender* came to mind as I returned him back to his dojo the hard way. The glass scattered on the padded floor like spilled popcorn at a movie theater. His students crowded around for their chance to see real martial arts in action. Miraculously, he stood up without a cut and says, "My code forbids me to fight you."

I responded with, "You won't fight me because you're a chicken baby." Disgusted by his excuse for cowardice, I swore never to be like the karate guy. He was too afraid to test his skills because of fear and doubt. He feared being pummeled and doubted his inefficient art form. The realization of wasted time and energy spent on karate was obvious to one of us. This is the fable of how a karate guy with a fragile ego turned into a chicken baby.

With the fable of the chicken baby in mind, I continue experimenting with technique. This exploration will unlock the closed doors to my personal evolution. Maybe my defiance will prompt Varla's return to interrupt my experiments.

I proceed in my experimentation by dispersing three-twenty pound bags of ice into five inches of cold bath water. Ice from the first bag crackles as it hits the water. The second bag has less crackling and the third bag creates a habitat suitable for penguins, if their living environment was a 1970s bathtub with white porcelain tiles. Reading the digital thermometer is unnecessary, but my curiosity with numbers demands answers. It registers in at forty-two degrees Fahrenheit. I slide into the tub of ice water to induce an adrenaline rush. The frigid water feels like the stabs of a thousand icy daggers. I reframe it in my mind as one thousand hands massaging me. After three minutes, I'm fully adrenalized and ease out of the tub with my body sporting a bluish complexion. Three hundred reps of jumping jacks at a vigorous pace helps circulate my blood, returns my skin color, elevates my heart rate, and spikes my adrenaline for the next step.

Immediately after adrenalizing, I subject myself to Pulsed Electric Magnetic Frequency inside a copper pyramid. For three minutes, I absorb and redistribute this extraordinary magnetic adrenaline power to my whole body. My body feels charged to the brim, glowing, buzzing, and strong enough to blast through walls.

Typically, an adrenaline rush doesn't last too long, but my protocol extends the duration. To prove it, I burst out the door wearing shorts and sneakers and sprint at top speed for twelve seconds! In comparison, elite sprinters can only maintain their top speed for six to eight seconds. Like a mad scientist or a crow, I let out a "Caw" as I regain my breath and rest for a moment. My recovery time is shortened too, and in twenty-three seconds I explode again, hauling down Veronica Springs Court. After multiple sprints, my jolt of energy has reached its expiration date. Normally, you could expect to crash from an adrenaline dump, but after AMPing myself, it's more subtle.

Covered in sweat, a third trip to the bathtub is necessary and scored as a win. The gentleman within me appreciates cleanliness. I pour a pound of Epsom salt into hot bath water and soak motionless and satisfied. Mentally, I review the day and express gratitude for meeting Varla, testing my limits in the AMP experiment, and for having a delicious lunch. I plan for tomorrow, dry off, read for a few hours, and go to sleep. Good night. Forty winks. Forty Henry Winklers. Whimsically, instead of counting sheep or the letter Z jumping fences, I'm counting Fonzies jump sharks. No doubt I'll be dreaming of Varla.

## Chapter 7 Training at the Library

The outside hasn't changed a bit. The Spanish Mission style architecture adorned with a series of tall arched windows, neatly trimmed hedges, triple decker fountain, and sporadic clusters of palm trees create a blissful sanctuary on the corner of State Street and Anacapa. I haven't been back here since joining The Foundation. My old stomping grounds, the public library. I doubt I'll recognize anyone, as they rotate the staff to suburban branch libraries due to burnout from dealing with the homeless. It's no coincidence I'm meeting Ladders at the library on a Thursday. Today is his first lesson about knowing your enemy. On Thursdays, the library has a head lice screening clinic or, as I call it, free government scalp massage. Normally, I don't like people touching me, but these lice patrols are acceptable. The tools to check for lice include chop sticks to part the hair and a fine-toothed nit comb to remove the eggs. It's funny, I routinely call humans nitwits, and it was only a few years ago a nurse trainee informed me a nit is another word for a lice egg. My scalp is always itchy; I suspect it's from salt water or another lice outbreak.

I've got enough time before Ladders' session to get a once over on my scalp. In the library breezeway, two twenty-year-old girls and one guy dressed in fresh scrubs welcome me with exuberance. These nurse trainees stand eagerly waiting for patients to treat for head lice, while the forty-year-old head nurse trainer rocks back in her chair half a sleep.

"Hi, are you interested in being checked for head lice or have your blood pressure taken?"

The enthusiasm from this young trainee is startling. And by God, what a courageous sales pitch. "Sure, is it going to hurt?" I can't resist a chance to tease.

"Oh, not at all, you'll barely feel a thing. Have a seat. It will feel like we're brushing your hair." The trainee smiles brightly with an uncontrolled giddiness of having her first contestant. She gently runs the tightly toothed metal comb through my hair, while the two other trainees crowd me to enjoy the spectacle.

Library patrons shoot concerned and disgusted glances as the threat of a head lice outbreak in their precious community sours their book gathering experience. The ammunition I've given them to discuss in their book circles and at the dinner table is priceless. I'm amused as one patron scratches her head on her way inside the library. The power of suggestion is real. On the first pass over with the comb, she lightly grazes my scalp and I experience the equivalent relief from scratching a mosquito bite.

"Mmmmm." I accidentally and creepily express my pleasure. I can predict what the trainee says next verbatim. Three, two, one …

"How can you tell if it's dandruff or lice?"

Bingo, we have a winner.

The trainer mumbles, "When in doubt, pick it out."

I get the feeling she's uttered the same phrase each semester for years. After the scalp massage, I receive a complimentary travel size shampoo and conditioner with bold capitalized words: MAXIMUM STRENGTH. Without question, I assume the laws of the Geneva Convention extend to protect the rights of head lice, hence my initial reservations to scour them with chemical warfare agents. I devise an alternative war plan and share it with the nurse trainee.

"What if, instead of bathing with harsh shampoos, I challenge the lice to breath holds in the Pacific Ocean?"

The head trainer perks up and springs out of her chair. I assume she's prepared for this line of questioning and says, "It's near impossible to drown lice. A louse can tolerate water for up to eight hours."

"Okay, I'll nuke them and thank you for combing my hair."

\*\*\*

Slightly disgusted with myself over my slack hygiene, I go outside and see Ladders dismounting from his fluorescent futuristic carbon road bike.

"Better lock it up, folks around here will nab that bike and pawn it."

Ladders does a quick survey of the area and notices the slew of seedy looking individuals. "Good idea." As he locks his bike, I notice he has the Mental Mind Force manual secured under his armpit.

"Tell me about your reading assignment."

"You were right; this manual changed me. No joke, it rocks."

I give him the full McGurski smile. "Welcome, Ladders."

"Did you write it?" he asks.

I give him the slightest of modest nods. "Before you ask, you'll experience the Adrenaline Magnetic Power (AMP) when you are ready."

"How did you know? Did you read my mind?"

"I figured you'd want to try it. On to another exciting subject." The art of redirection is an indispensable tool for teenagers and people with ADHD. "Come on inside and we'll talk."

"This place is pretty nice. What is it?"

"You've never been to the library before?"

"I was messing with you."

I'm as gullible as the rest.

As we walk through the library, I note nothing has changed except for the people and a few new book displays. We grab seats in the back and I ask him, "Ladders, can you imagine a technique that instantly gives you confidence with girls?" Obviously, this kind of statement to a teenage boy will grab his attention, but also trigger a defense mechanism to protect his ego. These techniques are not designed as a pickup, but to build confidence and more, which results in higher attraction.

"Dude, I can pull girls."

"Of course you can, but stillness of the mind and body will add to your charisma."

Impatiently, Ladders asks, "What does stillness have to do with girls?"

"Listen." As I say this, my pupils dilate on command, shooting a mystical cool gaze with intent and boundaries set. The message is do not interrupt. "Today, we'll tackle stillness of the mind and body. Are you commanding your knee to bounce?"

"No. Again with my knee. What's your obsession with my knee?"

"We've been over this. Your knee moved without permission from your brain. This means your body is in control and not your mind. Pointless energy burned on an unproductive tick, making you look hyper, nervous, and out of control. How can you be a leader if you cannot control your own knee?"

"I don't think people care if my knee is moving or not."

"A confident man is full of energy and directs it wisely." I lean closer and lower my voice to regain full attention. "Here is the reason you should listen. Would the sight of a hyperactive knee attract a woman?"

"I don't know?"

I manage his slight defiance with a stare until he complies with the right answer.

"Probably not."

I stop talking to ensure he can absorb this information and then throw a book at him to keep him alert. This technique re-engages and grabs his attention. He catches it and responds.

"What was that? Why are you throwing books at me?"

"This is primal. Our primal nature requires a man to stay motionless for long periods, to control his breathing, and explode into action when necessary. If you are tracking animals and you are fidgety, what will happen?"

"The animals will either see or hear motion and flee."

"Right! And the *hombres* in your hunting party?"

"They'd be pissed at me."

"Your tribe will not tolerate weakness. Females are hard-wired to detect men with skills. Behavior in today's world that translates into old world skills has sex appeal. Can you name some?"

While I await Ladder's answer, I realize I miss the library. Free of loud talkers and music, it's a tranquil and organized place. Ladders pauses for twelve seconds before he answers. The time he takes before answering is a clue he's unsure, but willing to try. In his first attempt, he meekly says, "Would having a cool car be one of these skills?"

I appreciate his introspection before answering, but his tone repels me. I decide not to coddle him. "You are answering a question with a question and no confidence. Answer with gusto."

"Not moving."

"You're missing the point about stillness. Don't be a barnacle. Is a lazy guy who watches TV appealing?"

A few seconds pass, and he answers assertively, "Providing."

"This is true." I follow my borderline compliment with a quick review. "Behaviors jeopardizing group survival are turn offs. What is your solution?"

"Eliminate unnecessary motion."

"Here's the contradiction: there is a time to be still and a time for action. Purpose is the underlying factor. You must believe in your definitive reason for stillness or action."

We've been sitting too long. When teaching, it's essential to incorporate movement every eleven to fifteen minutes. Activity stimulates blood glucose to the brain, inciting greater concentration. We pace the perimeter of the library, past rows of literature, and a disheveled man slumped in a chair. As we walk, I ask, "Ladders, have you noticed anything significant yet?"

"Yes, I have. I thought about this after our first session and then again a few minutes ago. When you stare, there is intention."

"Go on."

"It feels like when you stare you send some kind of message, but I can't understand."

I showcase my reflective listening skills and reply, "And why can't you understand it?"

"I'm not sure. I have a lot on my mind."

"Let's sort it out. What's on your mind?"

"I'm kind of dating this girl, but I want to hang out with my friends too."

Wow, he's sharing details of his personal life, which means I've gained his trust. It's obvious to me his concentration is split. Reprimanding him to clear his mind is not the right tactic. Instead of restating his problem, I'll guide him towards developing his own solution. "How is a library organized?"

"Huh, what are you talking about?" he asks.

"Trust the process. How is a library organized?"

"They have books on shelves."

"If you were to do a research paper on how to kill head lice, how would you find the books?"

"Ask the librarian."

I didn't anticipate this answer since I avoid people. I'll have to reconfigure a new line of questioning. "Right, and how does the librarian retrieve the book so quickly?"

"The books are organized into different categories."

"Go find information on head lice."

"I don't have head lice. And I don't want to ask the librarian about head lice, as they'll think I have it."

"Why would you ask the librarian, when you could ask the nurses in the breezeway?"

"What nurses?"

"We walked by four nurses, and a table full of brochures on head lice and you didn't notice. Why do you think you missed it?"

"I was excited to tell you about the Mental Mind Force Manual."

"At that moment, you gave me your full attention because you were excited. While you are with me, my attention is on you, but I am still aware of my surroundings."

"It's confusing; you want me to focus on you, but at the same time observe other things?"

"Life is a contradiction. Your brain is like a library with random books. Organize your ideas, categorize them and you decide when to give them attention. Stillness of the mind takes practice."

"I have to keep my mind and body still?"

"Think of it as a battle against the enemy within."

"What am I fighting?"

"Fight your disorganization, your impatience, and unproductive impulses."

"I don't get it."

"Question the purpose of your thoughts and movements. For example, if your knee moves without permission, it's not serving a purpose. Punish its insubordination and flog your thigh, and further relapses will dwindle. Your hyperactivity is a sign of desired change, an opportunity to expand your awareness. Your assignment for the rest of the week is to listen to plants as you slowly water them."

"What have you been smoking?" he asks sarcastically.

"It's not profound. Listening to an organism drink can be remarkable or unremarkable. It's your decision. Regardless of how you play it, this exercise will slow your pace. Attack your restlessness with a heavy dose of slow. When we slowdown we can enjoy the details. Awareness expands and then you can focus on the details." The slowdown also disengages the aging process.

"I want adventure."

His answer is full of impatience. "The best adventures are often in the mind." Mine is full of Zen. "Scram before I throw more books at you."

To avoid being a hypocrite, this week I'll immerse myself in self-awareness and concentrate on simple tasks. The challenge is not to drop anything, stub my toes, or bump into walls for a week. Leaving the library, I see an anthill and devise a devious plot for a future Ladders' session and chuckle to myself.

## Chapter 8 Varla Returns

Roosters don't wake up this early and neither should I. The incessant metallic clanking from the brass knocker forces my hand. Before answering the door, I throw on slacks and inventory my attire: no shoes, no shirt, no belt, but I am donning my golden amulet. It's presentable, and visitors at 6:30 a.m. are not greeted with formal wear. The irritable sound of the knocker becomes tolerable as I sense Varla on the other side. Is she here to bust me? Is this one of those booty calls I've heard about? Whatever the reason, it's serious enough to warrant an early morning visit. I stand tall and greet her with an inviting smile.

"We need to talk," she says.

"Come right in."

She peers around at my barren walls and dearth of furniture. "Don't you have chairs?"

"Sure, they're outside, but probably damp from the marine layer."

"Why don't you have chairs inside?"

"If I had chairs inside, I'd be tempted to buy a green felt poker table, and then I'd be obligated to host a poker night. Believe me, you don't want poker players in your house. They smoke, drink and don questionable jewelry. Don't you see how chairs can lead to gambling and guys wearing jade rings?"

I can tell by her perplexed look, she's not following my logic and I realize she didn't come here to hear about my issues with gambling.

We chat in the plant room and I listen to her chronicle a tale of an enormous muscular man on horseback who banged on her apartment door and handed her a letter. Her description of him resembles the cover of a romance novel, but from what I've heard concerning The Horseman, he's suited for the cover of Soldier of Fortune. I warn her, "His name is Jeremiah, and he goes by the code name The Horseman."

"What a stupid code name," she says.

"I agree The Horseman is a stupid code name. Speaking of code names, if you don't have a code name already, may I recommend ZZ Top Heavy?" A well-earned, playful but sturdy punch to the gut accompanies my recommendation. "*Ooooof.*" I gladly eat a gut punch from this buxom vixen just to feel her touch.

"You got any more wisecracks about my boobs?"

Deeply sucking in air, I say, "Nope."

"I'm not calling him The Horseman. What do you know about Jeremiah?"

"He's The Foundation's enforcer. In three years, oddly, our paths have never crossed. What I know about him is he has anger issues, and he writes the rules and enforces them. Two of my friends lift weights with him and spin stories of him bench pressing horses and shot putting refrigerators. Even Claude and Alexandra stay clear of him."

"When Jeremiah handed me the letter, I pretended to read it while he waited. But I couldn't read it. I think it's in Esperanto."

"Then what happened?" I ask.

"Nothing. He tied his horse to a tree and stared at me. I stared back until he left."

"Do you have the letter with you?"

"Yeah, that's why I came here. I know you can read Esperanto."

"Let me see it, and please pitch a squat on the rug. I have some pillows for you to lounge on. I can light some candles and it will be like *1001 Arabian Nights*."

"Easy, snake charmer, I'm not sure I even know what that means."

"I don't either. I associate floor pillows with Middle Eastern culture."

"Would you read the letter already?"

The Foundation members typically read letters at sunrise but I don't. I don't understand the purpose and attribute it to another stupid tradition that I'll boycott. I reveal the gist of the letter to Varla. "It's an outline of how to exile a traitor, a Traitor Letter. I think Jeremiah presumes you and I ransacked Johnny Santos' house and stole the Movement Letter. I bet Jeremiah will be coming for me next. When he delivered the letter to your apartment, he expected you to attack, and when you didn't you confused him. That's my guess," I say.

"What's our move?" asks Varla.

"Since you didn't fight, maybe he expects we'll run, but if we run, they'll chase."

"I don't run."

"You've heard of the fight-or-flight response, but have you heard of the other two options?"

"I fight."

"What does a cat do when a dog corners it?"

"Hisses and arches its back."

"Right, the cat postures and when a dog rolls over and exposes its belly, that is voluntary submission. We have four options: fight, flight, posture, or submission."

She poses with her hands on her hips, bust thrust out and answers, "We're calling their bluff and posturing."

"We'll go right at them. Plan A is posturing and Plan B is war." I pretend to scratch the left side of my neck with my right hand to conceal the lump in my throat I swallowed. The Foundation has been my meal ticket and if I'm excommunicated, it's back to van life.

"Why does The Foundation think we stole the Movement Letter?" Varla asks.

"A few days ago, they sent Darcy to ask me to inscribe a Letter of Action to find a journalist who maybe in possession of the Movement Letter. Maybe they suspect I stole the Movement Letter and you are covering for me. It's a stretch, but it is plausible."

"Huh, I know all of this already. Remember, I came to your house, genius?"

I divert her attention. "Hey, stay with me. We need to get in tune with each other for this mission. When things get hot we must respond together. Do you agree?"

She cracks her knuckles and says, "I'm always ready to bang, but I get your point that we need to be prepared."

"Have you ever centered your energy?"

"Yeah."

"If you lose your center, are you able to reset your balance point on the spot?"

"What?"

"If you get nervous, can you ground yourself quickly?"

"I don't get nervous."

I rephrase, "Have you ever been tuned to another person's vibration?"

"You mean spiritually or sexually?"

Trying to ignore her distracting comment is challenging. "Hold my hand. What do you feel?"

"Your body temperature is cooler than mine."

"Wait ..."

"Now your hand is warmer. How did you warm your hand so quickly?"

"It's a Tibetan technique," I explain.

The Tibetan monks sit on snow-covered mountains draped in wet sheets and have contests to dry their sheets the fastest. They concentrate on raising their body heat to unbelievable levels. It's G-Tummo Vase Breathing.

"I raised my body temperature to be in sync with you," I continue. "This next part is weird; we have to make eye contact and hum the vowels of the alphabet in unison."

"McGurski, is this necessary?"

"Yup, hum it with me and exaggerate the sounds. AAAAAAA, EEEEEEE, IIIIIIII, OOOOOOOO, UUUUUUUU."

I give her a playful wink and smile as I say the Os in a groaning fashion. She smiles and rolls her eyes. "The vowels are our set point to become in tune with each other. If flustered, center yourself and repeat the vowels in your head to reconnect with me." The vibration of vowels contains a certain power because they supply the energy for each word. They are the mitochondria of each word.

"The humming vibration kind of feels good."

"Suspending judgment is a sign of being in tune."

"By the way, why does your house smell like dead cat and mustard?"

So much for suspended judgment. I laugh and tease her back, "You are the worst investigator; it's trout and asparagus. Didn't they teach you to check the trash for evidence?"

She barks back, "Mix in a shirt."

I "shirt up" as requested and proclaim, "Time for action. Let's pay the big man a visit."

## Chapter 9 Posturing

We've decided to posture and challenge the leading representative of The Foundation. Claude's been like a mentor to me, but I need answers. With Varla prepped and me donning a black merino wool shirt and my favorite brown velvet blazer, we make tracks. A fifteen-minute drive to Montecito brings us to a decadent world. The guest houses here dwarf my ranch. A squad of landscapers meticulously tend the lush greenery and mature trees. At this hour, nobody is expecting us, so we park outside the gate and walk through the unlocked pedestrian entrance way. The sprinklers are on, and carefully set to prevent water from hitting the pathway. The staircase and balusters leading to the estate are imported Italian marble. My lips are moving and my index finger is pointing as I count the steps of the staircase. Varla notices.

"What are you counting?"

"I count twenty-seven steps to the door. Twenty-seven is 3x3x3."

"Haven't you been here before?"

"Plenty of times."

"Do you always count the stairs?"

"How else can you tell if the number of steps hasn't changed?" I answer her in jest to conceal my obsession with numbers. Twenty-seven is a significant number. According to Alfred Weysen, twenty-seven is a lunar symbol, indicating the light in darkness. It is the symbol of the divine light. My obsession with numbers and symbols is manifesting.

"You got a thing for numbers?" she quietly asks.

"They don't call me The Count for nothing."

"Hey, Count for nothing," she gleefully busts.

I expect Claude to be displeased with our unannounced visit and snicker at the idea of him trying to hide his displeasure under the front of stoicism. He's Haitian, so maybe Varla can speak to him in French to soften him. Before discussing this idea with her, the double doors open and Claude stares at me. I've deduced from the slightest narrowing of his eyes the hint of annoyance. As expected, our early morning visit has elicited a reaction from Claude. Our presence has pierced his stoic armor, thus shifting control to me. Remarkably, it's close to 7 a.m. and he's already wearing a suit.

His bodyguards flank him on both sides and there is also one behind him. There's Creole Eddy from Louisiana; he's the talker of the group and claims he's a six-footer. If he's six-foot, then I'm six-foot-three. In reality, I'm a real six-footer and not prone to rounding up. Rangi and Loto are the Samoan brothers and represent the heavy muscle. I train in self-defense with them and call them The Good Time Boys. They're a wild bunch and each of them has benefited from Claude. Rangi has been improving his speech impediment but rarely speaks, Loto is overcoming dyslexia, and Eddy is learning how to read. Claude hired them and The Specialist developed a specific program for each one.

A quandary pops into my head. For a champion of balance, why would Claude have three guards instead of four? My mind races, 1+1+1=3, the square root of nine is three.

Three 3s equal nine, and 3x3x3=27. Is this a coincidence or have I crossed a threshold searching for symbolism?

Varla sizes up the bodyguards, scanning for strike points, and makeshift weapons in the room. The presence of his bodyguards agitates her. I sneak a glance, intending to reconnect. She's moving her lips and slightly sounding out the vowels. Claude catches it too and cracks a slight smile. To me, stoicism comes naturally, although I actively rebel against it. Choosing an expression appropriate for each situation can be daunting, but with Varla, my emotions are fluid and evident from my unforced smile. I'm pleased she is practicing my lesson in an active environment.

Claude ends the smile fest with an unusually cheeky remark. "McGurski, have you been getting into mischief?"

I hand him the Traitor Letter. "Jeremiah, delivered this to the wrong person."

He defuses the tense situation by merely saying, "Interesting." He excuses himself with the letter to an eastern facing balcony.

There are hundreds of possible scenarios. Do they suspect I retrieved the missing Movement Letter from Johnny Santos? Is this a setup? I catch myself, as this worrying is unproductive. I re-center my chi and reconnect by gazing into Varla's eyes.

Claude returns and says, "Varla, in your interview, you stated you could read Esperanto. If you read this Traitor Letter, you would have known Jeremiah was calling you out. You don't strike me as the kind of person to back down from a fight."

"I didn't understand it, so I brought the letter to McGurski," says Varla.

"One reason we hired you is because you said you could read Esperanto."

"I can read the words, I just don't understand it."

That's actually pretty witty.

"As a consequence for misleading The Foundation, I'm giving you two choices: to be exiled, or study Esperanto and the metaphysical arts with McGurski."

I'm impressed with her poise and direct eye contact with him.

"Let's drink to this solution," she says. She draws power from her answer. In a delicate situation, she flashes style and style is rare.

In an instant, Eddy serves us mimosas in handmade champagne flutes. The precision of this blown glass betrays its origin.

In Esperanto I ask, "Been shopping in Venice recently? These glasses are handsome."

He breaks into a real smile. With much pride, he answers in Esperanto, "You have a keen eye."

When we first arrived, I upset him and it showed. I have pleased him with a compliment. I'm manipulating him like a chiropractor and adjusting him back into balance. I cut to the chase. "If Jeremiah visits Varla again, I will activate his dental plan."

Ignoring my bravado, he responds, "We appreciate your inscriptions. Deal with Jeremiah on your terms, but be wary of him. I've seen him punch through a brick wall." He then turns and directly addresses Varla. "Keep R. W. on the path. You two may leave."

We witness Claude securing the Traitor Letter in a file and head toward the front door.

I reflect on this encounter. We witnessed an unusual and full range of Claude's emotional expression and loquaciousness. Varla's female charms could have affected him. Her allure could topple a stern man of discipline, or maybe his light behavior is fueled from an obsession to create balance. He's shown us a light side of himself … so now he'll reveal his dark side. It all comes back to the symbolism of twenty-seven; the light in darkness! The lunar cycle or, in Claude's case, the lunatic cycle.

The front door shuts and Varla says, "That was intense."

"It's not over. My guess is that in twenty-seven seconds he'll release The Good Time Boys on us." Although I'm friends with Eddy, Rangi, and Loto, if Claude is making a point, it's business.

"Why? He likes us. He complimented—"

"This is different. Run to the trees." I run toward the staircase and jump over the balusters near the closest sprinkler. Landing on the grass, the water puddles around my shoes and bubbles. "They'll be coming out in a second, move."

"You're paranoid; nobody is coming for us. Go sing the alphabet. Remember, you said before if you run, the dogs will chase us."

"Move!" I shout.

"What am I missing?"

I torque the closest sprinkler head, readjusting the stream to point at the staircase. A blast of water hits Varla, and the water drenches her chest. She bites her lip, no doubt to stifle a barrage of curse words, and waves both of her clenched fists at me. Simultaneously, The Good Time Boys burst through the front door.

Her eyes open as wide as her mouth as she says the obligatory, "Oh boy!" She hastily hops over the baluster, firmly landing on the grass. Her soaked tight yellow blouse clings to her massive triple D chest.

We're in the middle of a dangerous OP and I'm rubbernecking to check her boobs bounce in a wet shirt. My breast fetish is as exposed as her chest. Eddy, Rangi, and Loto wipe out on the slippery marble staircase and land hard. My trap sprang us loose.

I knew once we were off his property, we would be safe. I'm relieved I didn't have to tangle with my buddies. We'd anticipate each of our moves and besides Sarrick, The Good Time Boys are my only friends.

We board the van and catch our breath.

"Our first successful mission together. We make a good team."

"Stop staring at my tits."

I flew too close to the sun, so my only response is full admission. "Oh, my bad."

It's time to brief Varla on some of The Foundation's dirty secrets. "Claude's obsession with balance is a cover for his bipolar episodes. I recall one scenario in which I delivered a letter to him and he released his four bull mastiffs on me. He loves technique applied properly and tries to pull my strings to force me into revealing what techniques are in my quiver. Knowing this, I rely on my wits to create alternative means to defeat the obstacles without resorting to technique."

"If Claude plays these games with you, why do you keep coming back?" Varla asks.

"Great question. It's a cat-and-mouse game. I come back each time to outwit him. Today, he tested to see if I would rely on the techniques from The Movement Letter. Running at twenty-five miles per hour would prove to him I had the missing letter. No tip of the hat to him. Ingenuity sealed the victory in this round. The win goes to McGurski and friends."

## Chapter 10 Intermittent Explosive Disorder

On the drive back to the ranch, Varla sits comfortably in the van with her legs propped on the dashboard and asks me how I joined The Foundation.

"Before The Foundation recruited me, I drifted and lived in my van. My disorders either prevented me from acquiring a job or retaining one. Claude knew my background and brought me to The Specialist. According to The Specialist, the right hemisphere of my brain had a deficient connection to the left hemisphere. This disconnection caused my antisocial behavior, hyperactivity, silliness, and aloofness. Given a choice between prescription medicine and a daily regimen to strengthen the connections, I chose the exercises. The specific exercises stimulate my right brain activity and resulted in reduced symptoms."

"Were they trying to fix you?"

"There is no chance of making me normal, but I gained more self-control."

Exploration and personal discovery is what compels me to continue this path. Before training with The Specialist, the only emotion I could identify was confusion. Confusion was easy to recognize because I caused it regularly. The rest of my emotions are no longer a mystery. Recognizing the range of emotions within myself and people has been a notable breakthrough. Throughout my obstacles, I maintain gratitude and awareness it could be worse. I continue, "Have you heard of the *DSM-5*?"

"Yeah, it stands for the *Diagnostic and Statistical Manual of Mental Disorders 5th edition.*"

Wow, she knows her stuff. "The *DSM-5* is The Foundation's playbook."

"What do you mean?" Varla asks.

"In order to be a member of their order, you must have a disorder."

"This makes sense. I have my share of disorders," says Varla.

"Besides ADD?" I ask.

"Oh yeah, I'm violent too. Have you ever heard of IED?"

"Isn't that a bomb? An Improvised Explosive Device? I once dated a girl on the Air Force Explosive Ordinance Disposal Team (EOD)."

"No, the disorder IED. It stands for Intermittent Explosive Disorder. IED makes bipolar look tame."

"Never heard of it."

"It's in the *DSM.*"

"Everything is in the book. What are the symptoms?"

"Extreme rage and an inability to resist aggressive, impulsive behavior. When I have an episode, I'm alive and energetic, but afterwards I binge eat and feel like garbage. I tried smoking weed to self-medicate, but the munchies wrecked my portion control. After a while, I didn't care and got nice and plump."

"I like a woman with meat on her bones."

"Good, because I have no plans on losing weight."

It's the best news of the day; her wide hips, juicy butt, and big bouncy boobs are not candidates for slimming modifications.

"I love to wear tight outfits. It gives men and women fits. That's why I have no friends. I move from one lover to the next, because once they experience an IED episode they leave."

A classic conundrum: men fawn over her and women are jealous. I could withstand anything this vixen could dish out. "When you explode, what kind of trouble do you get into?"

"All kinds, any kind, and every kind. When I was in the Army, one time in the break room, I was watching this movie, *The Naked Kiss*. In the opening scene, this chick beats the hell out of her pimp. Unfortunately, I didn't see the rest of the film because these two jerks kept laughing. They said no woman could beat them in a fight."

"The Army did a fantastic brainwash on those knuckleheads."

"Yeah, and I was there to dry them up. I emasculated them enough to step outside. Behind our dorm, the civil engineers were building a wooden fence around an electrical power box. On the weekends, soldiers cut loose playing football behind the dorm. One errant tackle knocked out half the power grid for the base. The half-built fence briefly served as a safeguard. When the first guy stepped outside, I side kicked him in the stomach, plunging him through the wooden fence. His friend scrambled to help him and got touched up."

"What did you do to his friend?"

"I bashed him baseball style with the flat part of a fence post to his chest. It's times like that I miss being in the

Army. I served what I called knuckle dustings to guys and they would never narc on me because they could not admit a woman beat them up."

Besides fisticuffs, she reveled in sharing stories of racing cars on windy roads, and accumulating speeding tickets, with enough moving violations to suspend her driver's license. The discovery of road rage fueled her passion for speed, reckless driving, and rumbles. Her variety of road rage surpassed the middle finger and shouted expletives. She achieved vindication on the road and turned her rage into an expression of art. The German-American poet Charles M. Bukowski said, "To do a dangerous thing with style is what I call art." I would not disagree with Bukowski or Varla. She pulled out a neatly folded police report from her purse and proudly handed her trophy to me. It read: "At approximately 11:55 p.m., California Highway Patrol assisted Santa Barbara Police with a road rage incident resulting in assault and aggravated battery on the side of Highway 54 in Santa Barbara County. An involved party was transported to The Santa Barbara Regional Emergency Center with critical injuries. The alleged perpetrator is a Hispanic female in her early twenties driving a white foreign sports car. Santa Barbara Police has an ongoing investigation. Santa Barbara Crime Stoppers is offering a $30,000 reward for information leading to an arrest."

My lone comment is, "They blame everything on the Mexicans."

"That was from my first road rage incident and I got a bounty on my head. This idiot pulled out in front of me in a yellow corvette."

I don't have to press for details, she's eager to share, and she captures my attention with the word, "Idiot."

"I slammed on my brakes and almost crashed into him. He kept driving through the canyon like nothing happened. I peeled out in hot pursuit. The roads are twisty, but I caught him: He couldn't drive for shit and he couldn't shake me. I flipped him the high beams, and he flipped me the bird. Craving the thrill, I pulled alongside him and gently nudged his back quarter panel. The fiberglass caved in on his tire and spun him out. This middle-aged man stumbles out of his hot rod and pretends to be tough. He wasn't so macho after I blasted him with a straight left jab and right cross, smashing his face. He curled into a ball on the ground to protect himself while I kicked him until my legs tired. When the fun wore off, I split."

"First road rages are always the sweetest."

"When you're fifteen-years-old, how do you relate to other girls when your role models come from the movies, *Faster Pussycat Kill Kill* and *Mad Max?* I mean, *Mad Max* is a movie about a prolonged road rage. I couldn't wait for my first road rage."

"Have you ever worn it, for the worse?"

"Once, a biker gang messed me up. Two bikers pulled out in front of me and then slowed down. I tend to escalate things fast, and cleaved them off the road. The six bikers behind me pulled along both sides of my car and smashed my windows with their helmets. Glass flew into my face, and I lost control of my rig. With my car smooshed in, the bikers lifted me out of the wreckage and got their licks in. The hospital held me for one week with a broken arm and shattered ribs."

Asking her if she is afraid of being shot is an unnecessarily silly question that only a normal person would ask. I figure out she's not worried about being shot because it is worth the risk. I imagine a scenario in the future where Varla comes home from work and I ask her, "How was your day today? Any good brawls?" and she replies, "Super, I road raged three guys." To which I respond, "Splendid, Muffin, I'll grab the hydrogen peroxide for your knuckles." She slugs me in the stomach and says, "Nobody calls me Muffin."

"In the Army, the medics had my height, weight, and birthdate memorized. How often can you attend drill with your face busted or your arm in a sling? The answer apparently is four. I never claimed to fall down stairs or off my bicycle. For three incidents, I wrote cage fighting as the cause of injury. My last excuse was alligator wrestling. When the Army officially launched an investigation into my conduct, they concluded I had unusual proclivities for violence and diagnosed me with IED. The Army's solution was to dope me with the equivalent of horse tranquilizers. The pills stole my identity. My drive and zest were chemically sedated."

"Did the Army medically discharge you?"

"No, they kicked me out for trouncing three officer's wives. You see, the medication wore off by night, and I went to the club wearing a tight outfit. I heard these chicken heads commenting about my clothes, so I thrashed them. I received an 'Other than Honorable' discharge. It would have been a dishonorable discharge, but the judge did not like those smarmy ladies, either. Try landing a job with Other than Honorable on your record."

"I betcha Alexandra and Claude tried to exploit that."

"Alexandra said she knew people who could expunge my record and change it to an honorable discharge. They said The Foundation would teach me how to harness my rage and hired me to be their investigator. Whoever heard of an investigator with ADD? It's funny but this job has helped me focus."

"The Foundation has helped me too," I add.

"My lifestyle isn't for the timid. I've gone through a lot of men, weed, cars, and a few women, but since joining The Foundation, I've been pretty chill. But I still harass Crime Stoppers with fake leads."

Is she warning me about the dangers of getting involved with her? How do I let her know I'm the man for her? I volley back her statement about crime stoppers. "I bet you shout at them demanding the reward."

"Nobody is stupid enough to cover that bet." She's hip to the crooked odds.

In my mental catalog, I list her hobbies as scrapping—not the scrapbook varietal—and road rage. We'll leave it to the travel agents to decide which countries are best to visit for road rage. What is atrocious to the masses is normal for us. Varla and I choose to surround ourselves with disorder because we can no longer tolerate the normal, cliché, and obviousness from the general population. We live outside of society. My slow burning resentment towards social norms and acceptance of disorder waits for someone to stoke my wild flame. Varla might be the one. Modest visionaries hang banners and hand out business cards with cute slogans geared at the masses, "Break free with me and you'll lower your cholesterol." As if lowering their LDL (Bad) cholesterol would solve their ordinary existence. Together, our treachery will shake the masses.

## Chapter 11 High Fiving Awesomers Report

We arrive at my ranch, although I don't remember driving at all as we were engrossed in conversation. Inside, we continue our chat, surrounded by my plants. The plants are the focal point of the living room. There is no need for a tour of the other living spaces. My office is furnished with a desk, a computer, and a swivel chair. In the bedroom, there are a few articles of clothing hanging in the closet and a bed. A spartan lifestyle is free of clutter.

Varla scans the assortment of plants and asks, "You got any weed?"

Déjà vu. "No, but it's ironic the purpose of these plants is to filter the smell of weed."

"Do you grow?" she asks in excitement.

"My neighbor did, before the police busted him. Overnight, the plants became orphans, and I've been fostering them ever since. My parents would be proud; they taught me the importance of fostering and adopting."

"Why is the purple flower with fuzzy leaves away from the rest?"

"The African Violet. It prefers solitude," I whisper to her, so the other plants don't hear. "It's my favorite, but it doesn't like to be touched. In fact, if you touch its furry leaves, that leaf will most likely wilt and fall off. It thrives with a bit a sunlight, water, and solitude."

Varla squeezes my shoulder. "You're no African Violet."

She has changed me.

Varla spreads out on the floor pillows and lays on her side. I sit a few feet away and have no problem maintaining my eye contact. After sharing details of our private lives, Varla responds with the perfect question from someone with ADD to someone with ADHD. "Is McGurski an Irish or Polish name?"

I laugh. "Unpredictability at its best."

She insists, "What's the story?"

"It's Polish; my grandfather arrived at Ellis Island with a bunch of Irish. When my grandfather said his name, the immigration officer wrote it as McGurski, instead of Magurski."

"Why didn't he change it back?"

"Too much red tape. Coincidently, he married an Irish woman."

"So how did you learn Esperanto?"

"My Polish grandfather and Irish grandmother fell in love, but due to pride or stubbornness, they would not learn each other's native tongue. They compromised and spoke Esperanto. When they moved to New York, I don't know why they didn't learn English. My father grew up speaking Esperanto at home and English everywhere else."

"Your dad taught you Esperanto?"

This brings back fond memories. "He taught me in a most unusual manner. Before tucking me into bed, I gave him my full attention while he recapped his entire day in Esperanto. It's a tough way to learn a language, but ... oh well. The first word I learned was *kafo*, which means coffee. His day began with *kafo*. From coffee to fluency. It sounds like a cheesy title for a language course. My father and I rarely spoke Esperanto outside of our house. Occasionally, we heard rumors of secret societies speaking Esperanto or hipster journalists chasing a cold lead connecting Esperanto to European cults."

"Besides speaking with your dad, did you ever speak Esperanto before you joined The Foundation?"

"There was one time, while pitching mail at the embassy in Kuwait. I overheard two dignitaries speaking in Esperanto. Without breaking stride, I walked past them, and said, *Saluton viro*. It's the equivalent of saying, 'Hey man.' At that time, their body language and facial expressions meant nothing to me. Although, what I said had to be noteworthy, because before turning the corner, one of them jotted notes in his planner while staring at me."

"I figured you'd be rusty. Was it hard to relearn?"

"Esperanto is part of my heritage, so there's no rust due to the simplicity. You'll see it's the easiest language to learn."

"What is this pyramid for?"

Her ADD is something else. "When you're ready, I'll show you."

"I like the name McGurski. It's a great name. Speaking of names, why did Claude say, 'Keep R. W. on the path?' Who's R. W.?"

I reply with zest, "R. W. is my name. R. W. McGurski."

"How did I miss that? Nice to meet you, R. W."

"I bet you twenty bucks there's a laundry receipt with my name on it in the trash."

"Again with the trash. Do you think all investigators rifle through trash?"

"I did."

"You were an investigator?"

"Yeah, but not for The Foundation. I handled investigations for a law firm. I didn't last long because I wrote a report called *The High Fiving Awesomers*."

"You gotta be kidding me. I've read *The High Fiving Awesomers*. All the investigation schools in California are using it as example. It's kind of the 'do not do checklist' of reporting. You're a legend."

"Infamous."

"Right from the beginning you set the tone, 'Narrating this mess is my service to you. You'll see, it's in my report.' And you wrote it in the first person narrative."

"You're over here quoting lines from my report, like a cool line from a movie."

"Every investigator in my class read *The High Fiving Awesomers*. We'd quote it throughout the day, 'If you don't buy lunch today, I will throw you through three sheets of drywall.'"

"Should I be flattered?"

"Absolutely. It's your opus."

"I've waited for the right person to share my motivation for writing *The High Fiving Awesomers*. Would you like to be the first?"

"Really?"

"Give me a back rub and I'll explain."

"Deal."

I'm no longer an African Violet; I can be touched. Varla's fingers dig deep into my shoulders. Her massage style can be described as a vice grip. "My cases involved workers' compensation fraud. There is an industry devoted to catching humans faking injuries. I solved most of my cases by rummaging through their trash. What these imbeciles throw away taught me more about human nature than the entire *DSM.*"

"What could you have possibly found in the trash?"

"I found receipts for indoor rock climbing, bowling, gym memberships, and golf scorecards. You present this evidence to the scoundrel, and they quit in lieu of court."

"I got to get my hands dirty more often," Varla says quietly to herself.

"Finally, the firm sent me on a different type of case. Our client insisted that a certain sales company had brainwashed their son."

"Juicy."

"I thought so too, and it turns out their son was the ringleader."

My hunch is Varla does not want kids, but if we have a son, we'll be proud if he masterminds a cult. We can't go to a justice of the peace to be married, as that would be too ironic. We'd have to go to a judge, but there'd be a judgment and maybe warrants.

"You mean the half-pint with his shirt aggressively tucked in?" she says, quoting more of the report.

"Drawing attention to the different levels of shirt tucking is a pivotal detail."

"I've read the report, but I need the backstory. What really went on?"

"It's a real horror show. They were everywhere."

"Who?"

"The High Fiving Awesomers were masquerading as salesmen from this company. It was a three-day sales retreat. To breach their inner walls, I filled out an online application and jabbered my way through a phone interview."

"Classic infiltration."

"The convention center concealed the motives of over three hundred High Fiving Awesomers and me, the interloper. For the first twenty minutes, we practiced our greetings. Smile, maintain eye contact, and firm handshakes to each of the nine High Fiving Awesomers at my table. At least three of the Awesomers ask me, 'Why are your hands so sweaty?'"

Varla reaches to touch my dry hands. Confirming her touch, she says, "Your hands don't sweat"

"They used to. But get this, I answered their question by saying, 'Yes.'"

"That doesn't make sense."

"I know, that's why it's the perfect answer. It takes your mind away from the sweat."

"Or they're thinking this guy is sweaty *and* weird."

"I went to the bathroom to wash my hands and before returning, I overhear my table mates say, 'He's so sweaty, it's gross. I don't want to shake his hand.'

"'Yeah, and he's always going to the bathroom, do you think he's doing blow?'

"'He's so weird and his breath stinks too.'

"'Did you see his dandruff?'

"'Give him a break. The dude is a mess. I think he's on the spectrum.'

"One guy sticks up for me, but being on the spectrum is not an excuse for poor hygiene. I want to kick them all in the nuts, the women included. When I get back to the table, I lighten things up by saying, 'Are we still practicing sweaty handshakes?' Crickets ... my self-deprecating humor sails over their low-brow intellect."

"I would have fought the entire table."

"I probably should have. Now, The High Fiving Awesomers might never be stopped. Their legions are spreading. In every situation, awesomeness flowed from their mouths, 'Male high-fiver wins an award for high sales numbers ... yeaaaaah! He's awesome! How awesome is that? That's awesome!' High fives all around. When the word awesome is said, they love to use the contraction 'that's' in front or in the rear. Like, "that's awesome!" or "how awesome is that?'"

"I remember this line in your report. It was hilarious: 'They could awesome a speck.' Now I get what you're talking about. These jerks awesome everything."

"It gets worse. To distinguish their varieties, I divided the High Fiving Awesomers into categories. High Fivers inexplicably slap hands to express their jubilance. While Awesomers resist their temptation for high fives, but their verbal expressions are limited to awesome and amazing. The High Fiving Awesomer is the worst combination of both traits. And finally, there is The Holiday Awesomer whose favorite question is 'Are you ready for the holidays?' They mimic the Griswold's super lit up house. When a Holiday Awesomer asks you, 'So, are you ready for the holidays?' what are you going to say?"

"Shut up."

"The direct approach. With eyes wide open, I like to say, 'I'm ready for anything.'"

"I think being ready is yuppie code for completing holiday shopping and stringing lights," she adds.

"Yeah, if a neighbor tries to shame you to hang lights and calls you Scrooge, that's a sign you're winning. It's not peer pressure if they're not my peer."

"What if an Awesomer told you, 'Have an awesome Christmas,' what would you say?"

"How would a crow respond to such verbal rubbish?"

"Huh?"

"Exactly. I'd resort to a PSY-OP mind-clouding technique. I'd torment the Awesomers with a well-placed, 'Caw!' The Awesomer would clearly hear me caw, but crow chatter is so distant from their expectation of a response, they'll pretend they heard me cough. Their desperation to rationalize my crow call divides us. There is no way for me or a crow to relate to them."

"You're nuts, but I like it. So, after all the awesoming, you found out that the half-pint was the ringleader. How did his parents react?"

"My boss never gave them the report."

"What! That's criminal."

"I was stuck; if I wrote a straightforward report, the clients would have been in denial and refused to pay. Either way, my greedy boss missed a payday. So, I wrote a retaliation against societal norms."

"Tragic. We should track down the client and give them your opus."

"I'm not sure if you're serious or not."

"Don't worry, I'm on the case."

"*The High Fiving Awesomers* became less of a report and more of a misanthropic manifesto. Throughout my life, humans mocked my eccentric behavior, so I gave it back to them in my report."

"Humans? What are you, a space alien?"

"Maybe. I distinguish between those that alienate, and call them humans versus people. I guess High Fiving Awesomers have the potential to be people too. My challenge is relating to them."

"I always saw *The High Fiving Awesomers* as comedy, but it's deep and relatable. My weight, having big boobs, a big butt, and battles with IED and ADD have been challenges for me, too. I've been judged and called a bimbo because of my curves and the way my brain is wired."

I'm not sure what to do or say, so I give her a hug and whisper to her, "You are exceptional." In a minute, she's digging for more details. For an investigator with ADD, she's tops.

"What did your boss say?"

"She first asked me if the report was a joke. Then she fired me for wasting time and money."

"You are a martyr."

The dialogue inside my head is saying two different things. One side says make a move and kiss her. The other side is saying to wait. At this stage of our relationship, we are building comfort and, for me, an unfamiliar thing called trust. Our foundation, so to speak, is being set for the enchantment stage. Delayed gratification will make the actual event spectacular.

"I'm a martyr? That's high praise. I've always seen myself as a mystic imbecile."

"Oh, you are that too," she says with a playful laugh.

"Thanks." And then I prove her point with my next question. "Do you think Alexandra wears pantyhose?"

"What? Why do you want to know?"

"I remember pantyhose were popular in the 1980s, but now, besides bank robbers and employees at chicken wing restaurants, do women still wear pantyhose?"

Varla rubs her thick thighs to her calves as if trying to stir up memories of wearing pantyhose. A simple but erotic motion. She gives me a wink with those gorgeous golden eyes and smiles, knowing she's in control. "I don't wear pantyhose, but I think Russian women do, because it's so cold."

Her answer is ridiculous. She's bluffing, she's as clueless as me. "I've got an idea. What do you say about seeing The Specialist together?"

"Why?"

"Trust me, it's going to be fun. I'll meet you outside her office on Tuesday at 9:00 a.m. Bring two pairs of pantyhose."

"I don't even know if I have pantyhose. What do you need pantyhose for?"

"You'll see. It's a surprise."

"I should be investigating the Santos case, but whatever. I'll see you Tuesday."

## Chapter 12 Ladders, the Destroyer

The sound of crunching leaves reminds me of my neglected raking and Ladders' session. I don't hear his bike brakes. But the thud of his bike being slammed is unmistakable. Before he can knock on the door, I greet him.

"Did you spray the brakes with WD-40?"

"Something like that."

"Come around to the backyard. I have an important question for you."

"I'm ready."

He's my protégé alright. The McGurski way is to be ready for anything. To be sure he's ready, I lightly punch him in the arm and say, "Go!" We race to the backyard. The forty-yard dash is lopsided. When Ladders reaches me, I ask him, "Are you a destroyer or a creator?"

Ladders sticks his chest out and answers, "I'm a destroyer."

"The world needs both. If you turn out to be a destroyer, I'll teach you the ways of combat. If you're a creator, I'll teach you to how to build."

"Build what? Cars? Houses?"

"Creating healthy relationships and then how to build an empire."

"In history, I read Genghis Khan conquered half the world."

This is a milestone in our relationship—he's sharing his knowledge with me. "You're right. What did he destroy?"

"Towns, cities, and people."

"What else?"

"Nothing."

"He also destroyed relationships and happiness."

"Why do you care so much about relationships?

I stop to reflect. At thirty-nine-years-old, I'm gradually appreciating the value of relationships. Varla's role in this development is obvious.

Ladders continues, "But a destroyer crushes people."

Everyone is a hypocrite. A deep thought triggers me. I wrestle control back from the distraction. "Yes, if that's what you desire."

"Awesome."

I tilt my head away from him and deliberately deep breathe through my nostrils in hopes to assuage the dreadful word awesome. "Please choose a different superlative," I say while clenching my jaw to accentuate my displeasure of this word.

"What's a superlative?"

"An adjective that describes greatness."

Ladders shrugs his shoulders and says, "Okay."

To regain his attention and prove a point, I chuck my shoe through the kitchen window. He's startled and turns to me with eyes wide open, as if he witnessed a crime. His expression hints that he might think I'm nuts.

"Whoa!"

"That's what I call an attention grabber. It took a second to destroy the window, but how long does it take to build a window?"

"I don't know."

"Guess."

"Two days?"

"What can you conclude from this costly demonstration? Answer wisely, or my other shoe is aiming for you."

He readies himself with his hands covering his face and answers, "It's faster to destroy than build."

"Right. Can anyone throw a shoe through a window?"

"If they are crazy enough like you."

"Not everyone can build a window. Destroying is easy and popular. Please explain this in your own words."

"Destroyers have competition, because it's easy."

"Excellent. To be a destroyer, you'll have to be creative with your destruction. This week's interesting assignment is spying on a colony of ants."

"Way boring."

"A successful destroyer is patient with his time and studies his enemy. If conflict is necessary, he directs his energy to destroy. Valhalla will await you or the ants."

"You lost me. What's a Valhalla?

"Valhalla is a mythical place where heroes killed in battle dine with the Nordic god Odin."

"Oh, that's nice. What does Valhalla have to do with ants?"

"My point is, under what circumstances would you destroy an ant colony?"

"Ants are stupid and they annoy me."

"Ah ha. If you spy on them, you might change your mind."

"Do you like ants?"

"Ants are explorers, survivalist, fearless, strong; they are nature's cleaners, creators, and destroyers. If you have no cause to destroy, then you don't destroy." Cripes, I gave away the meat of the lesson.

"Why would you kill ants?" Ladders innocently asks.

"In a survival situation, I'd eat them. Also, did you know you can use ant mandibles as stitches?"

"No, I didn't know that. How does that work?"

Wow, I can tell he is excited to learn about stitches because he is maintaining eye contact and patiently waiting. "You place an army ant over your open wound and squeeze its thorax so it will bite around the wound. When it bites, you rip off the rest of the body, leaving the head and mandibles clamped on the wound."

"Does that hurt?"

"Oh yeah, but less than an infection."

"McGurski, are you trying to talk me out of being a destroyer?"

"I'm teaching you the formula of what is worthy for destruction."

Ladders smiles a devious smile and shares, "Since there are countless destroyers and few creators, I should destroy destroyers."

"Countless? I hate this sad word, as it has lost its faith in numerology." He's probably under Alexandra's influence. I know she refers to the thirty-one annual festivals she attends as countless.

"I can't say 'awesome' or 'countless' around you? Any other forbidden words?"

"No high fives."

"Okay, but seriously, since there are a lot of destroyers and a few creators, I should destroy the destroyers."

"Listen you little psychopath, those video games are corrupting your brain," I say jokingly. "Check this out." I grab a phone book out of my recycling bin and provide an analogy. "A phone book serves no purpose anymore, it's a nuisance left at the doorstep. I will destroy this phonebook by ripping it in half and shall give it purpose. One, two, three!" Applying a firm grip, hands one inch apart, I bend the book and explosively pull my hands apart, popping my chest out for leverage. The paper splits as my hand pulls away in opposite directions to my waist. The two pieces of the ripped phone book dangle from my hands. I release my grip for dramatic effect and, *plop*, the paper hits the ground and my tribute to vaudeville (old time feats of strength) is over.

"That was awe—" he self-corrects before saying awesome, "I mean cool."

He's learning.

"You got to teach me how to do that."

"Go for a bike ride with your video games; they need sunlight and fresh air."

"Later."

After Ladders departs, I enter the kitchen and sweep the glass from the window into a small pile. Instead of throwing it in the garbage, I set it aside. As I duct tape a piece of cardboard over the window, I think about Varla. I'll see her again tomorrow morning. When and how should I make the first move?

## Chapter 13 Poet Von Squeeze

It's 9 a.m. on Tuesday and I'm standing tall, waiting on the sidewalk outside The Specialist's office. It's located in a typical strip mall on Cliff Drive that comes complete with a martial arts studio, grocery, family dentist, and more. Her office is on the second floor and is above them all in purpose too.

I hear what can only be Varla's car screeching tires around the turn. She drifts in to parallel park, the smell of burned tires accompanying her wherever she goes. My eyes fixate on her car door, I can't wait to see her. The door flies open door as she sticks one leg out seductively. She's wearing a tight short dress and pantyhose!

"This turn you on, buster?"

"Yes!" A simple answer for a simple question.

She exits her car provocatively, each motion a tease for my eyes, and then hurls an oval object at me. "Here's your pantyhose, freak."

I catch the plastic egg-shaped container and examine it with curiosity. "They're in here? Do I have to hatch it?"

"They don't call them pantyhose anymore. The old ladies in the department store called them nylons."

"Good to know." I tear my pair of nylons in half, ripping them from the middle of the crotch and give Varla one legging.

"What are you doing? Those cost eight bucks."

"Money well spent." I stretch the pantyhose over my head smooshing my nose and distorting my other facial features. I gesture for Varla to do the same.

"We robbing a bank?" she asks with alarming vigor.

"Even better; the plan is to bust through The Specialist's door wearing nylons on our heads and scare the crap out of her."

"I think it would be even more terrifying if we knock on her door wearing the nylons on our heads while holding helium balloons."

The second-floor window of The Specialist's office opens, and she sticks her head out. "I can hear you two; take those hose off your head and get in here."

Mama bear has spoken and foiled our plans.

We march up one flight of stairs to her office. It's less of an office and more of a cross between a gym, a laboratory, and romper room. The walls are lined with skill and strength-building equipment such as a Purdue Pegboard to increase hand-eye coordination and finger dexterity, a balance beam, a rack of free weights, and a fifteen-foot braided climbing rope hanging from the vaulted ceiling.

The Specialist greets us with a warm, "Hello."

I reply, "Greetings."

And Varla reciprocates with, "Hey."

The Specialist is unfazed by our attempt to rattle her and carries on with her business. I don't know her real name and don't care. She's a pro's pro, with the body of a gymnast. She's in her fifties but I bet she could still easily do a standing backflip. Her hair is in a French braid similar to the climbing rope.

"Go into the white room and follow the instructions; I'll check in on you two in an hour," says The Specialist.

Varla and I sojourn into the white room. It contains two desks, two chairs, no windows, a sheet of paper, and a pen on each desk. The instructions are to spend an hour on creative writing. We trust her process and without question we partake in the exercise in hopes of further unlocking our potential.

For thirty-nine minutes, the only sound in the sanitized white room is our pen nibs on paper. Periodically, I peer at Varla and draw a blank about how to make an advance on her. She breaks the silence with her declaration of a completed assignment and wants to share.

She stands to read to her audience of one. "I call this, *Varla's Book of Knuckle Sandwich Poetry.*"

Upon hearing the title, I turn away and bite my lip to prevent myself from laughing.

She proudly reads, "*Containing my rage, inspiring others, release, empty afterwards. I'm counting this as my rage.*"

I count my blessings she's in a good mood.

"*Today doesn't happen for everyone, get in line.*"

Standard angry prose.

"*It should be all here, because I'm not.*"

Attention deficit inspired prose.

"*Go chop wood.*"

Nice, I can imagine her telling me to, "Go chop wood." I act it out by trying to karate chop the desk.

*"The badge says 'Visitor, is that your name?'"*

I protest her plagiarism. "Hey you stole that one from my war journal. Have you been spying on me?"

"You were so quiet, so I was testing you to see if you were listening. As far as spying … maybe." She continues, *"Sometimes, I look in the mirror and don't know that it is me. Sometimes, I look in the mirror and am surprised that it is me. It is all impression."*

She's probably referring to what she looks like before and after a fight.

*"If I become a professional wrestler, here are the names for my finishing moves:*

*Burning Rubber*

*Slug Knot*

*Lariats of Fire*

*Hand of Doom*

*Ten of Clubs – the two-handed punch*

*Back of the Hand, Back to Land."*

Varla, as a professional wrestler, sounds reasonable.

*"If I drop an anchor on your face, that should slow one of us down."*

Ahoy, sailor, catch this.

*"Violence never solved anything, but it always made me feel better."*

There is power in the truth.

*"If there is a fire in the bathtub, don't expect me to take a bath."*

I'm an ice bath guy.

"What do you think?"

"That is the most aggressive poetry I've ever heard. Even your soft side is hard."

She takes a bow and a curtsy. "Thank you, let's hear yours."

I take Varla's cue and stand to read as well, while she lies on top of her desk and listens.

"*Escape from the Grip* by R. W. McGurski. I've been told I resemble a movie villain with my long face, goatee, big nose, arching eyebrows, and scar tissue between my eyes that enhance my devious traits. My athletic physique suggests I could carry out my mischief on humans with minimal effort. I've always had to initiate friendships. Friends confided to me before I introduced myself that they believed I was a killer. My features and mannerisms lend themselves to the diabolical. The villain in my story is based on me."

"In the climactic scene, the villain squeezes the hand of the hero and won't let go. The hero grabs a conveniently placed chainsaw with his free hand and intends to lop off the villain's arm. The villain lambasts the hero, 'They call my hands the Death Clutch; 300 pounds per square inch of pressure tightening around your appendage.' Hero drops the chainsaw because he concludes the impossibility of starting it with one hand. The villain tosses the hero to the floor and summons his three-man army to finish him off. Colonel Von Crush, Sergeant Van Squeeze, and General Von Grip emerge to pulverize the hero until he loses consciousness.

"The villain and his band of grip-strength mercenaries live on to terrorize society. As the years pass, they mature and do the Lord's work, opening pickle jars for the elderly. The End. If my treatment does not grease their wheels, the rewrite will include a romantic interest."

"You are so weird," says Varla.

I can be as quirky as her and redirect the conversation. "Are you Moroccan?"

She turns her head sideways, furrows her eyebrows, and shakes her head.

Her physical responses are magnificent. I chose misdirection to short circuit her brain. Those gestures are her way of rebooting her system.

She answers while laughing, "Moroccan, why Moroccan?"

I present my evidence. "The French accent and your dark olive skin."

"Honey, I'm Canadian." She delivers her line as if being Canadian is a letdown, not as exotic.

I tilt my head in disbelief. "What?"

She rebooted my system.

"I'm messing with you. According to the police blotter, I'm Hispanic, but actually I'm Lebanese."

"Hence the French accent, you sneaky Francophone."

She smiles and says *"Oui."*

I search my memory for all things Lebanese. Recalling the alleged Israeli jets breaking the sound barrier as they flew low over Beirut and shattered storefront windows is not the tone I desire to set. Nor will I remind her of the warehouse explosion in the port of Beirut. Those topics are the equivalent of mentioning cocaine and Pablo Escobar to a Columbian. When making an impression, do not rehash shallow and discourteous, sore subjects. My international diplomacy training is shining through. My choice is to comfort Varla with my familiarity and appreciation for her homeland.

"Lebanon, the Switzerland of the East. I once planned a trip to Jeita Grotto, Baatara Gorge Waterfall, and Cedars Ski Club."

"Wow, you studied the hot spots. No drinking at the famous cafes on Hamra Street?"

"Maybe a sip. I'm a nature guy."

"What happened, why didn't you go?"

I stall with the real reason. "I had to save the world."

"No, you're a villain. You'd be the one taking over the world."

I've shared a lot with her already, and she hasn't split. I might as well speak the truth; it's embarrassing, but also hilarious. "My passport was suspended for a while."

"What did you do?"

"The customs attaché at the embassy banned me under the suspicion of espionage."

"What? The customs attaché thought you were a spy? What is a customs attaché?"

"Customs attaché is a cool job; they work with the ambassador, law enforcement, and business trades."

"Pretty cool. But why did he call you a spy?"

"While pitching mail at the Embassy in Kuwait, my first sergeant reprimanded me for calling the diplomats by their post office box number and reading their magazines. Apparently, it is an unacceptable violation of their privacy, creepy, and not socially acceptable."

"They can't suspend your passport for being a creep."

"I'm not done. At an embassy party, I asked the customs attaché for travel recommendations to Libya, Lebanon, and Tunisia."

"An innocent mistake."

"He asked me if I knew who he was. I said, 'Yeah you're PO box 345, I look at your Busty XL magazines all the time.' Evidently, you don't make friends this way; especially in front of his modestly endowed wife. Since then, I've made progress with my impulse control."

She laughs hard. "You didn't. You have come a long way. Do you still like big busty women?" Her tone changes on a dime to lusty. "Let me test your impulse control." She rises, pushes off from her desk, slamming her chest into mine, walking me backwards until I'm against the back wall.

The sight of her chest bulging out of her dress top is provocative. No fight or flight here. I've chosen submission and arousal. She made the first move and can do as she pleases.

The Specialist walks in on us making out, without acknowledging our grope fest, and calmly says, "Leave your papers on your desks and I'll see you both in a week."

My, my is The Specialist, a cool customer.

We head downstairs giggling, and feel like a couple of teenagers that got caught in the act by the principal.

"I'll race you to the ranch," we say in unison.

## Chapter 14 Embracement

The first round was hot, fast, and sweaty. With my limited experience in intimate relationships, I struggle to find the right words to express my pleasure. Varla understands words are unnecessary and leads my hands over the curves of her body. I massage every curve to our mutual delight. The second round we taper our speed and increase our sensual touch. The rest of the morning, we indulge in each other.

I'm not known to be a master of transitions, so fortunately I'm excused from creating post coitus dialogue by my 12:30 p.m. alarm. "Varla, I got to jet, I'm meeting with my protégé at Francheschi Park at 1 p.m."

"Beat it."

Her response cracks me up. Her violent overtones mask her delicate side.

\*\*\*

I ride my motorcycle up the twisty turns of the Riviera and meet Ladders at Francheschi Park. I choose this place due to the proximity to his house. After today's session, he'll be too tired to pedal up the hills of the Riviera. He's early. I shake his hand, smile, and make direct eye contact. His handshake is firm, he's smiling, but the lack of eye contact is unreasonable.

"Something's missing. Do it again," I say.

He remembers the eye contact.

"Welcome, Ladders. Your knee appears well rested."

"I caught myself a few times and stopped."

I sense his mind is still cluttered and decide to probe. "What's going on?"

"I got into an argument with this kid at school. He's always busting on me because I'm Brazilian and don't speak Spanish."

"I can relate. What's his name?"

He turns away from me as if ashamed and gazes at the spectacular view of our beloved city below.

"Diego," he says quietly.

"If you could have beat Diego up and gotten away with it, would you?" This deliberate line of questioning will raise his energy.

He changes his tone, faces me, and answers with vigor, "Oh, hell yeah, I would have crushed him."

With this statement, Ladders has begun his emotional rollercoaster. I will guide his journey from somber to calmness, induced excitement, and finally release it into reflection. "Take a seat on the bench; believe me, you'll be better off sitting through this scenario."

A calm, suggestive state is achieved with a selection of carefully chosen words. I drop my tone two notches and hypnotically offer my invitation. "Pretend it's the weekend and you're watching your favorite movie. You're eating pizza and drinking soda. Feel the sensation of the chair underneath you. Focus on the chair, and describe it in your mind. How does the pizza taste? What sounds do you hear from the movie? A wave of relaxation is cresting over you. There is stillness within you. Your breathing has slowed. Your eyelids are heavy from concentrating. You are almost asleep."

Ladders' eyelids shut, and he teeters with the sleepy head bobs.

Before he attains slumber, I switch gears with a booming clap, raising the speed and volume of my voice, jolting him back into consciousness. "Picture Diego's face. Visualize your fist landing on Diego's jaw, feel your knuckles crush the bones." I use the word crush because it is a descriptive verb familiar to Ladders. Utilizing his familiar words allows me to slip past the processing part of his brain. "Hear him cry. Smell Diego's blood on your knuckles. You are a jawbreaker!" I clap my hands again, breaking his intense trance.

Ladders attempts to stand, wobbles, and grabs at the arm of the bench for balance. It's a typical reorientation from a trance. A personal goal of mine is to create the same disoriented wobbly response from an effective mind clouding. I stand tall. I walk tall, but I have occasional battles with doubt. Is my training ethical?

"You are cleansed," I say to Ladders, but also to myself. "What did you learn from this sequence?"

"Fighting Diego in my imagination can be as satisfying as in the flesh."

It's gratifying to hear my student's correct answer.

"At school, I'm always arguing. How do you do it? How do you stay calm?"

I answer from experience. "What I've learned from fighting, is I can take over an angry mind because that human is not in control."

"How do you takeover someone's mind?"

"Do you remember a kid in your kindergarten class who cried too much?" There's at least one in each class.

"My friend Josh cried every day. One time he cried because his shoelace was untied. I still rag on him about that."

"Nice example. I'm sure he loves reminders of his crybaby days. Does he still cry every day?"

"No, he's fifteen years old now."

"You could say he has better control of what?"

"His emotions?" Ladders realizes he answered a question with a question and corrects himself with a statement. "Sorry, his emotions."

"Kindergarteners can experience three different emotions in three seconds because they react to their environment and are out of control."

"So, how do I control my anger?"

"Anger is manifested from negativity. It is an out-of-control heat creature."

"Why a heat creature?"

"I'm glad you asked. What temperature do you associate anger with?"

"Hot."

"Anger is associated with heat because it burns through energy. You can harness your anger by channeling its power with quick-time breathing or tame it with blue calming energy and slow deep breathing."

"Can you control people?"

"First, you'll have to learn how to control your knee, before you can learn to control humans."

"My principal says to always avoid violence. Do you?"

"No, oh no. Does your principal practice karate?"

"I don't know."

I smile. If Ladders only knew about my background. "Conflict is vital to our growth. As I've gotten older, I seize control and determine my destiny. It's called self-determination. In other words, I make my own choices."

I walk Ladders to his bike. He's dragging as today's lesson was mentally taxing, but there is a teachable moment. People tend to remember the first and last part of a conversation, so I ask him, "Ladders, can you summarize what you've learned today?"

"It's like you said, control your emotions or somebody else will."

"Excellent, but it is crucial to sense other people's emotions and express our own. We must control the extent of our expression and how deeply we feel."

"What? I only understood about half of that."

"This will help. When Diego was yelling at you, what was his motivation?"

"He was angry because I don't speak Spanish."

"What was his motivation? In The Mental Mind Force manual, I list the four reasons people do things: to look good, feel good, be right, or in control. Which one was it?"

"It wasn't about looking good, feeling good, or being right. He yelled at me because he was trying to be in control."

"Bravo." I tap my right index finger on the palm of my left hand to show modest praise with my one-finger clap.

"When I responded in anger to his anger, he controlled my behavior. Now, that I know what he did, I'm even angrier."

"Tomorrow, when you see Diego, play the game. Speak to him in Spanish, and take away his power by saying, 'Hola, muchacho' or 'Hola, pollo niño.'"

"Saying hi boy or hi baby chicken is pretty funny."

"Let's call it a day."

"Oh, I almost forgot. Mom said to tell you and your friend Varla to be at Rincon tomorrow at 9 a.m."

## Chapter 15 ZZ Top Heavy

Varla and I wait under a rickety Tiki hut at Rincon. It's twenty-one minutes south of Santa Barbara, and a terrific location to watch surfers get barreled on primo point break waves. Another quintessential Santa Barbara day, partially sunny, a high of seventy degrees and low of fifty with no humidity, but everyone in the lineup is wearing a wetsuit. The Pacific never warms this far north. Not only is this an ideal surf spot, but if I was to ambush somebody, this is where I'd do it. On the one side of Highway 101 there are slightly sloped cliffs, and on the other the Pacific Ocean. Nowhere to run and a small bottleneck choke point. The overlapping noise between the cars zooming by and the waves breaking on the shore mask the sound of footsteps.

"Great spot for a trap," I say.

"Nobody is going to ambush us, you clown. By the way, what happened to your kitchen window?" Varla asks.

"I threw my shoe through it." I act it out by skimming a rock into the ocean.

"Oh."

I guess she doesn't need any further details. In her world, it probably makes sense to destroy things. "I'm considering sorting the glass shards as a dangerously sharp puzzle and gluing the window back together."

"Sounds like something you'd do."

I spot Darcy walking down a pathway towards us, I wave her over and whisper to her, "You got the papers?"

"What?"

"Did you bring the papers?"

"What are you talking about?"

"Anyone follow you here?"

I break character, and Varla and I bust out laughing, knowing the tightly wound Darcy will not understand my 1950s style film noir detective routine.

"McGurski, if I'm here, it (is) for business," says Darcy.

"I guess you two know each other?" I ask.

"We've met," Darcy robotically says.

Varla glares hard at Darcy.

"Since nobody else cared to further investigate Santos," Darcy says with a direct swipe at Varla as they stare daggers at each other, "I took the initiative and tracked what remained of Santos to a storage container in Goleta."

Goleta is a small city north of Santa Barbara and means The Good Earth. It was Santos' last stop on the Earth.

"I alerted the storage facility manager of a terrible odor coming from inside a container. The manager notified the Santa Barbara Police department, and they broke the lock on the container. Santos' corpse stunk. The desk was in there too."

It's funny how her narrative ended with "the desk was in there too." I'm grateful I can understand and cherish subtle comedy.

Darcy continues. "The police confiscated everything in the container. If no relatives claim it within two weeks, it goes to auction."

"If Santos' storage container goes up for auction, should we bid on the desk?" I ask.

"I'll be back in two weeks with details to let you know."

She leaves with no friendly banter. Throughout the brief conversation, Varla does not say a word. She listens and sizes Darcy up. It'd be a crazy fight of Varla's sheer ferocity and size versus the quickness, toughness, and Thai boxing skill of Darcy.

Varla has her hands on her hips and is flaring her nostrils. She showed restraint with Darcy, and I expect her to vent some steam.

"Have you ever noticed Darcy doesn't say the word 'is'? It drives me nuts," she says.

"I lived overseas for four years, so I'm used to broken English. It's kind of cute."

"Oh, you think she's cute. I see how you two get all giddy with each other."

"Giddy with Darcy? Are you out of your mind? Did you forget I like women with curves? I think you're jelly."

"You don't want to see me get jealous."

*** 

During the following two weeks, Varla and I chill at the ranch, practice technique, and bond. Here are the highlights of our interactions:

I catch Varla sun tanning on the lawn chair and pounce on her.

"You're like a puppy," she says.

I lick her face and pretend to sniff her butt.

"Gross."

"I wrote a new mind clouding phrase."

"How weird is it? Will it melt my brain?"

"Did you ever play hooky from school?"

"No, I was a good girl," she says in a playful tone, indicating this is a stretch of the truth.

"You ever shoot sweet corn in a field littered with deer? A vegetarian would shoot the corn instead of the deer. As long as the corn had a sporting chance."

"Are you on crack?"

"Rats, the mind cloud didn't work because it was too long."

"What is this mind clouding all about?"

"It's deliberately placing humans into a state of bafflement with irregular word construction and thought projections. The intent must be included to achieve maximum confusion. The target's brain temporarily goes out of focus and becomes fixated on figuring out the puzzle."

"What's so great about confusing people by saying weird stuff?"

"It's more than an assortment of weird words. Extraordinary combinations of words is sorcery. Couple these words with the right inflection and mental intent, and you've entered cosmic mojo. Mind clouding is beyond merely flummoxing people. Plus, it's good comedy."

"It didn't work on me."

"I bet the next one will."

"I don't get why mind clouding is important to you."

"Mind clouding is a necessary step in my quest to vanquish staleness. A full frontal assault on normal behavior."

"Full frontal assault? Again with the breast innuendo."

"While I'm here." I lay on top of her. "I've been meaning to ask you about your name."

"You've heard my name before, haven't you? A breast-man like you has spanked it to your share of Russ Meyer's movies."

She's referring to Varla, the name of the buxom star character in *Faster Pussycat Kill Kill*. She solved her problems through yelling, road rage, seduction, intimidation, and force. A powerful role model for boys and girls. They share the same name and problem-solving skills.

Nourishing my curiosity, I ask, "Did your parents name you after Varla from *Faster Pussycat Kill Kill*?"

"Yeah, and I'm just as brutal." She yells, "Kyaaaah!" flipping me over off the chair and landing on top of me.

"Oooof, nice reversal."

Who would name their daughter after a sociopathic woman from a movie? But I guess the crazies rarely fall far from the crazy tree. The name fits and I dig it.

She's laughing pretty hard.

"What are you laughing at?"

"You."

"What did I do?"

"You believed my parents actually named me Varla."

"They didn't?"

"Here's a secret; Varla's my code name. I picked it because I liked the character in *Faster Pussycat Kill Kill*."

"What's your real name?"

"Sophia."

"That's nice, but you'll always be Varla or ZZ Top Heavy to me."


At night, I've adapted to sleeping with Varla and her battles with sleep. Peace is the elusive commodity that escapes her during the day and night. While trying to sleep, she flips around from her stomach to her side to her back, as if an impatient amateur chef is testing a giant spatula and flipping Varla-flavored crepes for the first time.

"What the frig?" I say as I push her off me.

She replies, "I can't sleep."

"Did you try counting Fonzies jumping over sharks?"

"You are so strange."

"Do you have a dream car?"

"Yes, it's a Maserati Gran Tourismo."

"Dream about Maseratis jumping fences."

"Do you have a dream car?" she asks.

"No, I dream about big boobs and nine-handed massages."

"I thought you don't like people touching you."

"Massage has a purpose."

"And how did you come up with a nine-handed massage?"

"There's supposedly a one-armed guy in Ventura County, who is considered a wizard in the massage world.

Him, plus four other masseuses, could challenge the boundaries of massage."

"This is not helping me go to sleep."

"How about the letter Z from the alphabet? The letter Z has been linked to sleep in the comics. Count the letter Z riding sheep jumping over a fence."

"In *The High Fiving Awesomers*, you mentioned a comic strip taped to the conference wall that frustrated you and almost made you lose your cover. I always wondered what was on the comic strip?"

My God, is she random. "If I share the secret with you, will you let me sleep?"

"I promise."

"You asked for it. The poorly cut-out comic strip had a picture of a female climbing on the back of a male coworker saying, 'Is this what they mean by getting a leg up on the competition,' and the male says, 'I'll say.'"

"Those idiots awesomed that? My single urge is to throat punch them. Good night, McGurski."

***

Two weeks whiz by, and Darcy pays a visit to the ranch. I invite her inside, but she stays outside in the doorway.

"Today, be at the auction house at 9 a.m. and bid on item number 1080. The desk is valued at $500, but call Alexandra if the bids go over $15,000. By the way McGurski, Jeremiah challenges you to a duel. If you lose, you are out of The Foundation," says Darcy.

Before Varla or I can say a word, Darcy turns around and leaves.

"She's rude. Is she on the spectrum?" says Varla.

"We all are," I say.

"I think she has Asperger's," says Varla.

I've never been challenged to a duel before. From what I heard, Jeremiah's the wrong guy to mess with. I try to find the positive. Well, at least the challenge was not accompanied with a late 1800s French style glove slap in the face. We head outside and climb into my van. Varla serenades me and my van.

"It was an ordinary van

The van got bitten by a rock.

The rock wasn't even radioactive.

And now it's a creeper van.

Bed inside, creeper van.

Come inside, creeper van.

Candy inside, creeper van.

He was an ordinary man

Then he got inside of the van.

He's a creeper man

In a creeper van.

Creeper van, creeper man.

He's a man in a tan van."

I fake laugh Vinnie Barbarino style "Ha … ha … ha," and defend the van. "It's not a creeper van because it has windows along each side and the back. Creeps drive cargo vans with no windows." My tan van is a 1999 Chevrolet 1500 Express with 445,000 miles on its legendary 5.0 liter Vortec engine and is still making tracks. At 300,000 miles, I rewarded the rig with a $300 Desert Storm makeover. The paint on top is desert tan with black trim on the lower portion. I rummaged through a few junkyards and added a front brush guard and fog lights to lend to its urban assault, battle friendly appeal. I reminisce about my old headquarters, for if I lose this duel, I might be living in the tan van again. Would Varla stand by me if I was living in a van?

While we drive to the auction house, I wonder what will happen if Jeremiah is there. My reputation of being "ready" is a burden when facing off against a 6'4" goliath. With a man of his size, I can't afford mistakes. The ridiculous karate moves I learned peering through windows or watching the DVDs of charlatans boasting they could teach Dim Mak (death touch) through a video series won't help me. I'll have to stand tall and walk tall. The safe strategy is to dismantle him with low limb destruction. Kicks thrown at his calves, breaking his base until … timber.

Varla senses my concerns. "Are you nervous about the duel?"

I bluff. "Nah, I've decided how to handle this punk."

"With pleasantries, I am sure."

"He started it."

*** 

We arrive at the auction house. Fortunately, Jeremiah is not waiting outside and there are no places for him to tie his horse. Inside, I search the room for a large crazy guy. He's not here, but I stay sharp in case he pops in. My eyes oscillate to check both doors. Meanwhile, the human bidders cram inside. They sit with one leg crossed over the other on puny folding chairs to bid on the wares of the recently deceased journalist, Johnny Santos. I count forty-five humans in this 500-square-foot rectangular room. Plant him in the ground and let the bidding begin.

These dreaded humans pompously raise their numbered paddles to shoulder level so as not to make a spectacle of themselves. Their true ambition delights in being seen and being "in the scene." The treacherous bidders are our competition. On the positive side, I can see by their smiles they are proficient in oral hygiene and dressed in appropriate attire.

The cadence and urgency in the auctioneer's voice have no effect on me. However, the numbers are stimulating and trigger my numerical obsession. The dialogue inside my head surpasses the speed of the auctioneer's voice and sounds like this: The desk is item number 1080. 1080 is the average number of breaths a person takes in an hour. Breathing is the first significant movement of a newborn and is the foundation of everything else. 1080 is one zero away from 108. Internally, I shout myself "stop!" and control is restored.

Varla and I have been sent on this mission to ensure no outsiders acquire the desk. The bidding starts at a reasonable $500. It's a fancy writing table of old world craftsmanship and made of solid mahogany, which means it is a two-person job to lift. There are ornate brass fixtures and a fancy top with a carving of an eagle and grizzly bear tussling over a salmon. This modest creature of the sea will instantly join forces with either the apex predator of the air or a titan of the ground. A reversal of "you are what you eat." Perhaps you become what eats you. Triumph to either the speed of the eagle or the power of the bear. I'm betting on the eagle.

The bidders are ripe to be attacked with mysticism. I can sense their open, unprotected mental channels. I'll cast a negative energy blast to surround the desk with bad juju. My thought wave attack is simple, "This desk is rotten, this desk smells, this desk is broken." In seconds, the bidders lay their paddles on their laps. It's a basic technique requiring a message, a strong will, and belief. The results are astounding. Everyone stops bidding except for one bidder. He must be high on caffeine. I've found stimulants can disrupt the reception of mental vibrations. Varla hands me a note and gestures to the lone bidder. I hand him the note. He reads it and removes himself from the auction house without making eye contact with anyone. The bid is mine at $800, but this number lacks symbolism, so I out bid myself and bid $864.

"Stupid, you already won it," Varla berates me.

"864 is a better number. It's not out of superstition, but a tribute to the significance of numbers. The sun's diameter is 864,000 miles. In 86,400 seconds, the earth completes one rotation. And 864 is a multiple of 108. 108 goes into 864 eight times. $500, $550, $600, $650, $700, $750, $800, and $864 totals eight bids."

"You are so strange," she says as she grabs my paddle and smacks me on the arm with it. "No more bidding."

"Let's grab the desk and twenty-two skidoo."

She picks up on my unusual urgency and is ready to scram too. The gentleman would not rush, but the savage would. We did what we came to do. Lingering is for barnacles. She brings the van around to the back of the auction house and keeps the motor running.

"You look like you're ready to rob a bank," I say.

"Maybe I am," Varla answers.

One worker helps me load the desk into the side of the van. Setting the desk down, I rip a loud fart.

"Really? They don't pay me enough to do this crap," he complains.

"Pardon me," I say, while lightly chuckling.

"You savage, you better give that poor guy a good tip," says Varla.

Although I'm frugal, the value of hard labor does not elude me. I slip the guy seven dollars.

"You stink; stay in the back with the desk," says Varla.

\*\*\*

We cruise north west on Highway 101, enjoying the views and thankful Santa Barbara County is not grid locked with traffic.

"Maybe I'm here to teach you how to be a gentleman," Varla says.

"I'm sure I could learn a lot from you. Hey, what did you write on the note?" I ask.

"'Leave,' but I wrote it with belief and intention," Varla states.

"Nice."

Varla pulls the van over at a vista point to search the desk for the letter before reaching Gaviota. She is thorough, examining each drawer and possible secret compartments. She concludes the letter is not in the desk.

"What the hell? It's not in here."

My tone is indifferent. "Whoever has it is playing the game."

## Chapter 16 Beach Bonfire and Jesuita

We're back on the road and three motorcyclists zip by, and I swear one of them is Sarrick. I wonder if Varla rides motorcycles. Refocus, McGurski.

We arrive at Gaviota Beach and unload the desk in the parking lot and carry it on to the warm sand. Although it's heavy, we move it with grace.

As we're walking, Varla asks me, "Why are we delivering a desk to the beach? It's so weird. Sounds like one of your ideas."

I hold in my laughter and redirect. "The cliffs at Gaviota Beach are my favorite. The way the shale shoots out of the cliffs is like little fins."

"You're right. I've been here later in the day. When the lighting is right, the rocks turn a golden yellow color … it's gorgeous."

Our conversation ends as Eddy arrives, carrying a can of gasoline in his left hand and a sledgehammer in his right. Rangi and Loto are also each carrying sledge hammers. Varla's survival instinct kicks in, and she positions herself behind the desk with the van keys interlaced between her knuckles. I know we're safe. She is not aware of the prior arrangement made. I whisper in her ear, reassuring her everything is cool, and then greet The Good Time Boys.

"Greetings. Item number 1080 as requested," I say.

"You and Varla should stick around for the bonfire," says Eddy.

Without hesitation, they take turns at smashing the desk with the sledgehammers. They are having a blast destroying it. Rangi lifts his hammer, swings it sideways baseball style and says, "Key-yaaa!" as he decimates one corner. Loto upper cuts the top of the desk while yelling, "Bonsai!" Rangi hammers another sturdy blow, launching the top portion of the desk into a nine-foot orbit. Eddy goes last and, of course, says a speech before his turn. "Ladies and gentlemen, we are gathered to witness a mahogany desk be put to rest by brute force, Rhhaaaaa." Eddy pulverizes the remaining drawers with three overhand strikes, pummeling it into the sand. Eddy bows and gestures to Rangi and Loto to bow as well.

As he pours gas over the scattered wood particles and lights it, Eddy says, "Let's scorch this sucka."

Varla looks at me with the expression, "What the hell is going on?"

I act like I don't know, shrug, and then tilt my head, acknowledging The Good Time Boys and say with exuberance, "Yeah, daytime bonfires."

"We just wasted our morning and $864 on a desk they planned to burn, anyway? I don't get it," Varla says.

I appreciate the novelty of a specific act done differently. Having a bonfire during the day as opposed to the night pleases me. The five of us stare into the fire. It is $864 worth of firewood courtesy of an old desk once owned by Oscar, The Foundation's researcher, and briefly Santos. The water cresting on the shores, the airy sea breeze, the fire burning the wood table, and stones on the cliffs represent a swarm of elements adding to our satisfaction. I wonder if The Foundation will reimburse me for an $864 destroyed desk. We stay quiet and stare at the mesmerizing dancing flames until I break silence, "Is everyone ready for light sparring?"

Daytime sparring at Gaviota Beach in front of a bonfire is an unbeatable way to spend an afternoon.

"McGurski, go easy on us, we're a little banged up from your last visit," Eddy expresses.

I feign innocence. "What happened?"

"When you two left Claude's house in such a hurry, we came running to catch you and took a hard spill on the marble floor. Somehow, the sprinkler sprayed the front porch."

I bite my bottom lip, containing my laughter.

Varla chimes in, "We saw you running out the door. What was going on?"

"We were checking if you wanted to practice. You guys left in such a hurry we didn't have a chance to talk."

I clarify, "Oh yeah, I forgot our self-defense training."

"That actually makes sense," Varla states. She probably thinks I'm paranoid and makes her point by turning towards me with an exasperated expression.

Eddy answers, "It looked like you two were running from something."

"We were running from McGurski's wild imagination," Varla chides.

I chirp in with my newly revised version, "Nah, you saw me lapping Varla in a foot race."

For our self-defense drills, I partner with Eddy, while Rangi and Loto are matched. Varla is game to rotate in. Nobody stretches. The clean air and soft beach breeze are a spectacular juxtaposition of our combat training. Nature's beauty surrounds us, as we act like cavemen. We practice headbutts first. Eddy stretches out his palms to face me, simulating my opponent's head, while I ram my skull into his palms. When we train, we do fifteen reps before switching. The second drill is a flowing sequence, better known as Lift Off. Step in with the left foot, while swinging a right forearm to strike the neck, and with momentum, step behind, sweeping his right leg and trip him to the ground. Eddy and I do fifteen reps each in three minutes, while the big boys are on their sixth rep. Our last drill is a Double Straight Blast Takedown. I extend both of my palms into the inside part of Eddy's right shoulder, and even light force naturally spins his body clockwise. With the assistance of the momentum, I secure his neck and introduce him to the sand. Studying my first attempt, Varla is eager to try. Of course, Eddy talks a little garbage, so I coach her and enjoy watching her plant Eddy in the sand. She lets Eddy relish his turn on her as well, and I win fifty bucks from Rangi. I bet him with two-to-one odds that Varla would not complain about getting sand in her hair-easy money. We complete our drills injury free and with no loss of ego. Varla and I say our goodbyes to The Good Time Boys.

Will any of these techniques be effective against Jeremiah?

As we are walking back to the van, Varla confides to me, "I wasn't sure about Eddy, Rangi, and Loto at first, but those guys are fun."

"That's why I call them The Good Time Boys."

I'm glad she likes them. Hopefully, she'll like my friend Sarrick too.

"I figured out the letter was never in the desk. Someone else has it, which means the shenanigans with Santos were a distraction," says Varla.

She has figured out a key detail in this caper. But one I already knew. "What do you mean?" I ask nonchalantly, as if I didn't know, while I shake nine ounces of sand out of my shoes.

"Didn't you notice none of your cronies checked the desk for the letter before they smashed and burned it? They must have known it wasn't in the desk."

"Yeah, makes sense."

"Santos was a writer, and you are an inscriber. Maybe it's a symbolic message to you."

"Here's a message for you." I summon chi energy to my lips and lean over to give her a deep, passionate kiss. "Let's double down on nature and go for a hike," I suggest.

"We should hike the Jesuita Trail. Have you ever been there?"

"Nope, but I'm ready."

"This is my favorite hike in Santa Barbara. You'll love it."

"First, a quick detour to the thrift store."

"What do you need at the thrift store?

"You'll see, it's a surprise."

*** 

When we arrive at the thrift store, I head straight towards the stuffed animal section. These oversized, once heavily desired pieces of cloth with stuffing and googly eyes will serve our purposes nicely.

"What's this all about? Why are you buying these reject carnival prizes?" asks Varla.

"I've always loved carnivals, but despise the prizes. I never fell under the hypnotic spell to win a ridiculously large plush gorilla, teddy bear, or Rastafarian banana."

"So, why are you buying them?"

With a grin, I reveal my plan. "I recently bought a crossbow on Craigslist, and we need to test it out. I'd rather shoot these stupid stuffed animals than a foam target."

"Cool. I see where you're going with this. We'll scatter them in the woods and pick them off," Varla says enthusiastically.

Heading back towards the city on 101 south, close to downtown, we exit the highway and enjoy the scenery on Foothill Road. With lush landscaping and mature trees, it's a magical destination with ocean and mountain views. We arrive at the trailhead and there are two choices, the Arroyo Burro Trail or the Jesuita Trail. She informs me the Arroyo Burro Trail is a historic trail used in the past by hunting parties and prospectors. We choose the Jesuita Trail and arrange the stuffed animals in the trees, on rocks, and propped against berms and take turns shooting. Varla holds the record of nailing seven oversized plush toys in three minutes and forty-seven seconds. Shooting arrows into carnival prizes may be weird to some, but we act on a sheer impulse that insulates us from normal behavior. After waging war against the stuffed animals, we load the causalities in the van with the crossbow and hike.

***

The first part of the trail we bounce around on boulders, jump over the meandering creek, and appreciate the canopy of the large oak and sycamore trees. Gaining elevation, we leave the trees behind and zig zag around switchbacks. I'm having such a blast with Varla I do not count the number of switchbacks.

The top of the peak is named Inspiration Point. What a cliché. The sun is low in the sky two hours before sunset. Varla positions me in front of the sun and states she comes here to glow and wants to watch me glow. She steps back and observes my body.

"You have the glow," she says.

"Yeah!" I extend my hands out, making gentle sweeping motions as the golden ribbons of energy trails behind my hands.

"You can't capture the glow with a picture," she says.

"My buddy Sarrick says the same thing. Humans snap hundreds of pictures at vista points without truly appreciating the beauty."

"Who's Sarrick?"

"Oh, he's the owner of The Motorcycle Laundromat. We saw him earlier today riding past us on the 101."

"Best name for a laundromat. Being outside in nature is a nice way to process a case."

"Did you figure anything else out?" I ask.

"Jeremiah tried to frame us, and exposed himself in the process. Challenging you to a duel was his only option."

"Wow."

"In my experience investigating for The Foundation, I have found emotions are at the core of each case. Few people have control over their emotions. For example, Jeremiah's anger, my jealousy of Darcy, and you threatening to activate dental plans."

"I was being a tough guy, defending your honor."

"Psst, please."

Laughing, I change the subject. "What metaphysical technique should I teach you today?"

In a seductive tone, she says, "Ooooh, I hope my training starts soon, *maestro.*"

"We will listen to music and make unnecessary movements."

"Dancing?"

"Yeah."

"How mystical."

I must delay gratification and will dance with Varla later in the night. It's a sacrifice for the greater good. This can't wait. Until Jeremiah is dealt with, each moment is dangerous for Varla and I. I need information and visiting the ladies is where I'll begin.

## Chapter 17 Visiting the Ladies

I asked Varla, for my sake, to keep the doors locked at the ranch while I hunt for answers. My first stop is Alexandra's villa. In her formal tea room, we sit on two ornate antique Italian chairs. My hypocritical lesson with Ladders is haunting me. No unnecessary movement is a challenge when sitting on ancient chairs that feel like a rock. I resist the urge to complain, squirm, or readjust on these decidedly stylish-over-comfort sitting apparatuses. There are benefits to stillness, but I still contemplate excusing myself to rip a set of fifty-three bathroom sink pushups.

We sip on green tea and chat before I shoot for straight answers. Varla would burst out laughing at the sight of me placing my teacup on a doily.

"Did you know Jeremiah's father threatened Claude and me? He said if we didn't care for his son, he'd set our house on fire," says Alexandra.

"House or houses?"

"You caught my slip. Years ago, Claude and I lived together."

"Interesting."

She describes Jeremiah's father as a six-foot tall, 230-pound homicidal maniac plumber with hands that could crush rocks. Must have been from the wrench turning. Raising Jeremiah as a single dad overwhelmed him and caused him to abuse his son. I guess it was a coping mechanism. He saw the writing on the wall when fifteen-year-old Jeremiah already weighed 215 pounds and was close to six feet tall. His days of bullying his son would end in a few years. He deemed his son unmanageable.

"How did he know to bring Jeremiah to you?" I ask.

"Back in the seventies, we had positive results reforming and rehabilitating people with substance abuse and people without homes. The community embraced us. The word on the street was we were miracle workers or a cult."

"Not much has changed."

"Very funny. With my background as a clinical psychiatrist, and Claude's in physical therapy, people called us a power couple, black and tan, or, my favorite, yin and yang. We concluded our moderately effective methods needed a proactive approach to aid our target audience. The necessary research required us to close The Foundation for a while. The community did not respond well to the surge of people with addictions living on the streets. In addition, mental wards closed across the country due to their inhumane conditions. Thousands of people with disabilities were abandoned and unleashed upon the streets. The majority could not hold a job, so they self-medicated and became homeless."

"Let me guess. It became a never-ending cycle of you and Claude cleaning the streets, and LA County giving the junkies and homeless a bus ticket to Santa Barbara."

"That's accurate. They'd bang on our doors seeking refuge. To dig deeper into our research, we had to eliminate the distractions, so we spread rumors we were a cult. I came up with the name The Foundation because it sounded ominous. Claude did his part too, sprinkling in a dash of

Haitian voodoo to scare people. Young Jeremiah intimidated the rest away. We each tried to outdo each other with absurd titles. Mine was The Overlord, Claude's was The Minister of Justice, and Jeremiah was The Horseman."

"Claude told me The Foundation evolved from the teachings of Hermes Trismegistus. Is that a bunch of bologna?"

"Well, it's not all bologna. We do follow the teachings of Hermes."

"And Oscar, what did he do?"

"Same thing as he's always did. He collected books in seclusion, read, and occasionally recruited. During our years of research, we discovered a pattern in most of our clients. There was a disconnection between the two hemispheres of the brain. They had relatively healthy brains, but processed whole brain functions incredibly slowly or incompletely. In tasks involving a connection between both hemispheres, we noted a delay or sometimes a total misfire. It took us decades to figure this out and years to develop a healing protocol. Along the way, we experimented on people like yourself, Varla, and Darcy to test our theories.

"Our main goal is detecting and treating at a younger age. At three years old, the schools test for exceptionalities. Combining aspects of physical therapy and psychiatry, we developed a system to rebalance the brain to have both hemispheres firing congruently. Our program embraces and enhances the beautiful symmetry between the physical and mental stimuli."

"This is fascinating and thank you for experimenting on me, but I need input on Jeremiah or I'm toast."

"Jeremiah was kicked out of numerous boarding schools for misbehavior, so we decided to homeschool him. His terrible attitude drove a wedge between me and Claude. We separated and took turns raising him. Since he came from a home where he had no power, we gave him a taste of power. He became our enforcer. His father was a stickler for rules. So, we let Jeremiah create his own rules. This is how he became the enforcer and writer of rules for The Foundation. He created the corny ceremonial reading of letters at sunrise. The idea of early morning ceremonies was to spite me because I'm not a morning person. You can blame Jeremiah for his juvenile ideas and absurd titles. I'll give him credit; it takes discipline to write the rules. He had to learn to read and write in Esperanto. His dyslexia made it tougher. He persevered and conquered what he believed his toughest obstacle. His triumph over dyslexia does not compare with his lifelong battle with anger.

"I attempted to teach him manners and fine culture, while Claude gave him a physical outlet. He bailed hay and tended to the horses on his friend's farm. The quiet farm life suits him and he loves to spoil the horses. The only time I've seen that psychopath show affection was for those horses.

"To give you an idea of what you are up against, here's a crazy Jeremiah story. He once saw a video of a famous karate guy, named Mas Oyama. In the video, Oyama killed a bull with one punch. Jeremiah became obsessed with killing a bull with one punch. He asked the farmer to buy a bull so he could punch it, thankfully the farmer passed on that idea. Without bulls to punch, he practiced hitting wooden beams, bricks, and trees to hone his power. His only weakness is that he's slow, but what he lacks in speed, he makes up for in brute strength.

"Why do you think Claude has three bodyguards? It's because of Jeremiah. You came seeking answers on how to beat him in a duel. It's an impossible task, and I doubt anything I told you is of value. We played a role in creating this monster, but if you're lucky, perhaps he can still be reformed. If you beat him, promise me you won't hurt him. He has potential and only needs one last push for realignment."

Realignment must be the latest term in mental corruption. I mean psychology. "Great, you build a one-man gang, and now I have to beat him in a duel, but not hurt him." She's delusional.

"You should pay Darcy a visit. She can help you."

"Aren't you curious how Jacob is coming along in his training?" She already knows how Jacob is progressing, because I suspect she's been spying on me. I won't provide her with details.

"Oh yeah, I've been wrapped up in all this craziness. I forgot to ask."

"He's a good kid. Well, it's been an interesting history lesson." The Specialist taught me a drawn out "well" is a fine transition prior to departing.

"My pleasure, R. W. Good luck against Jeremiah."

\*\*\*

It's 7 p.m. and I've got a caffeine buzz from the tea. It's my turn to drop in unannounced at Darcy's house. She lives in Carpinteria, a small city fifteen minutes south of Santa Barbara. Avocado and orange trees surround her two-bedroom, one-bath bungalow. The lingering odor of a skunk is a clue the avocados are ripe. Avocados are a delicacy for skunks. I heard a rumor Jim Morrison of the Doors spent a month eating avocados and oranges. I survey my last chain of thoughts, which jumped from avocados and skunks to Jim Morrison, and guess my ADD is kicking. Before knocking on her door, I revisit an old habit and check her trash. There's an electric, gas, and water bill addressed to Suchada Tang. She lives alone and her last name is Tang, so is Suchada an alias? I knock on her door. Darcy opens the door and rolls her eyes. She's expressing herself naturally, at my expense, but I can handle it. In a short time she's made significant progress in social skills and English.

"I'm making house calls too," I say as a way of greeting.

"Please tell me you are challenging me to a duel," she says.

"No chance. But I brought the rope hand wraps. Alexandra said you could provide tips for my duel with Jeremiah."

"Muay Thai style," she replies.

Muay Thai is the art of eight limbs because the attacks come from your two shins, two knees, two elbows, and both hands equaling eight. "I'll do whatever style to beat Jeremiah."

"I'll be right back. I need to change into workout clothes."

She returns eventually wearing a tank top, revealing a tattoo on her shoulder. It has five rows of vertical Asian characters/letters with the top and bottom coming to a spiraled point.

"Is there symbolism behind your tattoo?"

"A well-traveled guy like you has never heard of Sak Yant?"

"Nope."

"It's a spell to bring good fortune and acts like a force field to deflect magic."

"Interesting. Does it work?"

"If you believe."

I wonder if it would deflect one of my famous mind clouds. "By the way, who's Suchada?"

"I'm Suchada. You would have known if you checked my trash."

"I did check your trash."

"You ever hear of a Thai girl named Darcy? Darcy (is) my Americanized nickname."

"I just had this same conversation with Varla."

"Maybe Varla can turn you into a gentleman."

"I'll always be a savage at heart. But I'm not vicious. In my duel with Jeremiah, throat, neck, and shots to the eyes are off limits."

"There's more room in the backyard, let's practice there."

The consequences of living in paradise and having avocados to pluck off your backyard tree comes with a hefty price for real estate and a violation of your sense of smell. The skunks have left their mark. My nose is wiggling and has intentions of jumping off my face and making a run for it.

"Wow, does it reek back here."

"Sorry, you get used to it. I cook with a lot of curry and hot sauce to neutralize the skunk smell."

"You need another plan."

"Enough of your whining. Let's train.

Darcy wastes no time and begins to bark orders.

"Do this technique and he won't register the strike's path because it (is) under his eye line. He'll suffer intense pain for a few minutes, but there will be no lasting damage."

Register the strike's path? She's been practicing her English. I guess what target she's referring to and say, "I'm not slugging him in the balls."

"It's not the balls; we don't punch balls in Thai boxing. You won't damage your fist either because where you'll hit him, there are no bones. When you hit your mark, his diaphragm will spasm and he'll gasp for air. You'll be aiming for the spot right below his sternum, but don't stare at it or you'll clue him in. The key to this technique is closing the gap and then transferring the weight from your back foot to the front foot at the same moment you land your punch."

She explains this Thai boxing technique as if it's a riddle for me to solve. "That's a lot of moving parts," I say.

"Are you paying attention? What spot on the body causes those responses?"

"The solar plexus … it's genius." Hooray for solving the riddle. It's only a decent plan if I can pull it off.

"Let me show you and then you'll know how it feels."

She's quick, and before I can stop her, she wallops me square in the solar plexus. Bam! No effect on me, but I can't say the same for Darcy. She shakes her hand while in impulsively dancing in a small circle. Ice is a better remedy.

"Damn, McGurski, what are you made of?"

I lift my shirt, revealing my dented gold amulet.

"You better hope Jeremiah (is) not into disco jewelry too, or you're dead."

"Good one, Suchada. I'll get ice."

"I'm okay. Look at these knuckles, they've seen worse. This one girl I fought had the uncanny ability to block punches with her forehead. Her head was even harder than your amulet. I broke every knuckle in both hands and managed to win."

We practice with light contact to perfect my form. Then she has a clever idea. Inspired by my protective amulet, she asks me to duct tape a hard cover of the *How to Speak English* textbook to her chest in order to withstand my full power shots. It's an impressive display of devotion and passion. She is tough and enthusiastic about spreading her national sport. Upon the completion of our training, I demonstrate gratitude by placing my left hand over my right fist and bow. She's no shogun, but I'm bowing out of respect.

"It's been my pleasure training with you."

She reciprocates and adds, "McGurski, if you do this right, you'll discover the ninth limb of Thai boxing."

As I head back to the ranch, I wonder what the ninth limb of Thai boxing is. I'm guessing it's a head-butt. What if Jeremiah is waiting for me at the ranch? Even worse, Varla is home alone; if this maniac provokes her, there could be a bloodbath of epic proportions at the ranch. I call her phone, no response. My imagination, combined with the potential for violence, triggers my urgency to speed home.

The lag time between pressing the gas pedal through the floorboard and faster movement is jokingly referred to as mail order acceleration. The lack of speed embodies Varla's moniker for the van, Slowpoke Van. Upon review, Slowpoke Van actually sounds creepier than Creeper Van. They'll be no gentle coaxing of the van, no "Come on, girl." No, "Come on, Bessy, you can do it." The tan van gradually builds momentum without resorting to motivating a machine. Its burly V8 rumbles to 70 mph. At 75 mph, the dashboard shakes in response to the irregular request of horsepower. I blast the radio to drown out the miscellaneous rattles a van churns out when racing at top speed. A gravity-induced decline motors the tan van to a personal record of 83 mph! It's peculiar zipping past cars in the fast lane. I beep my horn, smile, and wave as I pass a dumbfounded human driving a Porsche. At this rate, I'll be home in minutes to ease my wild imagination or settle a score.

## Chapter 18 Dressing Contest

Are those hoof prints? No, that's a stick. No hoof prints on the lawn or imprints of large cowboy boots. The tempo of my breathing changes accordingly, and I settle my negotiated terms with adrenaline. My emotions are a mix of relief and disappointment at the absence of Jeremiah. It's been awhile since I've been in a good scrap, but if this duel doesn't go my way, I'll be hurting. Varla greets me at the door and I embrace her with a thirty-second hug. We both are rank from our respective busy day, but overlook the odor and appreciate our bond. In mutual agreement, we hit the showers. Before my shirt lands on the floor, Varla is naked. There is no striptease, as she wanted out of her clothes. She comments on the dent in my amulet. It's too early in our relationship to share with Varla the meaning behind the two-headed eagle on my amulet. I recount how a woman named Suchada dented it with her fist.

"Oh, Darcy helped you train for your duel with Jeremiah?"

It's a bitter tone, and she's a better detective than I gave her credit for.

"Ooooh, the water pressure is firing. Get in here. Hey, the shampoo is almost empty."

The frugal miser in me states, "Pour water into it."

"You are so cheap."

Tripping over myself to shed the rest of my clothes, I open the shower curtain and witness her glory. Her chest is thrust out as she arches to rinse her hair. My left hand, without warning, begins its journey at her hip and eases up to her breast. "Mmmmm."

She tilts her head forward, presses her body against mine for a kiss. My hands naturally reposition themselves to caress her juicy butt. She pivots us both sideways in a considerate gesture so that I may soak in hot water, too. In our two-step pivot, she steps on my feet.

"Really? Socks in the shower are not sexy."

Memo to self, socks ruin a mood. In my haste, I left my socks on and never closed the shower curtain. Water sprays onto the bathroom floor. I hit my mental reset button and persist. I rip off my socks, whip the curtain closed, and reach around her back to pull her in for another kiss. She turns and places my hands on her breasts and asks me to squeeze. "I love a man with strong hands." Her head tilts back, resting on my shoulder, exposing her neck. A gradual nibble is coaxed into a bite. She orders me to get on my knees and I'm rewarded with breasts in my face. I tell her, "Let's make some heat." We set each other off like fireworks.

***

We both sleep hard until a knock on the door occurs at 6:00 a.m. Another early morning visitor. Before answering the door, I inventory my attire. No shoes, no shirt, no belt, but I am wearing dark slacks, and my dented golden amulet. It's presentable. Visitors at 6:00 a.m. are not greeted with formal wear. Déjà vu.

I look back, expecting to see Varla in bed; to my bewilderment, she's fully dressed.

Noticing my reaction she asks "You okay?"

"You won the dressing contest," I respond.

She answers with over the top giddy excitement, clasping her hands, elbows flaring out, and jumping with a huge smile. "A dressing contest? What do I win?"

Her pony tail is bouncing alongside her ample chest. She is deliberately acting silly, and it is super sexy. "It's funny; I have not thought about this in years. My father would sing a song to motivate my sisters and me to dress quicker. The song went like this: 'This is the dressing contest, let's see who will win and when I blow the whistle, we'll all begin.' And then he'd whistle."

"Pretty cute."

Another knock on the door.

Varla jokes, "That's not the milkman, is it?"

Before answering the door, I sense who it is. "No milk today, it's Ladders." I open the door and say, "Ladders, you didn't bring the milk, did you?

"Nope, no milk." As he says this, he leans his head and torso to the left, peaking a glimpse at the beautiful woman behind me.

Ladders is not scheduled for a lesson today, so I calmly ask him, "Who sent you?"

"Huh?"

"Anyone follow you here?"

"What?"

"You got the papers?"

"Jacob, don't mind him, that's his new spiel. He thinks he's funny," says Varla.

Varla knows his real name, which means she's working for Alexandra.

"What are you doing here, especially this early?" I ask.

"My mother says our family has a history of achievement early in the morning. She said to be productive today, so I came over," says Ladders.

"Oh, she's messing with both of us. Since when does Alexandra like to get up early? But forget about that for a moment. Varla, did you hear what Ladders' said?" Flattery from a teenager is gold and having a witness hear it is platinum.

"What part?" she asks.

"To come over here to be productive," I say.

"All I've seen you produce is a bunch a crap," says Varla.

Ladders asks Varla, "You here to decorate?"

"Zing. Nice one, Ladders," I say.

"You're right. McGurski's ranch could use a woman's touch. We should have Alexandra come over and decorate," says Varla.

"No!" Ladders and I exclaim.

"Ladders, if you want to be productive, go to the plant room and water them." Immediately, I reevaluate my directive and decide to provide extra clarification. "Ladders, remember when you water the plants, listen to them drink. Put your ear close to the soil and slowly pour the water. When you are tuned into their vibration, you'll sense when they've had enough water."

"I'm getting used to your weirdness," he says.

"I'm billing your mother triple for a 6 a.m. unannounced drop-in."

Ladders retrieves the watering can and fills it in the kitchen.

He is noticeably walking tall. "If the movement one selects is walking, then walk tall. Stand tall when provoked," are direct lines from the Mental Mind Force manuscript he has tucked into his back pocket. He's implementing and I'm proud of the early return on the Ladders' investment.

The events of the past few weeks are swirling around in my brain. I'll duck outside to the backyard and carve out a space to manage my ruminations. On my mental scorecard, I rate meeting Varla a triple plus. Mentoring Ladders is a single plus, interactions with Claude are neutral, the death of Santos is a triple minus, and the duel is a triple minus. I'm organized, but will have to purge one of those minuses. Defeating Jeremiah in a duel will declutter my mental filing cabinet. Luckily, they'll be no weapons in our duel. The first person to be knocked down loses and he will fall first.

Although my array of plants inside provide ample clean oxygen, nothing beats outside air. I'll practice a simple breathing exercising from *The Stockpile*. I raise my arms above my head and breathe deeply for six seconds, hold for six seconds and exhale for six seconds. It's more effective than coffee. This morning there is no breeze, no sounds from the neighbors, and no odors to cling to my heightened senses, so I'll focus on the sensation of touch as I pace barefoot on the backyard grass. The marine layer has made the grass damp and greets my feet with an introductory cold wet handshake. Compulsively, I proceed with my introduction ritual and look the grass in the eye and smile. Maybe it's the early hours that have brought me to the point of greeting grass or I maybe I have lost my mind.

I snap out of it and remember I forgot to ask Eddy for the inside scoop on Jeremiah while we were at the beach. He's always ready to talk, so I shoot him a call.

"Hey, Eddy, did I wake you?"

"McGurski, we keep early hours. What's up?"

"Did you hear Jeremiah challenged me to a duel?"

"Claude told me. You're crazy enough to fight that hay stacker, aren't you?"

"Any advice?"

"I wouldn't want any piece of him. He's 285 pounds of dense muscle tissue. What did you do to piss him off?"

"He thinks I stole a letter."

"Good luck, buddy. Hey, if you need more practice, me and the boys will pitch in."

"Thanks, man."

"We had fun destroying the desk on the beach. Do you have more furniture for us to break? Does Varla have a sister? Claude was pissed that we left a trail of sand in the mansion."

I solve Eddy's barrage of pointless questions with, "I don't know. Later, Eddy."

Speaking with Eddy is fruitless and reconfirms the war stories I've heard about Jeremiah. I'll have to keep Varla and Ladders busy while I tussle with a giant, and I know how to do it. I go back inside to the kitchen where Varla is perched on the countertop, snacking on coffee cake.

"I'm getting used to this no chair thing," says Varla.

She cracks me up with her teensy feet dangling a few feet above the floor, "Varla, have you ever heard of Wet Sheet Pack Hydrotherapy?" I ask.

"Yeah, I thought they stopped doing that in the seventies."

"We're going to give Ladders the Wet Sheet Pack Hydrotherapy Treatment. He's never been detoxed before. Would you please collect sheets and wool blankets from the linen closet?"

Ladders hears his name and comes in.

"Did I hear my name? It's hard to hear over the chatter the plants are making."

"Zing. Nice one. You're on fire today. Which is ironic because today you detox," I say.

"I'm fifteen, I don't drink."

"Great, that means fewer toxins to pull out," says Varla as she comes back with a pile of sheets and wool blankets. "I dipped the sheets in cold water and rung them out a bit."

"Excellent, thanks, Varla."

She lays the wool blankets on the floor and positions two of the wet sheets on top of them.

I coax him, "Go ahead, Ladders, and lay on the wet sheets."

"It's wet," he whines.

"It'll toughen you up, pansy," Varla says to challenge his masculinity.

Her alluring charm wins out and Ladders lies on the wet sheets as we wrap him up tight. To create the sauna effect, we wrap multiple wool blankets around him so he is wrapped like a wool burrito. The coldness from the sheets constricts his blood vessels near the surface of the skin, resulting in blood rushing to his core. The extra volume of blood in his core will increase his body temperature, while the wool blankets act as insulation and lock in the heat. In five minutes, this generated heat brings the blood back to the surface of the skin, improving his circulation. His increased body heat will open his pores and releases the impurities through induced perspiration. Sessions can last fifteen minutes to nine hours.

"Feeling snug?" I ask.

"It's pretty tight, I can barely move."

"Did you complete your ant assignment?"

"No, not yet."

"Varla, grab his legs and I'll grab his upper half and we'll carry him to the anthill in the backyard."

"No, come on. Let me out of this. Come on, man."

"We'll place you near it, so you can finish your assignment. Then you'll get the benefits of detox and completing an assignment. You're lucky to have such a creative mentor."

We easily hoist him and place him three feet away from an anthill.

"Would you keep an eye on Ladders, while I run a quick daytime OP."

Varla whispers to me, "How long should we keep him wrapped?"

I look her in the eyes with an intense stare and say, "You don't like pasta."

"What? Huh?" She's confused.

"Got you! It's my new mind clouding phrase."

She playfully bashes me on the arm. "You are nuts."

I whisper in her ear, "Keep Ladders bundled for thirty minutes." And then I turn my attention to my protégé. "Ladders, I'm heading out. I hope you survive the ants."

"You're the worst mentor."

Time to tangle with a lunatic.

## Chapter 19 It Can Happen Fast

Darcy gave me Jeremiah's address. He lives on a farm in Buellton, thirty miles away. It's not his farm; he rents a stable for his horse and lives in the loft above the stable. Turns out The Horseman is a minimalist as well. I park the van on the side of the road, hop over the wooden fence, and creep across the open field for three hundred yards. It's a grand pasture for grazing horses and for me to launch a 7:30 a.m. ambush.

My intentions are direct. I'm looking for you, Jeremiah, and when I find you, I will punch right through you. Psyched up, I envision an image of my fist splattering his solar plexus and him crumpling to the ground. In a flash, I send a direct message on a magnetic current to Jeremiah's brain waves. "I command you to fall; you will fall before me." Mysticism is most powerful when the purpose is clear and simple.

I close in on the barn and hear him brushing his horse. The sweet aroma of hay smells like molasses. He keeps an orderly barn, and I would too if I slept in the loft above the horses. Advancing forward, I'm within twelve feet of him. For a moment, I contemplate weaponizing myself with the pitchfork hanging on a hook on the side of the barn. I banish that weak thought and clear my mind. My heart rate hasn't changed; I've trained the buck fever out of my system. He is unaware of his impending doom until he turns to brush the other side of his horse and spots me. He knew I'd come for him.

He drops his brush and says, "So, you're McGurski."

The quick step technique enables me to close the gap to him. In a snap, my mind goes from deliberately being clear to one of definitive purpose. My fist connects with a solid right cross to his solar plexus. As I physically punch him, I accompany it with a mentally projected fist scattering his chi. His slack jaw and wide-open eyes respond to both my speed and the pain from the thunder of my punch. The brunt force staggers him three steps backwards. "*Uhhhh,*" he groans, as the air is sapped out of him. I follow with a flying knee connecting flush under his jaw. His head rocks back. Oh cripes, he's taken my two best shots, and he's still standing. He's dazed and throws a desperate, lazy haymaker. I overreact and duck into a squatting position at the height of his knees. It's fortuitous; the gods of war have blessed me with an impromptu battle plan. I grab his pant cuffs at the ankles and lift, leveraging him off his feet backwards. His massive body is upended onto his head and speared into the ground. His face turns pale white—he's out.

## Chapter 20 Discovery

Now I know what Darcy meant. The ground is the ninth limb of Thai boxing. My idea of combining the quick step with the solar plexus punch won the day and scrambled him good. It happened fast; he lost the duel, and his horse did not even stir. Do not boast, belittle, or linger after a skirmish. This, however, is a duel, a bit different from a regular brawl, and we are supposedly gentlemen upholding the rules. In nine seconds, color returns to his face and I spot what I believe is a glint of happiness in his eyes. Proving I am not a total scoundrel, I offer my hand to help him, but he waves me away. He's not in a condition to stand yet.

He tries hard to speak in between coughing. "Thanks, McGurski. I haven't been hit that hard since my father tried to knock the stupid out of me."

Is he trying to evoke pity? I answer him, "Sounds terrible."

While holding his chest, he discloses in a weakened voice, "I guess when his beatings didn't work, he believed The Foundation and their techniques would cure me of being a cretin."

I offer a modicum of sympathy. "You're no cretin."

"My whole freaking body hurts, but losing to you in a duel releases me from The Foundation. No more rules, no more early morning letters, and no more ceremonies."

"Didn't you make the rules?"

"I made all kinds of crazy rules to frustrate Claude and Alexandra. I guess we'll both be hanging it up."

"How do you figure, sodbuster? You lost the duel."

He changes the subject. "Man, you're fast."

I let him in on a secret. "I recently learned how to move fast." He's earned my admission. "You were right."

He has a mixed expression of satisfaction and fear when he asks me, "Did you do it?"

"Do what?"

"Did you kill Santos?"

I'm not briefing him on the whole story, so I finally admit, "Nah, lack of discipline killed Santos. I mean, you were right, I stole the Movement Letter."

He exhales deeply, and the tenseness in his face subsides. "Can you do me a favor and teach me the quick step technique? It looks fun."

"It is fun, but if I taught you, your heart might explode like Oscar's and Santos'. Plus, The Foundation would bring you back in."

"You're right. Forget about it."

"I respect your discipline and the fact you took my best Sunday punch." Once more, I offer my assistance. Whoa, is he heavy, I double down and lift with both hands.

"I'm not saying it was nice to meet you, McGurski, but under different circumstances, who knows."

"Likewise *hombre*." This mission is complete. I walk back to the van through the large stretch of farmland, relieved

I avoided injury. The reality is the person who attacks first usually wins. After ambushing him, I controlled my adrenaline, which allowed me to diffuse further hostilities. Real world results for the AMP experiment.

Jeremiah's size intimidated me. I understand the expression "the bull is always bigger when you are in the ring with it." His personality did not match my expectations, either. Perhaps the abuse from his father led to him becoming a bully himself. Losing the duel humbled him and changed him for the better. He's freed his demons and can go on with his life. In a way, The Foundation is partly responsible for his cure.

Varla is in the distance standing beside her car wielding binoculars around her neck. Instead of asking her why she's spying, I bounce over to her puppy style and say, "Did you see my knockout?"

The crossed arms across her chest are the first signal. As I'm close enough to see her eyes narrow and nostrils flare, I can feel her rage in the atmosphere.

She saw me move and solved the mystery. "Nobody moves that fast, which means you stole the Movement Letter."

I address my guilt. "Yup."

The decibels in her voice increases. "All these adventures we've been on, and you had it all along."

I change the subject. "Hey, did you leave Ladders wrapped?" Hopefully, this stalling tactic will distract her long enough to cool off.

"Sure, I fed the brat to the ants. Of course, I unwrapped him. Ladders must have been pretty toxic because he discolored those white sheets."

"I'll have Sarrick bleach them; how did Ladders act afterwards?"

"Pretty good."

"Cool. Thanks for running the detox."

"I'm going to need a detox soon, too. Hey! Quit changing the subject. When did you steal the Movement Letter?!"

"After Darcy told me it was missing. It's a long story. Let's talk about it back at the ranch."

"Deal. I'll race you."

"It's on."

I hop into the van and burn out, kicking dirt over the road. The race is a joke; a twenty-nine second head start is not enough, and there's no way for me to outrun her speedy little Alfa Romeo. In seventeen seconds, she pulls alongside the van, beeps her horn, sticks her tongue out, and then passes me. I flip on my high beams to taunt her, and she flips me the bird. Flying down the 101, she is out of sight in a blink. The drive will give me an opportunity to collect myself and explain my case for stealing the Movement Letter.

It's fascinating how one impulsive act can lead to mayhem and change the course of people's lives. I believe Varla is twisted enough to appreciate the calamities caused by the theft of the Movement Letter. If I'm wrong and she's upset, it shall pass. In the words of Doris Day, "*Que sera sera*. Whatever will be will be, the future's not ours to see." However, influencing the future is on my current agenda. To be a free spirit, riding the wind and living the dream, I've learned to trust mystical forces. I'll frame the outcome I desire in my mind. I develop a thought wave pattern and send it out into the ether: "The story of me stealing the Movement Letter is funny, laugh it off." Linking the wavelength to Varla's personal channel is a snap because we are connected.

## Chapter 21 Truth with Varla

I arrive at the ranch and Varla's in the backyard reading a mixed martial arts magazine on a chaise lounge chair. She changed into a tight white t-shirt a couple of sizes too small and yoga pants. Her glorious curves are on full display. I'm saluting her in my own way, but not with my hands.

Varla greets me, "Welcome back, slowpoke."

"Wait until we go camping and then you'll appreciate the tan van."

"I gotta hear your defense; I don't know why, but I expect it's a funny story."

She specifically said the word "funny." That means these mystical thought waves are legitimate. I got to remember to use my mysticism more often. "How am I supposed to concentrate with you wearing a tight white t-shirt? Those curves are driving me nuts."

"Come here," she says in a seductive voice.

I quick step to her and create a gust of wind blowing her hair back.

"You move faster than your van. Tell me the story later. Tend to my needs."

I mount her, nibbling my way to the side of her neck and whisper, "Let's do it right here."

She groans with pleasure. My right hand is cradling her neck while my left hand moves its way from her waist to her ample breasts. What an unexpected and thrilling twist. She arches accentuating her breasts, which allows me to move my left hand to slide her pants off and then she suddenly stops me.

"Hey, blue balls, tell me the rest of the story."

"Ohhh, you're sinister. You can't do this to me." I stand literally and figuratively. The aching in my loins is brutal.

"You earned it."

"I'm going inside to ice my balls. My nuts are reporting you to human resources. Do you want a drink?"

"Sure, how about a Shasta or a TAB?"

I shuffle into the kitchen, hunched over as if I took a shot to the groin. I yell back to her, "Sorry, I'm out of stock of 1980s soda. I'll surprise you." My ice supply is depleted from the AMP experiment, so I grab a bag of frozen broccoli to ice my nether regions. The refrigerator is stocked with Perrier. It occurs to me Varla has been to the grocery store, and that coupled with her clothes in the closet suggests she's moved in. I hand her a bottle of Perrier sparkling water.

She examines the bottle and then at me with suspicion. "Did you shake it?"

I gingerly sit on the adjacent lounger and place the chilled bag of broccoli on my man parts. "Ahhh, the mysteries of life. To shake or not to shake that is the question."

She fires back, "If this water explodes on me, shaking is all you'll be doing." She opens it slowly, with no fizzy eruptions.

"I heard Frenchies like Perrier."

"I'm Lebanese, and it's pronounced Perrier." She annunciates Perrier with a proper French accent.

"True, you don't smell like a Frenchie."

"You kind of do."

I sniff both of my armpits. "You saying I need to musk up?"

"Your nut sack bag of broccoli smells better than you."

"You'll love the beef and broccoli fricassee I'm cooking for lunch."

"Gross."

"Give me a sip."

She hands me the bottle of Perrier.

"On with the story, numb nuts. I've waited long enough."

"All right, Darcy gave me Santos' address. I went to his house and tossed it, looking for the Movement Letter."

"What's so important about this letter?"

I hesitate for a moment, but since Varla already knows me pretty well, this won't be a shock. "I thought it might explain how to levitate."

"What are you, six-years-old?"

"I was still tossing his house looking for the Movement Letter when Santos came home. When I heard his car pull into the driveway, I slid out the back window, and casually strolled to the front of the house. I presented myself as an agent from the auction company and fed him a line about a mistake in the desk's value. He invited me inside and freaked when he saw his house had been torn apart. I led him to believe auction thieves ransacked his house for the desk and he should part ways with it to avoid further invasions. With a bit more manipulation, he informed me the desk was in a storage container. I flashed cash, told him I'd buy it for triple the price he paid, and followed him to the storage unit in Goleta. Once he opened his container, I found The Movement Letter in the top drawer and studied the quick step technique. Within minutes of reading, I practiced traveling short distances of nine to fifteen feet."

"Why did you practice the technique in front of him? You could have waited and practiced in private."

I'm about to find out how flexible Varla is with rules. "Santos seemed like a pretty cool guy. He had a Dodge Viper in the garage and a Harley Iron 883 motorcycle. I figured he's the kind of guy that would be astonished with the quick step."

"You are the only person who says the word astonished."

"It's better than saying amazed."

"Go on."

"When I demonstrated to Santos how fast I could move, he flipped. He begged me to teach him. I taught him the movement, but forgot to teach him how to stop. On his first attempt, he blasted off, but when he tried to stop, he fell and slid six feet. A nasty spill, but it didn't discourage him. He laughed off the scrapes on his side and tried again."

"He learned that fast?"

"Yeah, it's pretty easy once he learned how to stop. He did a couple of runs yelling, 'This is awesome, yeee haw!' Santo's goofy smile and joyous fist pumps are etched into my memory. It's easy to share with someone who appreciates. I ignored his awesoming, but I halted his attempt to high-five me."

"He tried to high-five you!? That's too much."

"When I abruptly shouted, 'No high-fives,' he responded with the familiar scrunched nose and head tilt reaction, the calling card of confusion. After his third run, the sweat poured off his forehead as he labored with heavy breathing. His last words were, 'One more time.' Then his heart exploded."

Varla is laughing. "It's tragic and all, but I clearly picture you two zipping around and Santos trying to high-five YOU." She tries to catch her breath from laughing and talking at the same time. "Then what did you do?"

I exhale a stream of relieved air out of my lungs, grateful she appreciates my position. "I shoved his body in the storage container, wiped my fingerprints, and scrammed. When I returned to the ranch, I secured the Movement Letter and laid in bed, wondering how I could have taught Santos without him dying. The next morning, I delivered the Letter of Action to Alexandra."

"Your fingerprints must be everywhere. You mean to tell me you wiped down his house and storage container?" Varla asks.

"I started to wipe the container down and then remembered, I don't really have fingerprints anymore. After years of suffering from sweaty hands, my fingerprints are almost nonexistent."

"Leave it to you to find the silver lining in having sweaty hands. What about the auction and smashing the desk on the beach?" Varla asks.

"I stole the Movement Letter before the auction."

To lighten the mood, I playfully look around, as if checking for eavesdroppers. "As for the beach, smashing a gaudy desk seemed fun. I asked The Good Time Boys to bring sledgehammers and gas. I owed it to them because I flaked out on our last training day."

She gawks at me with her big, golden eyes and raised eyebrows. "Wow, you're an outlaw. I knew bringing a desk to the beach sounded like a McGurski thing."

"I tried not to laugh when you said that."

"I understand why you shared the letter with Santos. Have you ever read the book, *The Kybalion?*"

"Yes! *The Kybalion* started my mystical journey."

Her energy rises. "Me too! This quote explains everything, 'The ears of understanding are open to the lips of Wisdom.'"

"Think about the thousands of uninitiated people who can benefit from this knowledge."

"The problem with Alexandra is she only shares letters with a select few. It drives me nuts."

"How would you select candidates?" I inquire.

"Oh, I've given this a lot of thought. I'd pick the naturals, the uncontrollable, and the exceptional. We'll be a diverse pack."

"The Foundation is pretty diverse."

"True, but where The Foundation is stingy with selections, I'll be generous. Where The Foundation is careful, I'll be reckless. I'd also propose an amendment to The Foundation mission statement and add cleaning the streets of the un-roadworthy."

I add an amendment, "Humans who chuck cigarettes out their car window need to be road raged."

"I like it," she affirms and adds, "drivers who turn without using the turn signal get smashed."

"One more; humans who litter unlucky lottery tickets and fast food wrappers, must suffer thirty lashes."

We widen the net of acceptable excuses to road rage.

I fill her in on a secret, "Hey, crusader, the inside scoop is The Foundation has big plans soon to step out of the shadows again. Hopefully, their selection process is better than mine, as my first initiate didn't last too long."

"You and your initiates need impulse control." As she leans on the word impulse control, I squeeze her breasts.

"*Ooooh*," she lets out.

I smile and say, "I'm an uncontrollable."

"You're exceptional too."

I stand behind her and rub her shoulders. Carrying those breasts around is grounds for a free massage. Exploring the versatility of my hands that have the power to caress and tenderize, I whisper to her, "Get some rest, tomorrow morning we've got a crazy mission."

## Chapter 22 The Little League Follies

Elings Park sits on top of the summit, 400 feet above sea level, and is famous for its majestic views of the Santa Ynez mountain range and Pacific Ocean. It's a popular destination for weddings, picnics, hang-gliders, mountain bikers, and youth baseball. An ornamental three-foot stone wall curves throughout the picnic area and keeps the meadows of wildflowers at bay. Gnarled oak trees are scattered in the park and are especially pleasing in the pavilion, where the wooden deck is built around twisted oaks. There are three baseball fields on a plateau. Our challenge is to find which one the Motorcycle Laundromat Batters are playing on. The team wearing orange and white with a motorcycle patch on their sleeve is a giveaway.

"Our mission is at a little league game? What kind of OP is this?" demands Varla.

"Support mission. Sarrick sponsored a team. I told him I'd come to cheer for them."

"I hate kids."

"We all do. But these aren't normal kids. Each of these little boogers has a slapstick comedian inside of them. Sarrick is not big on kids either. He's in his mid-fifties and has no plans of creating offspring. In lieu of kids, he's sponsoring this team to pass on knowledge and get more customers. I applaud his efforts on both endeavors."

"What do you mean? How do the kids become comedians?"

"As soon as the game starts. The kids will entertain us with standard little league misplays, overthrows, dropped balls, players running into each other, tripping over shoe laces, its absolute follies. Only 1940s movies can relate."

"I'll take a nap."

Maybe this angle will change her mind. "Cool, I'll wake you when the parents get out of control."

"Do they fight?"

"Mostly argue, but if you're lucky, they'll throw down."

She scans the parents in the bleachers, the umpire, and the monarch butterfly whirling around her face for their inherent potential for violence. "The lady in the green top has an edge to her." The butterfly and umpire earn a pass.

"Where? Which one?"

"The blonde wearing the green shirt. The one with D cups."

A large cup size always grabs my attention.

"Oh yeah, what makes you think she's feisty?"

"She's got the look. I know it when I see it."

"I'll keep my eyes on her. Did you see the pregnant guy in the red shirt inhaling those hotdogs? Twenty bucks says he spills ketchup on his shirt."

"You and your gambling. I'm not touching that action. He'll catch it with his bottom shelf."

"My gambling has won me thousands of dollars. What's your fighting got you, a wanted poster in the post office?"

"If we went to Vegas right now, what would you do?"

Chills. Oh, the lure of the casino. In my heyday, Vegas meant a joyous playground, a house where adrenaline and numbers danced into the wee hours of the night. It's not the chance of winning big that fueled me, it's the thrill of overcoming the probabilities. No other place offers this intoxicating mix of numbers and adrenaline.

"That depends on what hotel we're staying at."

"They're all the same with flashy lights, no clocks, and cigar ridden money traps."

"No, no, no, no, not true. Each one has its own personality."

"How many have you been to?"

"On the west side of the strip, I've been to Mandalay Bay, Luxor, Excalibur, New York New York, Bellagio, Caesars, Mirage, Treasure Island, Circus Circus, and Stratosphere. On the east side, Tropicana and MGM Grand. Twelve in total."

"You're a degenerate."

Little does she know, I recited the hotels in their precise order. "I can mathematically prove I'm not a degenerate."

"You're too much. You've got a degenerate formula?"

"Every trip to Las Vegas, I split my action. I gamble for three days and then I drive two-and-a-half hours to Zion National Park to hike and camp for three days. A degenerate would not balance nature and city life."

"Not bad. I almost buy your bullshit formula. For our next vacation, we're going to Lebanon, not Vegas."

"Is it safe to drive in Lebanon?"

"Not all Lebanese are nuts, just me. In Lebanon, it's normal for strangers to invite you into their homes for a seat at the dinner table. We'll take a vacation from the numbers, gambling, and road rage."

"Uh, yeah sure." I'm somewhere else, not distracted, just zoned in. I'm not looking at the blonde in the D cups, or Varla's triple Ds. I've found a mark. There he is, the grown man with his hat on backwards. He's sitting on the lower bleachers, too lazy to climb the stairs, ripe for the pickings. In the cartoons, I'd have dollars signs for eyes. He's a bored father, fulfilling his Saturday morning obligations.

Varla smacks me in the shoulder. "Are you listening to me?"

"Easy pickings, I've found our mark."

"A who?"

"A chump, sucker, sitting duck, dupe, stooge, in other words, an easy guy to fleece."

When I approach this moron, I expect and will endure his obvious canned phrases. His comments regarding the little league game will be along the lines of, "Beats mowing the lawn" or "I'd rather be fishing." I'll tolerate this chatter in order to rip him off.

Before Varla can interfere or object, my long strides down the bleachers advance me to my target. If I could slither over to him to accentuate my intentions, I would.

I ask him, "Is that your boy on deck?"

"Yeah, how did you know?"

"Good looking kid, he looks just like you."

"Thanks. He's having a rough day out there. It's tough to watch but beats cutting the grass."

Internally, I cringe. I predicted it was coming, although he did say cut the grass instead of mow. If he said pulverize the grass, we'd become lifelong chums. He's played his role, and now I'll spring my turmoil on him.

"I bet you twenty bucks he strikes out."

"Excuse me?"

"I'll give you three-to-one odds."

He rocks back and forth to get his weight moving with upward momentum to stand. "Listen, I'm not betting on my son to get a hit."

I've grown accustomed to an escalation in voice volume when I confront humans. "He doesn't have to get a hit; he could pop up, line out, get hit by a pitch, work a walk. I'm betting he'll strike out."

"What's your problem?"

"It's a win-win for you. If your son does anything but wiff, you win sixty bucks. If he wiffs, you're fueled by embarrassment to practice with your son and you'll bond."

He turns his head a few inches, which means he's processing. Varla's behind me snickering and hopes this guy will snap. I haven't pushed him that far.

"I'm not betting on my son," he firmly states and probably believes this is the conclusion of our conversation.

I push him a little further. "It's a meager twenty-dollar wager."

"I said no!"

I double down and try another angle. If Varla won't take this action, maybe this stiff will. "See the pregnant guy over there in the red shirt? Twenty bucks says he spills ketchup on his shirt."

"If you don't leave me alone, I'm calling security."

In desperation, I offer him one more piece of action. "How about even money riding on the left fielder to trip on his untied shoelaces?"

Varla interjects, "Nobody is taking that action, not even this slouch. Let's just watch this boring game. Don't make me call your sponsor."

Varla, the voice of reason. An interesting turn of events. We all have our weakness. I love baseball, the numbers, piles of statistics, sporadic action, and, of course, the endless opportunities to gamble.

*** 

Sarrick's team of wiry clowns are fast, but can't hit the ball out of the infield. They're not sluggers. Milk is not cutting it for these weaklings. I'll chat with Loto and Ragni about little league group discount rates for steroids. The Surfside Auto Muffler team members are massive. They might be on the juice. Their first baseman is growing a beard, and the catcher is as big as me. In today's matchup, power is outmatching speed.

Sarrick sees us accosting the little league dad and waves us over near the dugout. His team is up to bat and each kid on his team holds the bat like a cricket mallet. They are all swinging with massive exaggerated undercut swings, as if playing cricket.

"Sarrick, your team sucks," is my informal greeting. Varla smacks me on the shoulder again, a gentle reminder to introduce her. "Oh. This is my girlfriend, Varla."

He shakes her hand and says, "Nice to meet you; stick with this guy and you'll get mad discounts on laundry service."

"Nice to meet you, too. You see right through me, I've been using him all along for those sweet discounts on dry cleaning. I'm always getting stains on my top shelf," says Varla.

He steals a glance at her chest, and his predictability is met with laugher from Varla and me. I can't blame him.

"Did you forget to teach the kids how to swing a bat?" Varla asks.

"It's not cricket, but close enough. We're trying to class up the game Indian style."

"Try giving the kids steroids and chewing tobacco," Varla jokes.

He laughs, but is probably unsure if she's serious or not. "Glad you could make it. I've got to get back to coaching and nice to meet you Varla."

"You too."

"I'll hook them up with the roids. I've got a connection," I yell.

"Geeze, man," Sarrick quips.

I guess I yelled it too loud, as seventeen humans in the bleachers are giving me odd stares. We go back and perch ourselves on the bleachers.

"Is it me or is the only dialogue I seem to hear is, 'How are the wife and kids?' and 'How is he doing in school?'"

Varla nods in agreement and says, "These saps are lame."

"In Varla POV, how should they act?" My question puts an incorrigible grin on her face as her imagination has been given free rein.

"They'd act uninhibited. Jugs in the green shirt should flash these nimrods and give the crowd what they want to see. Set those mammary glands free. They should have incense burning, fog machines, a snake handler, a fortune teller with a crystal ball, a hotdog eating contest, a fire breather, no holds barred wrestling, a parade of elephants, and a leotard wearing muscle man lifting dumbbells while riding a unicycle."

Her rebranding of the little league atmosphere combines the best elements of The Coney Island Freak Show and the set of any 1980s music video.

"They'd sell out every game; maybe The Foundation could sponsor it."

"I'm hungry. Do you want anything from the concession stand? Can I leave you alone for a second?"

"I'm good. I'll be a good boy."

Six rows away, I hear baseball banter. An irritant with a mustache and shirt with words on it is clamoring about balls and strikes. "Hey, ump, where's your dog and cane?" The cliché banter rattles me. I can't tune him out. For all my mental skills and tricks, this incessant gnat of a human is renting space inside my head. I send thought waves to him with the message "shut up." To no avail. I counter by yelling, "Good call, ump."

He persists with his obviousness, "Hey, ump, did you forget your glasses?"

Varla is back with a plate of buffalo chicken wings, "A second ago, I swear I heard you yelling."

"I was congratulating the ump."

"Yeah, right."

"Hey, let me have one of those drumsticks."

"I asked if you wanted anything, you said no, you had your chance, get your own."

"I guess I'll have to do this." I swoop in and snatch one seagull style. "Too slow."

"You take one more, I dare you," Varla hisses at me.

"I just wanted one." I've got plans for this wing; once I finish the meat, this bird will fly again.

"Come on, blue, get your head in the game. Are you blind?" the irritant barks.

"What's that idiot yelling about?"

"Balls and strikes."

"He's annoying. Did you tell him to shut up?"

"I've got a better plan."

The bleachers are no place for this crumb and his generic banter. Time to activate operation Freedom Bird. I chuck the remains of the chicken wing bone like a tomahawk and watch its glorious flight path as the wing sails through the air end over end until plugging the irritant in the back of the head. Mission accomplished!

"What the … who threw that?" He stands surveying the audience until he locates Varla, the only person eating chicken wings.

"Did you throw that wing at me?" he yells.

"No, but what if I did, what are you going to do about it?" she yells.

My face must be red from cackling, and tears pour down my face as I try to catch my breath.

"What are you laughing about?" he asks me.

Varla shouts, "LEAVE HIM OUT OF IT. I ASKED YOU A QUESTION. WHAT ARE YOU GOING TO DO ABOUT IT?" With each word, Varla advances a step closer to the irritant.

I try to warn him, "Hey, tough guy, she's not the type to sell wolf tickets."

"You got a big mouth, lady, almost as big as your fat ass."

He ignores my warning, and oh Nelly, he's doomed.

Varla plasters the nitwit with the plate of hot wings, pie in the face style with the force of an Olympic shot putter. His neck snaps back, and he is unconscious even before tumbling down the bleachers. Ding, ding, ding, throw in the towel, it's a knockout.

"Fuck! There goes forty-three days," Varla yells at herself.

"Forty-three days of what?" I ask.

"I've been punch sober for forty-three days. It felt good though, I needed that."

I wasn't aware of punch sobriety being a thing, but with Varla it sounds right. The crowd swarms to check on the numbskull as we drink a whole glass of scram and vamoose.

## Chapter 23 Why High Fives and the Word "Awesome" Suck

We make our getaway in the tan van down the curvy road as we hear the distinct sirens of an ambulance, followed by police sirens to rescue the nitwit with the face of wings. A minute later, the ambulance and police cruiser zip past us up the hill. Meanwhile, Varla flips her hair in a carefree manner. After committing assault and battery, Varla's biggest concern is the strand of hair that flopped back into her eyes. If I was a strand of her shiny dark hair, I would get in line because defiance might evoke violence. I imagine her karate chopping her unruly hair into crooked bangs.

I ask Varla, "You hungry?"

"Yeah, I didn't finish my wings."

"You ever been to Sumo Burritos on West Victoria Street?"

"Sumo Burritos? What is that, Mex-Asian fusion?"

"Let's find out."

The pay-to-park meter in front of Sumo Burritos no longer vexes me, as I have the adequate funds to park. I'm sliding out of the van about to deposit money in the meter when I hear Varla mumble something.

"What?" I say.

"I said before we order our food, give me a back massage. Those bleachers with no back support are the worst." She lies prone on the van bed and waits.

"Alright, I'll give you a three-minute massage, then we eat."

I straddle her waist and dig into her shoulders, kneading them.

"That feels good, but go lower, it's my back that's sore." Her stomach growls, and she tells it to shut up. While squeezing and rubbing her lower back, her moans guide me to the sore areas. Two minutes later, her ADD kicks in. "Why do you hate high fives so much?"

Other people have asked me this question before and I pounce at the chance to answer. "High fives are childish and condescending. When you have a disability, teachers smother you with awesomes, good jobs, and high fives. A bulletin to teachers, please mix in surrogate superlatives and don't slap my palms with yours."

"You can't fault them for their enthusiasm and encouragement."

She may have a point. I explain further. "You've seen the puzzle pieces representing Autism Awareness?"

"Yes."

"I view myself as a puzzle piece that doesn't fit into the rest of the puzzle. A true outlier. I'm the piece that does not need teachers to coddle me. I honed my thick skin on the playground. If I got teased, I fought and became more durable mentally and physically." As I'm speaking, I stop massaging her because I'm animated and expressively using my hands while making my point.

"We're a lot alike. Hey, don't stop," she says, referring to the massage. I reengage with the massage and she tilts her head back, smiling and says, "You should post on school bulletin boards a moratorium has been placed on good jobs, awesomes, and high fives."

"The irony is I've never done a good job or had a good job until now," I lament.

My ADD kicks in. "What's the real story with Alexandra hiring you to investigate me?"

"Oh, that's private."

I raise her arms, exposing her armpits, and warn her I will have to tickle it out of her. She squirms sideways, laughing, and folding her arms to shield her armpits. I regain my top position and practice the top control ground game I passively absorbed from watching the Ultimate Fighting Championship (UFC).

"I'll tell you if you get off me, your breath is awful."

I disengage from my stellar ground control, pull a cellophane bag out of my pocket, and pinch two fingers' worth of mint sprigs to chew.

"Are you eating an actual sprig of mint?"

"Yes, would you like a sprig? Your breath doesn't stink." Fortunately, I replenished my stock and have extra to offer her.

"Sure I'll try it." I hand her a sprig. "I've never had real mint before, but this taste's pretty good,"

"Quit stalling."

"I've never seen you this impatient before."

She teases me. I tease her back by sitting in the lotus pose, pretending to meditate.

"Alexandra was suspicious of your relationship with Claude. Especially after he suggested you mentor her son," she answers.

"Did you know Alexandra and Claude lived together?" I add.

"Alexandra told me they were married for years and Jeremiah ruined their marriage."

"Because he bullied both of them. Nobody in The Foundation likes Jeremiah's bulling style or his rules."

"I'm guessing she adopted Jacob (Ladders) to correct the mistakes they made trying to raise Jeremiah."

"Have you noticed nobody in The Foundation has natural offspring?"

"When you have a disorder, a part of you is resistant to pass it on to the next generation because you understand the trials they'll face," she reflects.

"Removing yourself from the gene pool is the ultimate sacrifice. It's shepherding the well-being of the future herd. For me, mentorship is the way." As evident with Ladders.

"I hate kids."

I can't discern if she's joking or not. "Did The Foundation really want me to back off practicing technique?"

"No, I said that to screw with you."

I shake my head and a few flakes of dandruff fall on my shoulder. Next time I'm at the store, I need to buy a different brand of shampoo as my hygiene is a mess, but at least it's not head lice. Am I talking to myself again? Internally, I have checked out, spaced out, and unplugged from reality. Regain focus, McGurski, and reenter the conversation. "Freaking dandruff," I say. It's a nice recovery, and I doubt she caught me spacing.

"You were right. None of The Foundation members appreciated Jeremiah's intimidating approach. Especially Claude. Also, the flamboyant horse riding gimmick attracted too much attention."

"Jeremiah did crazy stuff on purpose to rattle them."

"Claude told Jeremiah you stole the Movement Letter, and I covered for you."

"Who told you that?"

"Eddy told me when were at the beach."

"Claude set me up. He must have known after accusing me of stealing, Jeremiah would challenge me to a duel."

"But you stole it."

"Yeah, but they don't know that."

"What are you going to say to Claude?"

"Jeremiah is done."

"And the Movement Letter?"

"Oh, I'm keeping it."

"You're quite the Dickens."

The smells of soy sauce and toasted corn from Sumo Burrito permeate the van, a blunt reminder of our hunger. Before getting out of the van, I notice two dainty tourists in their thirties strolling on the sidewalk close to the van. The gentleman has his hair neatly parted to the side and wears a polo shirt aggressively tucked into his blue trousers. His girlfriend is holding his hand and has a blue ribbon in her hair. They are dull candidates that need some spice in their overprotected lives.

"Varla, let's give these preps a show."

She plays along and screams, "Give it to me harder. Sock it to me, baby!"

I rock the van and peep out the window to see the aghast look on the young couple's faces.

Varla yells to them, "Hey, want to join us?" as she swings open the side door and laughs devilishly.

Needless to say, their stroll became a light jog away from us. After our interaction with the tourists, we order a couple of Yokozuna Street Burritos. Their advertisement weirdly boasts burritos the size of a brick and heavier. They live up to their sumo moniker. The Yokozuna Street Burrito is the kind of meal you eat outside if there are street cleaners nearby. A crow caws from an adjacent tree, spouting he will devour our fumbled crumbs. The flour tortilla is no match for the overstuffed contents inside, a weird combination of sushi, ground beef, black beans, and cheese. I can't place the taste, so I'll cop out and declare it to be edible.

"How is it?" I ask Varla.

"Uhhh, edible?"

"Same pager; you read my mind."

Lunch has been a pleasant respite from our adventure, but things are adding up. After lunch, I'll piece together this mental puzzle and meditate on this caper. I've got a hunch there will be huge revelations.

## Chapter 24 Meditation Chamber

It's midafternoon and I'm meditating inside my copper pyramid. The infused pure oxygen from the plants stimulates my mind. I check Jeremiah off my mental checklist. Checking boxes normally is a satisfying event for me, but this check didn't have the expected impact. What's bothering me is his relief to be finished with The Foundation. He said the early mornings sucked, but that's not enough to leave this type of gig. The money is great for the work we do, but the real work is on ourselves. He complained about the rules and he wrote the rules. Maybe Alexandra was right about Jeremiah needing to be realigned. When I knocked him out, something inside of him shifted.

I've been so preoccupied with Jeremiah, I have not properly paid my respects to Santos. In retrospect, maybe I should have high fived with him. Before his heart exploded, he tried to connect with me and because he tried to high five awesome me, I denied him of a compadre. He chose to celebrate in a common way, but being a friend means respecting different styles. Who cares if people say the word awesome, amazing, or good job? These are positive words, albeit overused. I've been negative. Maybe The High Fiving Awesomers limited their expressions to fit in.

For years, I struggled to share my sentiments and could not grasp why a person would deny themselves diverse avenues to express their emotions. I viewed Claude's stoicism and the limited vocabulary of The Awesomers as self-imposed disabilities. In return, I mocked them for being normal. I said before, "We're all on the spectrum." The self-imposed rules are the boxes we build to conceal ourselves. To be open and expressive is to be vulnerable.

I liberated a part of myself by sharing The High Fiving Awesomers report with Varla. She understood it and could identify with the comedy and the plight. When I shared the Santos tragedy with Varla she revealed the lighter side of herself. She never met Santos and therefore had no remorse for his death but also acknowledged the comedy of that situation. It's a healthy viewpoint to find laughter in untraditional places. Maybe my mystical wavelengths influenced her or it's her carefree nature, but she handled the discovery of my theft of the Movement Letter quite well too.

In meditation, you allow your ideas to flow, and often there are no clean segues between thoughts. It is kind of like letting your ADD run wild. For a moment I reflect on ridiculous titles: Mr. Mrs. Miss, ma'am, sir, doctor, The Horseman, The Specialist, The Minister, The Overlord, The Count, Ladders, Varla, and ZZ-Top Heavy. Titles are strange.

My muscles are unaccustomed to sitting still for this length of time, but the clarity with which I'm seeing things today is unmatched. I'll remain motionless until I determine what my next step will be.

At Alexandra's house, my eyes were opened to the true nature of The Foundation and Jeremiah. It amuses me they pretended to be a cult. They share similarities. With my knowledge of cults and Varla's support, we could overthrow The Foundation and turn it into a real cult. We could run The Foundation better than them. Sarrick's philosophy is right. Working at a job is training to run your own business or, in this case, form a cult.

Claude enticed me into the organization with outlandish made up stories of Bruce Lee and General Patton having an affiliation with The Foundation. His background knowledge in my interest in the martial arts no doubt fueled those outlandish claims. We'll utilize the same strategies to hook new recruits.

My visit with Darcy taught me to self-advocate. In the past, when I've sought guidance, it has paid dividends. I can't take over The Foundation by myself. I need Varla, Darcy, and The Good Time Boys on my side.

I express my gratitude for my development and dedicate myself to guiding people with disorders on their journey. They'll be indoctrinated the McGurski way with no high fives and no awesomes. Our cult will be different, but that's what they all say. There's a chance assisting others will allow me to maintain my balance between being a gentleman and a savage.

A revelation occurs to me. Three members run The Foundation: Claude, Alexandra, and Oscar. It's obvious they are not a worldwide force, and I had not realized that until now. Perhaps those sneaky rascals have been grooming Varla and me for Oscar's position. When Varla and I upend The Foundation, our mission will remain closely aligned; share the wisdom with the ones who will benefit from it, while adding a McGurski spin.

The dangers of this takeover do not elude me. This is a big home run swing; if I miss and strike out, it's back to living in the van or worse. A gamble of a lifetime with high stakes. I'm not gambling with house money. Not only is my future at stake, but Varla's, Darcy's, and The Good Time Boys, too. I'll feel lousy if it backfires and my crew is exiled, but if I don't take the swing, I'll regret it for the rest of my life. High risk equals high reward, and low risks aren't worth the squeeze. I'm rolling the dice.

I'm grateful to everyone in The Foundation and the next move is to confront them, thank them in person, and share my new vision. I exit the meditation chamber, proud of my patience to sit still for over twenty-three minutes and solve multiple equations. Throughout the whole session, I tuned out noises and powered through distractions.

Back to reality, I hear Varla munching kettle-cooked potato chips and a roast beef sando (sandwich). A dollop of mustard splatters on the upper part of her shirt. "My top shelf catches everything," she mutters, without an attempt to remove the stain.

"I'll clean it off," I say, but she restrains my lecherous offer with a stare.

"How was your trip to outer space? Did you come back with any prophecies?" she sarcastically asks.

I'm convinced she'll remain curious and skeptical of the pyramid meditation chamber until she has her turn.

On the ride over to Darcy's, I share my revelation with Varla in the McGurski way. We're ready to visit our constituents, and shake The Foundation.

## Chapter 25 Another Visit with the Ladies

I spring out of the van, eager to boast to Darcy regarding the outcome of the duel.

"Are you coming?" I ask Varla.

"No, go ahead, I'll wait in the van."

"What's up?"

"There's too much temptation in there, and I might deck her. Plus, her house stinks."

I haven't really seen Varla fight yet, and blasting the loud mouth at the baseball game hardly qualifies as a fight. But I do know from play wrestling with her she's plenty strong. "I'd buy ringside seats for that fight."

"If it ever happens, bet on me. I'm staying in the van and preparing for our overthrow of The Foundation. Say hi to Stinky for me, I mean Skunky, I mean Darcy. Take a deep breath before you go inside."

"Rough."

Darcy meets me at the door, and the smell of skunk pushes me back one step. It's more than skunk; her house is a membrane containing the funk of chili powder, curry, skunk, and incense. Darcy does a cursory scan from my head to my toes for injuries before inviting me inside.

"Well?" she inquires.

I cough a few times to clear my throat of the odor and tell Darcy, "The ninth limb of Muay Thai is the floor." I reach to shake her hand and thank her, but she gives me a hug.

"The sensation when you fully connect and knock someone out … it's ineffable," she replies.

Her vocabulary is expanding; a while back she had used the word uncanny and today ineffable. She's rehearsing these lines or using *The How to Speak English* textbook for more than a chest protector. I admit to her I have no idea what ineffable means. "Ineffable?"

"It means too great to be described in words."

I clarify my reactions. "It felt ineffable when I hit Jeremiah, and then I felt a weird connection with him. One minute I'm punching a hole through his chest, and then we're chums."

"You're not a villain after all. Sharing a battle you earned each other's respect."

"It's funny, that's what I told Jeremiah, 'I respect your discipline.'"

In an unprecedented gesture, she asks me to sit on her couch. She sits next to me and opens a well-worn red scrapbook. There are newspaper clippings, magazine articles, and multiple photographs of her Thai boxing matches. Of course, she's probably felt the same feeling in the battles she's endured in the ring. She's not so robotic after all. This is not her bragging, and in multiple pictures, she is bowing or hugging her opponent.

"These moments meant more to me than the titles. The comradery and electricity I shared with these girls in the ring is something I've been chasing since I've retired from boxing."

"Have you tried gambling?"

"You are hopeless."

"I'm joking. But I think I understand. For over a week, the image of Jeremiah punching through brick walls has captured my imagination. Strangely, battling the constant worrying outdid the dread of the actual dual. Now that it's over, it's a fond memory."

"I take it back, you're not completely hopeless. I suspect Jeremiah will heal from this loss and become better. Just like my knuckles. My hands (are) all better."

They still looked pretty mangled. Do I correct her and say, "My hands are better." No, now is not the time for an English lesson. "I hope Jeremiah heals from it, too. Varla's in the van waiting for me. We're heading over to Alexandra's and then Claude's for a victory lap."

"She's an ornery one, don't keep her waiting."

In the background, maybe in her backyard, I hear a *pa-wush* and *ping* noise. I've heard it a few times while we were talking. "What's that noise?" I ask her.

"What noise?"

"The *pa-wush* and *ping*."

"Oh, I pay the kid next store to shoot the skunks. He's practicing, shooting targets with his air rifle."

"Are they still eating your avocados?"

"Yes, and now a family of skunks moved in under my back deck. Nobody wants to visit because my house smells like a skunk."

"Well, good luck with your skunks, and thanks again for the battle plan."

"My pleasure, see ya."

She is becoming personable. Her dialogue and tone are warmer. My guess is Alexandra is mentoring her. Returning to the van, Varla is sporting a devious smile.

"Are you pleased with yourself?" I ask.

"While waiting for you, I've been planning how to tell Claude about us taking over The Foundation. My idea is simple and direct."

As long as she doesn't punch Claude in the face, I'll smooth it out. I notice she doesn't ask about Darcy. There is clearly tension between the two.

Next stop is Alexandra's house. I hate driving the van around these mountainous roads. Each twist and turn is too tight for a big van. "Cripes, I can't make this turn." I have to back up because the van's turn radius and length can't turn sharp enough.

"Hmmmf." Varla holds her tongue, trying not to criticize my driving.

"Are you kidding me?" I exclaim, as I have to do the same thing around the next turn. It's not so much the effort of backing up that creates the tension as the anticipation of Varla berating my driving. This must be eating her up, so I'll show her sympathy and provide a target for her wrath. "Three, two and one, let me have it, Varla."

Varla breathes in deep and exhales in relief. "You don't know what you're doing. Let me drive."

"I got this. The van's not built for these twists."

"You're not cutting it right. The Fed Ex trucks do this every day without having to back up. Here, let me show you." On the following turn, she grabs the wheel and gradually turns nine feet before I would have. She makes the turn easily, looks at me in the eyes, smiles, and sits back in the passenger seat with her fingers interlocked behind her neck. It's the leisure/gloating pose. When it comes to driving, Varla knows her stuff.

We park on the street and gaze at the Pacific Ocean, rows of tall, slender palm trees, and the rest of the city from a high vantage point only the Riviera can provide. Alexandra greets us at the door and is wearing a Lilly Pulitzer style pastel green and pink floral dress.

I goof around and say, "Afternoon tea for three?" Alexandra has schooled me, and I know afternoon tea is between 3 p.m. and 4 p.m. while high tea is after 5 p.m.

I'm here in one piece with no marks or bruises, and she instantly deduces my victory over Jeremiah.

"You did it!" Alexandria exclaims. "Come in and sit. The water is already boiling for afternoon tea. Good to see you too, Varla. Did you just finish working out?"

Her commentary on Varla's tight white t-shirt and yoga pants is her form of light scrutiny. Her formal manners are clear as she offers Varla an unsolicited shawl to cover her melons. She politely refuses the shawl and projects confidence in her skin. Varla wins this battle of wills.

"Oh, it so good to see you two together, you make such a sweet couple."

"Are you sure sweet is the right word?" Varla challenges.

Ignoring Varla's remark, Alexandra presses on. "May I recommend a caffeine-free spearmint, peppermint, or chamomile tea?" She remembered and is considerate of my issues with caffeine.

"Spearmint," says Varla.

"Spearmint, please," I echo.

We sit on her ancient rock hard furniture and chat while sipping tea. With the three of us choosing spearmint, the aroma is multiplied and invigorating.

"Is Jeremiah okay?" asks Alexandra.

I respond in a cavalier manner. "He'll be fine. I took your advice and trained with Darcy. She taught me a special technique to drop him."

"Physically, I'm sure he'll be fine. How did he behave afterwards? Did he seem mentally stable?" Alexandra probes.

"He said he was happy to be leaving The Foundation."

"Did he say why?" she asks.

"Yeah, he did. He said there are too many rules and the early morning ceremonies are stupid."

"Ah that." She straightens the fabric in her dress, sips her tea, and clears her throat before continuing, pivoting the conversation with her dignity intact. "He created those childish rules!"

"I think Jeremiah will be fine. Before we left the farm, I saw him tending to his horse," says Varla.

"You were there too?" Alexandra asks Varla.

"From a distance, watching with binoculars. My man needs constant supervision, he's incorrigible."

"We all must care for someone and for me, I guess it's Jeremiah. I hope he's okay."

She guesses that she cares for Jeremiah? Even Varla raises an eyebrow at that statement of quasi indifference. Her hypocrisy begs me to scrutinize. "You called him a maniac and sociopath."

"No, I called his father a maniac for threatening to set our house on fire, and Jeremiah a psychopath for punching Claude," she clarifies.

"Whoa, you didn't divulge that detail," I say.

"Claude appreciates his privacy," says Alexandra.

"Why did Jeremiah punch Claude?" I ask.

"It was years ago, in the middle of an argument, Claude called me a disparaging name. Jeremiah heard it, flipped out, and broke Claude's jaw. His jaw had to be wired shut and has never been right since," Alexandra says. "He stood over him shouting, 'This is what you get. This is what you get. This is what you get.'"

This is valuable Intel, and it signifies Jeremiah squanders the power of his adrenaline rush. During the excitement of a confrontation, blood is diverted from the brain to the extremities to deal with impending physical harm. The repeating of a basic sentence such as, "This is what you get," implies low level reasoning.

"Is that why Claude is so quiet?" I ask as Varla sips her tea while she inventories this acquired news. In true investigation mode, she's listening over speaking.

"He tries to use stoicism as a cover, but the real reason is it hurts for him to talk or smile. Why do you think he hired those three bodyguards? Jeremiah left the same day, and has been living above the stables ever since," says Alexandra.

"How ironic, since Claude is a physical therapist and has access to old world healing techniques. Why doesn't he heal himself?" I say.

"He chooses not to heal himself as a reminder of his failure with Jeremiah. It's a self-imposed sentence," Alexandra postulates.

"Wow, his constitution is strong," I remark.

"And would you believe throughout the madness, Jeremiah continues to attend The Foundation ceremonies, enforce rules, and write rules. He separates the wild side of himself from the business side. I should go check on him," Alexandra babbles.

I reply, "I'm sure he'd appreciate your company."

"Thank you, McGurski, this meant a lot to me," says Alexandra.

Alexandra walks us outside and gives us both hugs. "I see you still drive that big van. How on earth do you manage the turns?"

"With help from me," Varla teases.

"I have the feeling we'll be seeing you soon." I say. I don't imagine Alexandra will challenge our takeover. After we break the news to Claude, we'll inform her and the rest of the crew.

Varla and I leave with our heads full of information to digest. This has been an enlightening tea party. Our pending visit with Claude and the bombshell we'll drop in his lap will truly shake The Foundation.

## Chapter 26 Third Position

Claude greets us at the door and invites us inside. The Good
Time Boys are absent. This is unusual, so perhaps he fired
them. Does he already know Jeremiah is finished? No matter,
Varla and I will hire them as recruiters. He leads us to his
lounge. It's an upscale mix of wooden walls, a large flat
screen TV, a bar from the 1930s, and expensive leather
furniture. Varla and I sit close together on a worn in leather
couch. I imagine The Good Time Boys lounging on this couch
watching rugby. The smell of leather is comforting and
masculine. Claude stares across at us from a large leather cigar
chair. We inform him of the duel.

He is pleased and asks, "Did you hurt him?"

I answer coolly, "Does it matter?" But I have
discovered his angle, and I know he hoped I hurt Jeremiah.
The vengeful side of Claude presses for the details. I share
with him the angst of anticipating the duel, contrasted with the
apex of the solar plexus punch. I savor the glory of the
mission.

"Where's the desk?" Claude asks.

My first thought is "no chance for a bonus." That's the
old small way of thinking. If we play our cards right and

follow our big plan, we'll be cutting our own checks and bonuses.

"Where's the desk?" he asks again.

Instead of mind clouding my way out of this pickle, I sell him a version of the truth. "We brought the desk to the beach and burned it. We ditched the evidence tying us to the death of Santos." When I think about what I said, it makes little sense. We bought the desk at the auction like anyone else could have, and there is no implication of foul play by buying or having a desk that once briefly belonged to Santos.

He's squinting and darting his eyes to comprehend if there is any logic to my statement. Inadvertently, sometimes my normal conversations can be an accidental mind cloud. Will he buy this line? By his account, the Movement Letter is unaccounted for. Nope, he's not buying what I'm selling because he's staring at the worn out soles of my shoes and connecting the dots. My reputation has grown. I've eliminated Jeremiah and without The Foundation's enforcer, he has no power. Honesty will be my excuse. I succumbed to temptation and I will learn from this ordeal. Witnessing Jeremiah's emergence after being humbled motivated me. I too, shall emerge stronger through controversy and confess to stealing the Movement Letter. The Foundation found my weakness: curiosity.

Claude moves his head slowly, inspecting my shoes with a long gaze. "Been running fast with those shoes?" he asks.

"I have it," I reply, and with this simple, three-word statement, I relieve myself of the burden of my deception.

"I figured." As he sternly presides over me, he breaks the uncomfortable silence that lasted about three seconds, but felt like three minutes. "When I heard of you years ago, I knew you'd be a comparable fit for The Foundation. Oscar described you as a slightly autistic, six-foot veteran with ADHD who is prone to violence and gambling. Those traits qualified you for The Foundation. Speaking fluent Esperanto entitled you to our experimental fast-track program. You've been an excellent protégé. I never formally mentored you, but you knew I've been mentoring you."

"Oscar must have been the guy at the library asking if it's possible to punch through brick walls. He played the role of a half-drunk social worker real well. He never mentioned I was being recruited," I reveal.

"Oscar was mysterious and didn't get out much. He preferred to read. When he did recruit, he brought us the ones with the best potential, like yourself. In your case, he tracked you down and placed an invitation under your windshield wiper."

"I remember being so happy it wasn't a parking ticket."

Over the years, Claude had showed an unusually keen interest in my development. Because of him, six months after recruitment, I went from living in my van to buying a small ranch house. He referred me to The Specialist, and through cutting-edge therapeutic techniques rebalanced the right side of my brain. This resulted in improved focus and the ability to quell my obsessive compulsions. I overcame my social awkwardness and could maintain direct eye contact with people. Combined with the surgery to cure my hands from sweating, I gained confidence in social situations. It seems implausible this was an elaborate plot to groom me to remove Jeremiah.

I confront him to be sure. "You did so much for me. Why did you set me up to duel with Jeremiah? Why did it have to be me?"

Claude gradually lifts himself with his arms and legs in unison to ease his way off the chair. The rubbing of the leather makes a noise similar to a fart. Varla and I glance at each other, testing our will and our lips to hold back our juvenile-level amusement from turning into full-blown laughter.

Meanwhile, Claude has shuffled his way to the bar and is cleaning a glass with a hand towel.

He diverts his attention from his cleaning to speak. "McGurski, we chose you because of one of your favorite topics … probabilities." He gives us ample time to think about what he said as he squeezes tongs together to grab ice cubes and place them into his glass, *plop, plop, plop.* "Varla, you missed your opportunity to fight Jeremiah because you lied about being able to read Esperanto. In hindsight, that was fortuitous. After all, you are supposed to be controlling your temper."

Varla simply nods in acknowledgement.

I can tell he's satisfied and relieved with Varla's acceptance of his reasoning, as he slowly pours a drink of the hard stuff.

After pouring his drink, he continues, "In my estimation, Darcy and Jeremiah would have fought to the death and we wanted neither to perish." He holds up the drink in the dim lighting to cherish and observe the interaction between the ice and aged bourbon. "The Good Time Boys are a unit and would have fought amongst themselves in order to be the one to battle Jeremiah, but individually each would have failed." He takes a long sip. He's in control of his pace, with his words carefully chosen. The last time he spoke in anger resulted in a broken jaw, and with Varla, he knows anything is possible.

"McGurski, since you identify with villains, I provided the chance for you to taste the hero glory. Your three traits, speed, discipline, and sympathy, suited you for this mission."

"Oscar handpicked me, you mentored me, and surrounded me with resources to finish Jeremiah. Did you really care if I was sympathetic to him? You dreamed of me hurting him, didn't you?"

He sits back in his chair with his right arm dangling straight down, holding the drink and slightly swirling the ice in a clockwise motion. Keeping his cadence slow and deliberate, he says, "I'm indifferent."

The vagueness of his answer betrays his intention. He places his drink on the coffee table and misses the coaster. In poker, that's considered a "tell."

He repositions his glass on the coaster and says, "Perhaps you think Alexandra and I are two eccentrics treating and hiring people with disabilities to do tasks. That we are the creators and controllers of a fantasy land. It had to be this way to get you off the streets. You two, Darcy, Jeremiah, Eddy, Ragni, and Loto represent the 0.05% of the people with disabilities who are prone to excessive violence."

He's right. The rap sheet on The Good Time Boys alone is as thick as a Tolstoy novel. I snap back at him with statistics, "According to the U.S. Department of Justice, the rate of violent crime against people with disabilities is double the rate the general population experience. Violence is a two-way street. In our defense, our population needs a few champions of justice to answer with violence."

Claude rubs his jaw gingerly, absorbing my message.

"Maybe you don't have complete control." I point to his jaw.

Varla chimes in, "We'd like to hear the story behind your busted jaw."

"I've spoken too much today," he says.

"Then I'll speak and forewarn you of the Santa Barbara takeover. McGurski and I are taking charge of the third position," Varla asserts.

She picked her spot well. Her timing to blast him with our plans has him off balance.

"What do you mean, the third position?" says Claude.

Varla fires back, "The vacancy. Oscar has no offspring, so McGurski and I are nominating ourselves."

His pause and deep breath are his way of recalibrating. He didn't expect such boldness. "Interesting. What is the plan for running your third of The Foundation?"

This gives me chills, as he's already conceded … it's a sign of things to come. I can relax and stop worrying about living in my van again. I share our plan. "The Good Time Boys will do massive recruiting. They will unleash the Combat Letters to legions of their buddies. With these secrets of fighting tactics, pressure points, and striking techniques loose in the public, there will be an uptick in street fights, a surge in popularity in the Ultimate Fighting Championship, and expansions of trauma wards due to the public's tendencies for overconsumption. Blood and broken bones will be our first contribution. The Healing Letters will follow and in our system, the last letters we'll reveal are the Breathing ones."

"That's backwards," the traditionalist in Claude claims.

"It's the new model. The inverted pyramid," I state. Deliberately leering at Varla, I say, "I like the idea of a top heavy foundation."

She rolls her eyes at me.

"But you can't expect people to balance on such a tiny base," Claude affirms.

"A pyramid is built for stability. True balance has high stakes. An inverted pyramid provides a chance to balance with risk. Value is determined by risk and difficulty," I state, challenging his ideology.

"Yours is truly the vision of a madman … I love it."

His response is unexpected, and I have the perfect quote to support his words. "Isaac Newton said, 'I can calculate the movement of the stars but not the madness of men.'"

"No eyes will raise to heaven. The pure will be thought insane and the impure will be honored as wise. The madman will be believed brave, and the wicked esteemed as good. Hermes Trismegistus," Claude volleys back a fine quote.

"With Jeremiah gone, we'll be eliminating his needless rules. McGurski and I will collect the money from Oscar's estate to finance our agenda," Varla states in a businesslike manner.

"Oscar's estate is entrusted to The Foundation," says Claude, protecting his stake.

"We are The Foundation, and unlike you and Alexandra, Varla and I aren't going underground for research. Varla, lay out the proposal you came up with."

"Alexandra will be in charge of the youth division of The Foundation. McGurski and I will be in command of recruitment. The Good Time Boys will be our recruiters, and your chain of physical therapy practices will be flush with new customers to rehabilitate. Everyone gets what they desire," Varla states, deliberately omitting Darcy from the proposal.

"And Darcy's role?" Claude asks.

In Varla's world, there is no position for Darcy, but I see her value and potential. "She'll fill Jeremiah's role of the enforcer and also run various missions," I say, keeping my eyes on Claude, but I feel Varla shooting imaginary daggers at me.

Claude accepts my answer with a nod. We shake on it.

"Monsieur Claude, did you ever release bull mastiffs on McGurski?" Varla's question comes from left field and breaks the businesslike atmosphere.

Both Claude and I slightly chuckle.

"Yes, I did, as a joke. Those dogs love McGurski. They galloped after him; if they had caught him, they would have licked him to death."

"I thought so, *au revoir, monsieur*," Varla says with a sense of vindication.

"*Au revoir, mademoiselle*." Claude turns to me and says, "McGurski, my boy, you've found your rudder, you have a direction in life, and have become an expert in the art of bemusement. Keep it weird."

I share with him a quote from Hunter S. Thompson, "When the going gets weird, the weird turn pro."

*\*\*\**

Right as we were leaving Claude's house, Alexandra rushes in, out of breath and in a panic. "I'm glad I found you all here. It's not over," she exclaims. "I visited Jeremiah; his favorite horse died, and he's blaming you." She points at me.

"I didn't touch his horse."

"He claimed you traumatized his horse."

Alexandra's panic has reactions and emotions running high. Perusing the room is a stimulus overload. Besides viewing thousands of video on human emotions, The Specialist taught me how to apply mathematics to solve emotional equations. For example, Claude's physical motions plus his words do not equal calmness. He's standing beside his cigar chair and if you pay attention to the tight grip he has on the arm of the chair, causing discoloration on his knuckles, you'd call his bluff.

"Everything will be okay," he says, trying to play it cool.

This equation showcases an example of physical gestures not in congruence with his pacifying statement. No, it won't be okay with Jeremiah back on the scene and angry;

he'll be screaming for vengeance from me or Claude. Maybe he figured out Claude played us.

Varla's body language is overt, and if she had sleeves, she'd be rolling them up. She cracks her knuckles with a confident smile on her face, as a proclamation of readiness. If Jeremiah busts through the door, Varla is primed for battle.

Alexandra goes to the bar and downs a shot of something in a hurry. My anticipation adds to this dramatic stew. Here we go again with those butterflies in my stomach. I have to fight self-doubt and Jeremiah again.

These thoughts bombard my brain. This is the result of my specialized treatments. Before my training, I tuned things out and now I am acutely tuned in. When you're repeatedly shocked for missing the slightest twitch of emotion, you adapt and catch the smallest details.

Alexandra regains her composure after a second shot and announces she's off to the Jazz Festival to relax. Claude asks Alexandra if she runs into The Good Time Boys at the Jazz Festival to have them call him and that he needs to speak with her in private. Claude and Alexandra excuse themselves. This party has met its expiration date.

My takeaway is there is no cure for everyone and no fairy tale ending. I'd bet the house Jeremiah will be waiting for me at the ranch.

## Chapter 27 The Horseman Rides Again

The sun is setting on the drive back to the ranch. When we arrive, it will be dark, and I won't be able to incorporate the sun into my fighting strategies. I would have positioned myself with my back to the sun while I launched a slick angle of attack, simultaneously blinding Jeremiah with the sun in his eyes. This match pits my speed versus his power and this time he has the advantage of already tasting my best move. If I was in Jeremiah's shoes, I'd want to fight me, too. He blames me for the death of his horse. Fair or not, if he comes to my ranch, I'll be ready to rumble.

A funny notion occurs to me that Jeremiah and I can't both be villains, or can we? In my eyes, he's a small town heavy handed bully and I'm the abominable one letting loose my inner demons. I'm the world shaker, the one taking over The Foundation, the one with the master plan. The pressure is mounting; I must win to enact the Operation Santa Barbara Takeover.

We're almost at the ranch and I can feel in my gut Jeremiah will be waiting. As I turn into the driveway, I wonder if he's stupid enough to block my path. If he does, I'll plow him over. No such luck. He stands enormous, guarding the front door of the ranch. His left arm is bent, shielding his solar plexus.

Jeremiah yells to me, "I hope you're not a one-trick pony. If the solar plexus shot is all you got, you're done."

A guy with the ludicrous title The Horseman is calling me a one-trick pony. My decision is to dismiss the premise of a witty comeback and focus on the task. To be clear, this is not a duel. I do not know to what extent Jeremiah will go to avenge his horse. My sole mission is to prevent him from harming me or Varla. I'll do what's necessary, including fighting dirty. I feel the surge of my trusty adventure compadre, mister adrenaline. The sun's down, but there's another way to blind him. I know from experience, fighting blind is no picnic. I flip on the high beams, jump out of the van, and sprint towards him diagonally to ensure I don't obstruct the light on his face. He covers his eyes with his right hand and still shields his solar plexus with his left. Attacks to his upper body are not an option. I tuck and roll to sweep his legs. He falls onto his side and pops up angrier. Good, he'll burn through his energy faster. He charges and runs past me as I merely side step matador style. As he passes me, I slap him on the back of the neck. *Whap.* Bears use this same technique, but the difference is they have the power to snap his spine. How ironic. Maybe if I practiced high fiving, my slap would have had a greater impact. My quickness is too much for him. I can do this all night and he knows it. His anger and frustration lead him to advance towards Varla.

There are a few ways power beats speed: predictability, timing, close quarters, luck, deception, and anticipation. He lures me in with the threat of attacking Varla. Quick stepping to the passenger side of the van to intercept him, my solar plexus is met with a fist the size of a lunch box. Where my amulet protected me from Darcy's relatively small hands, it only partially protects me from Jeremiah's meat hooks. My forward momentum amplifies his daunting strength and staggers me backwards a few paces. I exhale the wind punched out of me with a, *"Uuuooopmf."* My controlled adrenaline short circuits the pain, but I foresee an ice pack on my chest in the near future.

"How do you like the solar plexus punch?" Jeremiah gloats.

His confidence disintegrates as he rubs his swollen fist, unsure of what he hit and why I didn't fall. Those stories of him punching through brick walls were exaggerated. He shakes his head and fist to clear himself of the doubt creeping in. We both know I withstood his best shot. I declare round one a draw, and I'm ready for round two.

Varla doesn't give us a chance. She exits the van and says. "Your horse was sick. You had the vet over to the ranch three times this week."

I guess she's been busy investigating him, too.

"The vet said he'd get better with rest and then McGurski traumatized him. He's going to pay for killing my horse. He's going to pay for …"

Varla knows there is no reasoning with him. I suspect she has devious intentions, but their fleeting exchange of dialogue allows him a chance to collect his breath before his next attack. Puffing out his chest and slapping his forearms is the equivalent body language of a gorilla pounding his chest. Psyching himself up is his way of combating self-doubt. My adrenaline rush induces tacky psyche, and everything is clear and moves slow. I notice the bulging veins in Jeremiah's neck and it reminds me of when my ex-boss Mazetti would get angry at me.

I watch as Varla positions herself to his left side and raises her arms in the universal sign of submission and tells him, "You don't like pasta."

Instant confusion. It can happen fast. She capitalizes on his disorientation, leveraging her entire 190 pound frame into her effort, karate chopping the side of his neck. She must have hit his vagus nerve, because his knees buckle. Her follow up left hook lands flush on his nose. A six-foot cone of liquid sprays out his nose, painting the grass red. He's incapacitated while she launches an onslaught of hammer fists on the left side of his jaw. I cringe at the sound of his bones breaking. The impact spins him forty-five degrees and has him bracing with his right hand on the ground like a tripod. Varla's last hammer fist comes straight down, obliterating his collarbone and sending him face first into the turf. The barrage of punches has turned his face into a spaghetti dinner.

She winks at me, licks the blood off her fist, and says, "I'm a destroyer."

She called herself a destroyer. That statement is not sitting right with me, but before I can analyze it, Varla perches one foot on Jeremiah's back and poses as if she killed a wild animal.

"Alexandra can scrape him up," she says.

I reply in McGurski fashion, "Is it weird this is turning me on?" My girl robbed me of my fisticuffs with a mammoth, but I forgive her. "You owe me one."

"The pasta line did the trick," says Varla.

"Remind me to reward you with an imaginary mind clouding black belt."

Faking submission to advance an attack is a brilliant strategy. The art and science of befuddlement. Varla and I flip him to his side to check if he's breathing.

*** 

Ladders comes outside and says, "Could you guys keep it down, the plants are trying to sleep."

"What are you doing here?" I ask.

"Checking into the McGurski bed and breakfa—" He drops his sentence, mesmerized by the massive bloody man lying on front yard. "You did this to him? Whoa, is his jaw broken?"

"Varla's handy work."

"Whoa."

I remember what Varla said in the heat of the battle and it confirms my suspicions Ladders has been leaking information, so I press him, "Have you been recording our lessons?"

"What do you mean?" Ladders stalls.

"It's a straightforward question. You recorded our private lessons and shared them with Alexandra and Varla. Didn't you? And now you are inside my house without permission."

Varla jumps in to protect Ladders from my accusations and postures, "How did you—?"

I stare directly into her eyes while casting a thought wave of cool blue energy with relaxing intentions as I explain, "You said, 'I'm a destroyer.' Destroyer is a private term between Ladders and me."

Varla's face is flush, she's radiating heat, and her upper chest is heaving in and out rapidly as she wipes the sweat off her forehead. She's in the mood to brawl and acting overly defensive, she shouts, "No harm done."

She doesn't realize she's shouting, as the adrenaline is possessing her. I guess it would be normal to feel betrayed by my protégé and girlfriend, but it doesn't bother me. There is a trend of betrayal in my life. My mentor betrayed me, setting me up to fight Jeremiah. In return, I'm overthrowing him to rule The Foundation. Trust is not part of my constitution. After all, I'm part scoundrel. I can't trust anyone, and maybe that's why I'm a scoundrel. When you choose to self-identify as a villain, being a scoundrel is a way of life. I've come to terms that nobody can be trusted. Even with Varla on my side,

I'm alone. She spied on me, she spied on Jeremiah, and you can't trust a spy. Catching them is the enjoyable part. As Claude enjoyed catching me stealing the Movement Letter, I relish catching Ladders and Varla.

In a jocular manner, to lighten the atmosphere, I address their treachery by saying, "You're spies."

With her adrenaline levels peaking, she's not reacting to jokes. Her will is strong, the mystical cooling energy waves are not affecting her. There's a better way to subdue her, and this method will rock her world. Before dealing with Varla, I prioritize and divert my attention to the bloody behemoth. He requires medical assistance pronto.

"Ladders, call your aunt and tell her to come over. She can take Jeremiah to the hospital."

Meanwhile, I convince Varla to try out my AMP experiment.

She quotes a line from her namesake in the movie *Faster Pussycat Kill Kill*, "I don't try anything, I just do it … want to try me." It's a scary spot on impression.

The plant room welcomes her as she exchanges her mass exhalations of carbon dioxide for clean oxygen courtesy of the plants. She lies on the Pulsed Electric Magnetic Frequency mat inside the copper pyramid as I coach her through the different breathing modalities for maximum retention of adrenaline. Her entire body has a slight vibration to it, and the untrained eye would perceive it as shaking. Her state is enhanced as I whisper empowering commands into her ear, "You are full of energy. You are the bringer of war. Your body is being magnetized."

She'll stay in the meditation chamber for three minutes. The AMP will assist her in harnessing her energy in a controlled manner and then she'll relax in a hot Epsom salt bath. On my way back from drawing her bath, I peer out the window and observe Ladders and Jeremiah sitting on the grass together. The left side of Jeremiah's jaw is hanging by a flap of skin while he sits in his own pool of blood. Ladders is talking to him like it's nothing out of the ordinary. It's beautiful.

"Varla, come here."

"Is it okay to leave the pyramid?" she asks.

The AMP experiment and plants have softened her edge. "When have you ever asked for permission?"

Interestingly, it appears the AMP has a different effect on Varla. She is, dare I say, mellow. She stands beside me and watches the odd couple sitting on the grass. I place my arm around her sweaty shoulders and hold her close enough to smell marijuana on her. That explains her behavior; the pyramid, and Pulsed Electric Magnetic Frequency mat combined with a marijuana cigarette amplified her to a state of chill. I'm amused at the image of Varla inside the pyramid smoking a joint.

I tell her about my discovery. "We're the villains."

"What?"

"I ambushed Jeremiah, traumatized his horse to the point of death, and stole the letter. We pummeled him into a bloody pulp and left him lying in the front yard."

"We flipped him over." She defends what little virtue we have to stand on. "So what if we are villains? We're good at it." And then she concedes.

"I'm not saying that being a villain is a bad thing. Villains are proactive optimists."

"What do you mean?" she asks.

"They create plans to better themselves and their crew."

"You mean hatch schemes," she adds.

"The hero merely reacts and attempts to thwart the villain's scheme. There is no forward progress or regression with the hero. They strive to maintain the status quo. The hero has no personal ambition except the vain glory to save the day. The villain carries the burden of sustaining the hero."

"As villains, it's our challenge to change the world," she states, confirming she's on my side.

"And we will." I open the window and yell to Ladders, "Where's Alexandra?"

He responds, "She's not answering her phone, she's at the Lemon Festival." He corrects himself, "No, this week is the Jazz Festival. Your friend, the big guy, needs medical attention, so I called Claude. He'll be here soon."

I turn to Varla and say, "This should be interesting."

She responds, "Let's bring the chaise lounges out front for human theater." She's referring to them as humans now, too.

"Good idea."

***

We lounge, sip Perrier, and wait. You can't hear a Phantom coming. In the distance, you'd expect to hear a trace roar from such a powerful engine, but silence is also a sign of fine craftsmanship. The black Rolls Royce drops anchor diagonally on my front yard with a haphazard park job reflecting an urgency. Varla bets me twenty bucks Claude came here to stick it to Jeremiah. I counter with twenty dollars, riding on him to mend Jeremiah. His loyalty to the Hippocratic Oath will prevail. Although I'm twisted, I'm still an optimist.

While removing his tie, Claude rushes over to Jeremiah. He wraps the tie under Jeremiah's chin like a makeshift sling and has Ladders hold what's left of his jaw in place while he ties a securing knot on the top of his head.

We've added a new spin on the Norman Rockwell painting. Please, someone commission this painting: Two maniacs sharing a bottle of Perrier on lounge chairs watching an elderly man in a three-piece suit and a fifteen-year-old boy tend to a giant with half a jaw on blood-soaked grass, with a Rolls Royce Phantom in the background. Varla hands me twenty bucks.

Claude bends over and makes eye contact with Jeremiah and says, "In a few weeks, we'll be fine. We'll heal our jaws together." And pats him on the shoulder.

Jeremiah nods and gives him a thumbs up.

Ladders is in awe and says to Claude, "You can fix his jaw?"

"Everything can be healed."

It's pretty deep declaration. I believe he's referring to their broken jaw's and their broken relationship. A few years ago, I would have only understood the literal side of his statement. My personal growth has granted me access to this subtle, invisible dimension.

Claude asks me to bring out water and hydrogen peroxide. When I hand him the supplies, he says there's a special gift for me and Varla in the trunk of his car.

Did he booby trap his trunk? Will the car explode when I open the trunk? Dismiss the paranoia, he is above sabotage. I open the trunk with my body shifted off to the side, tilting my head back and holding my breath, just in case. There's no explosion or cyanide gas, so I wave Varla over. His trunk is full of Oscar's books. There's also an envelope addressed to me and Varla. We'll open it later. Presently, we are too busy unloading the books and placing them on the lounge chairs. We expect Claude will leave with Jeremiah soon.

My neighbor Amelia approaches with her two Afghan hounds, Cliffie and Alfie. The dog's body language is straightforward. Their nostrils are picking up the metallic scent of blood. Amelia is curious too, but hesitant. At first, she keeps away, but curiosity finally compels her to peek at the carnage in her peripheral vision. I can relate to her avoidance, but for different reasons. All it takes is a quick peek and Amelia is sucked into my world.

I wave to her and say, "Good evening, Amelia, did we wake you? Sorry, our Canasta game got out of hand." There's no way she'll comprehend my warped card game humor.

Amelia turns ninety degrees and bravely absorbs the totality of the spectacle taking place in my front yard. Her life will be forever enriched by this moment. This is my gift to her.

She grabs both leashes with her right hand and places her left hand over her mouth. "Oh my, R. W., is that gentlemen okay? He's bleeding everywhere," she says.

Varla chimes in, "I've seen worse."

Amelia recognizes Varla's statement is her social cue to keep on moving.

Meanwhile …

"Can I help?" Ladders asks Claude.

"Yes, please do," says Claude.

They assist Jeremiah to his feet and into the back seat of his Rolls. Ladders sits with him.

Claude climbs in the driver's seat and motions Varla and I to come over. He says, "It's how you described it, McGurski. There will be blood in the streets with you and Varla at the helm of the third position."

"You didn't have to deliver the books," I say to Claude.

"Psst please, I had The Good Time Boys load them when they returned from the Jazz Festival. Knowing you, you probably checked for booby traps."

Cripes, he played me. Does this mean I'm predictable? "Nice of you to pay us a visit," I say.

"Heed my warnings regarding these books," he states with grim overtones.

"What warnings?" I ask.

He backs up, tearing more grooves into my lawn, and peels out. There is no wave or goodbye from Ladders, as he is busy comforting Jeremiah. Varla is preoccupied admiring the bloodstains on her t-shirt, the mangled front yard, and hundreds of books on the lounge chairs.

I stare at her, not caring that she can't be trusted. She is who I desire. If a normal relationship struck my fancy, I'd be content with the weather forecast. The phrase, "The weatherman said today your umbrella will be your best friend," horrifies me. Varla would never utter a sentence with that assortment of words. While math is linear and clear, Varla is deranged and unpredictable, and the balance they achieve together nurtures me.

## Chapter 28 The Deal with Number Three

It's been a long day. Varla and I are slumped on the grass and share a beer. The night has cooled to sixty degrees.

"Do that thing where you heat your body up," she asks.

"G-Tummo Vase Breathing coming right up." A few short breath holds with abdominal contractions, combined with the mental image of a fire burning throughout my body, and I'm radiating heat.

She grips me tight. "Oh, that's better, you're like my personal heater. I've been meaning to ask you, what's your deal with number three?"

I disclose a layer of my madness. "Nicola Tesla said, 'If you only knew the magnificence of the three, six, and nine, then you would have the keys to the universe.' I'm not sure what he means, but I've incorporated those numbers into my life with the chance of understanding the universe. Throwing people through three sheets of drywall and making proclamations of fighting people six times has been part of my pursuit to discover the keys of the universe."

"Have you lost it?" she jokes.

I dig deeper into the wormhole, unsure of the clarity of my ideas. "Another thing Tesla and me have in common is we both turn our backs on the LETTER five."

"The letter five?"

"Yes, I disrespect the five, it belongs in the alphabet."

"You got a problem with the alphabet too?"

"It's not in the same league as numbers. Kids don't ask what's your favorite letter, they ask what's your favorite number or color."

"Is there more?"

"Sure, I don't consider five a number anymore. Its association with the high five and inability to be divisible by three are my main gripes."

"A, B, C, D, E, F, G, H, I, J, five, L, M, N, O, P," she has fun reciting the alphabet with her special addition of five.

"It never occurred to me to place the letter five between J and L. Well done!"

"Did you know five is the third prime number? How is your cozy relationship with the number three now?" she taunts.

She's right; in the past, three and five have formed alliances. The .357 magnum is an example of a three and five in a harmonic state of destruction with the assist from seven. "You're jealous of the three."

"It can't compete; the number three doesn't have boobs like me."

"*Au contraire*, the number three is voluptuous, too. A bird's-eye view of three (3) is the proof."

"You act like you're three."

"Association with the number three is a compliment."

"Have you ever heard the song *Take Five* by Dave Brubeck or *25 or six to four* by Chicago?" she asks playfully.

I'm no zealot. I'm hip to those tunes. My phone rings, and I expect Alexandra, but it's not.

"McGurski, it's me, Ladders. I figured out I'm not a destroyer or a creator. I'm a healer. I've been helping Claude fix Jeremiah's jaw. It's like magic."

"It runs in your family. I'm glad you found your path."

The idea of being a healer never occurred to me. What other avenues have I overlooked? I yell at my internal self, "Extinguish the doubt and move forward."

"Would it be okay if I trained with Claude? He has a chain of physical therapy practices around the county I could intern at. It's a good way to learn the craft."

"Healing is what you are meant to do. Good night, Jacob."

Jacob found his path and climbed to the top of his ladder at fifteen-years-old. At thirty-nine-years-old, my status, according to Claude, is one of a madman. Embracing the madness and turmoil is where I shine. It's better to be a bright shiny villain than to be dull. The shine attracts attention. The envelope Claude left has a shine too. It's grabbed our attention. Currently, it serves as a bookmark.

"Hey, it's getting late. Let's move the books into the house," I say to Varla.

"Uhh, I was almost asleep. What time is it?"

"11:07. You're crashing from your adrenaline high. When we get all the books into the house, we'll open the letter together."

"Deal."

Between trips of carrying stacks of books from the chaise loungers inside to our new "floor" library, I contemplate opening the envelope. Varla takes a wide berth around the envelope, as if to avoid temptation, but keeps her eyes fixated on it, like there could be money inside. The warning regarding the books must be in the envelope. It's hard to imagine what we could fear from books? I'll read it before the night is over.

Our new library consists of 324 hardcover books, some as old as 200 years, and they come with their own musty smell. We've arranged them on the loungers in thirty-six stacks containing nine books. In the rush to carry the books out of the trunk, I didn't have a chance to examine them. I flex my discipline muscle, prolonging the opening of the envelope and leafing through our inherited library. The activity turns into an equation: If McGurski and Varla carry nine books on each trip, with the average trip lasting forty seconds, how long before they have removed 324 books from the loungers and are free to read the contents of the envelope? It's a practical word problem. My self-restraint will be tested for twelve minutes.

Varla has stopped carrying books and is sitting on the grass, reading with intensity. It's an aggressive form of reading. She flips through the pages with an accompanied noise testing the book's binding.

I didn't include breaks in my practical word problem, so our projected completion time is compromised. Oh well.

Varla slams the book shut and stomps inside. What could she have been reading to elicit this response?

The book stands out amongst the rest, and it has the brand new book smell of fresh paper and glue. I'm compelled to open it. Why would this book be a part of the collection? I read the title, *The Diagnostic and Statistical Manual of Mental Disorders 5th edition*. I smile and shake my head. On the first page, an exquisitely written message in Esperanto garners my attention. It reads, "Happy recruiting, may this powerful book guide you in choosing your candidates. Love always, A."

Alexandra came through with a classy touch. Who else would write Esperanto in calligraphy?

My guess is Varla read about IED in the *DSM-5* and opposed what the eggheads wrote. The books can wait. How do I comfort Varla? Cripes, I'm unsure how to provide comfort. She reminds me of a rattlesnake. If you tried to pet a rattlesnake, the outcome might be fatal. I'm unsure if it is normal to compare your girlfriend to a venomous viper. Scanning my memory for acts of comfort, I chuckle. Ladders' sitting with Jeremiah is an example of sympathy. In a mentor/protégé relationship, both are supposed to learn. I had gleaned this nugget from my student and will go inside and sit with Varla. I will not wrap my arm around her or console her with words. I will sit and wait until she is ready.

She's in the plant room with her head between her knees, tears rolling off her face. I've never seen her cry before and it never occurred to me she could produce tears. I sit next to her and keep my promise to remain quiet. I don't offer her a tissue or a hug; I just sit.

During part of my training, The Specialist had me watch thousands of strangers cry to catch the subtleties of human expressions. I reacted to their plight with indifference, but as Varla cries, my instinct is to care for her. I'm not the kind of guy to utter the phrase, "There, there," and if I did, Varla would punch me. I'll wait until she is ready.

Varla breaks the silence. "I researched IED in this stupid book and hoped to read examples of what people with my condition do."

Interpretation: she's researching samples of other people with IED for creative ways to inflict her brand of havoc. It's the equivalent of a serial killer taking notes from murder mysteries.

"It says people with IED are prone to aggressive and destructive behavior towards people and property. I mean, doesn't everyone enjoy fighting and destroying property? But in the fifth edition, they say people with IED typically have physical aggression towards animals."

I choose not to correct her, explaining authors don't "say" things in books, their words are just written. I also resist the urge to mention it's the dreaded letter five causing her strife. The publishers missed an opportunity to skip the fifth edition and proceed to the sixth edition. It's not absurd when you consider hotels skip the 13th floor.

"My love for animals is one of my few connections with people. I can't be associated with IEDers if they are animal abusers."

"But you obviously love animals and don't hurt them."

"When we fired the crossbow at those stuffed animals, I enjoyed it."

"You can't compare shooting a stuffed animal to the real thing. That's like saying I like the taste of root beer, so I'm probably an alcoholic."

"It's different."

I clasp my hands against my chest, close my eyes, and bow my head. This news hits harder than a blow to the beef bologna. Varla, tough and gritty, has a warm spot for animals. Sharing her vulnerabilities is proof she trusts me. From one savage to another, I comprehend the love for animals. We've removed animals from the wilderness and tamed the beast out of them through care, trust, and love. In the wild, where a mere thorn in their foot could disable them, their remedy is a tongue bath. Quit licking your wounds; we'll remove the thorn, and you'll provide the unconditional love. Rule breakers of this sacred code ought to walk the plank. Besides the physical abuse, there is also the mental anguish of being summoned by names like Fifi. On a familiar feline note, what is the determining factor between naming a cat Boots or Mittens?

Prominent psychiatrists have gone on record, stating mental abuse has a longer lasting negative affect than physical. I'll speak for the pets and disagree. Being chained to the side of the house, beaten, and given the same food every day is crummier than being called Rufus, Spot, or Biscuit. How are these random thoughts going to cheer Varla? They say making love heals wounds, but this isn't the right moment. I've also heard laughter is the best medicine, but I can't remember any good jokes. Violence seems to cheer her, so I shop this angle, "Would you like to cruise for animal abusers?" In my proverbial back pocket, I've been waiting for the right moment to revisit Alexandra's neighbor, Fletcher. I have to be certain he is not tugging on his dog's leash anymore.

"Nah, thanks for trying to cheer me up. I'm hitting the sack."

Even the way she describes the act of sleeping has violent overtones. Fletcher is lucky Varla's not in the mood, otherwise she would have smashed him into bits.

"You heading to sleepy times? Sleep pup, sleep pup-eroni, sleeper doodle do."

"You say one more goofy term of endearment and I'll elbow slap you seven times."

## Chapter 29 Stakeout

While Varla sleeps, I carry in the rest of the books and finally open the envelope. The anticipation is not the same without Varla to share it with. Claude's note is written in Esperanto.

*Dear Varla and R. W.,*

*There are 972 books in The Foundation's library; my collection is 324, Alexandra's 324, and Oscar had 324. We impart Oscar's literature to welcome your partnership. It is a marvelous assortment of letters from the alphabet forming words in sequences. The value is in determining the right sequence for the right audience, otherwise it is a mere pile of books. Alexandra and I will embrace your changes and explore where it goes. A new day, a new way.*

*The Foundation.*

*P.S. Alexandra threw in one extra book to fast-track your recruitment.*

On the surface, it appears to be a very cordial note, unless you have a slight obsession with numbers. Did Alexandra believe she could pull this off? My nickname, after all, is The Count. In the note, Claude states each library is 324 books and Alexandra threw in an extra book. So, the total should be 325 books, which means either she swiped one or The Good Time Boys did when they loaded Claude's trunk.

*The Stockpile* is missing. It's the core of The Foundation's knowledge and where the real techniques come from, all the juicy stuff like The Movement Letter, the breathing techniques, and martial arts techniques. These practices shaped my development. The rest of the books are swell, but without *The Stockpile*, it's like eating mashed potatoes and broccoli without a steak. To recruit, you need bait. You don't bait the line with broccoli; you reel them in and feed their bellies with steak and fill their imagination with *The Stockpile*. I dismiss my sudden hunger and join Varla in bed. When we wake, we'll devise a plan.

"McGurski!"

"What? Who's at the door? Did you remember to feed the fish?" How can I feed the fish, I don't have any fish? Varla is at the edge of the bed, sitting with her legs crossed.

"Nobody is at the door."

"Do you think a cobra would drink a tuna fish smoothie?" Sometimes I say weird things when I'm groggy. "I had a dream about tuna fish."

"When are we opening the envelope?" Varla asks, ignoring my jibber jabber.

"What time is it?"

"Five a.m."

"I only got four hours of sleep. Let me sleep."

She pounces on me, "Come on, open the envelope."

"Yeah, the letter in the envelope is garbage." I flip over to my other side to judge her reaction.

"How so?"

"I read it last night." I pause for her reaction.

"You sneaky bastard. Lying, stealing, scoundrel."

She playfully hits me as I evade her punches under the covers. Now I know why I was dreaming of tuna fish smoothies—it stinks under here. We should have showered before going to bed last night. I pop my head out to get fresh air and say, "These things are all true. You knew I was a savage." By accepting her volley of attacks, I diffuse the situation.

"What does the letter say?"

"I'll translate it for you." After reading it, I wait for her outrage.

"It's pretty straightforward to me. Why is it garbage?"

She misses the discrepancy in the number of books.

"They shorted us *The Stockpile*!" I say with animosity.

I get the impression Varla is trying to hold back her laughter, but I don't know why. Before I can ask her opinion on the possible culprit, she's already drawn a conclusion.

Varla and her companion, logic, convince me Alexandra confiscated *The Stockpile*. The Good Time Boys wouldn't steal the book because they wouldn't betray me and Claude. Claude wouldn't withhold the book from me because I am his protégé. The evidence points to Alexandra. She has the motive. Her perception of being squeezed out is accurate; we negotiated the third position without her. This is her way of gaining back control. She knows if I have any allegiance at all, it's with Claude. Also, she's been mentoring Darcy, so perhaps she's been grooming her for the role of the third position. Varla is adamant we conduct a classic style stakeout of Alexandra's house. We'll track her movements and note if Darcy pays her a visit.

Varla is swift with this plan. The rental car agency by the airport opens at 6 a.m., and we're there at 5:55 a.m. The tan van is too recognizable for this undercover OP. To my dismay, it's a compact car, and although it has tinted windows, it resembles a roller skate. The seat is as far back as it goes and the steering wheel remains in my lap. If I close my eyes, it's the same sensation of being on a budget airline with the seat in front fully reclined. Kneeing the steering wheel does not manifest the same satisfaction as kicking a reclined airline seat.

In one hour, I went from comfortably relaxing in bed to running a stakeout, brimming with an unreasonable amount of boredom. Before leaving the rental car agency, Varla hands me an extra musty book on wild animal mating habits, binoculars, two liters of water, an empty plastic bottle, and volunteers me for the first shift. Varla leaves in my van and I'm left to drive to Alexandra's villa in this puny rental car.

I park across the street from Alexandra's house and place the sun visor against the windshield, instantly transforming into cloaking mode. Between the dark tint on the window and the sun visor covering the front window, I'm invisible. Twenty minutes in and I'm starved for action. The first sign of life is Fletcher, the douche dog walker. He's tugging too aggressively on the leash again. Discipline prevents me from breaking cover and rescuing the dog. I resist and table the fiendish ideas I have in store for him. Guessing where his dog will produce a squat cobbler is the highlight of my morning. The pooch is regular and lays a moist ground turd on Alexandra's easement, and of course Fletcher does not pick it up. My self-restraint is being tested.

For three hours, I alternate between reading and counting the hair on my forearm. Reading on a stakeout is unlike normal reading. On a stakeout you read a half a page and then check your surroundings. If you are too engrossed in your story, you could miss the target. Therefore, the literature should not be too interesting. Although, this article on the unusual mating habits of flatworms is intriguing. Turns out flatworms are hermaphroditic and joust to play the male role.

Penis fencing determines the outcome. The two flatworms stab each other with their penises until penetration and insemination has occurred. The recipient must then carry and lay the next generation of flatworm eggs. That exhausts the topic of flatworms, unless you have a team of late night talk show comedy writers at your disposal. They surely would craft a mildly funny quip on flatworm mating.

While staring mindlessly out the car window, I wait for any movement to occur. At this stage of the stakeout, I'd settle for a leaf blowing in the wind. It's Ladders! He's exits the house and is unaware of his surroundings. An unfamiliar crappy car in this swanky neighborhood should at least warrant a double take. He hops on his bicycle and pedals down the Riviera.

An hour and a half later, I hit the jackpot. Alexandra's garage door opens and her shiny silver Lexus backs out. Of course, I'm in the middle of peeing in a container when she decides to leave. I finish my stream and fumble as I try to tighten the lid back on. The lid slides between the center console and driver's seat. Meanwhile, Alexandra is slipping away. My hands are too big to retrieve the lid. A split second decision must be made; I could toss the pee bottle out the window or leave the topless pee bottle in the cup holder. My personal code does not allow me to litter. I'm in such a rush to catch Alexandra, I forget to remove the sun visor and drive for 100 yards peering through the side window. When my brain catches up, I rip off the sun visor and tear through the windy roads. Each turn, I sneak a glance at the pee to make sure it is not splashing over the top of the container.

This little roller skate of a car handles the turns better than my van, but that's not saying much. Alexandra's car is not in sight. There are only a few ways up and down the Riviera, but once Alexandra reaches the city, I need to be on her tail. If I lose her, the stakeout will be for nothing. The urine is splashing higher and higher on the container as I accelerate. I'm scrutinizing the urine instead of the road. This

next turn is a doozy, and I'm contemplating a drift move with
the emergency brake. It's a rental. Half way through the turn, I
pull on the emergency brake and delight in the sensation of the
back end of the car whipping around. The screeching of the
tires fills the car with the smell of burned rubber. My
adrenaline is charged. Will the car skid into a tree or will I pull
out of the spin? Varla would be proud. I maneuver through the
turn and bask in the one second of drifting glory. However,
yellow liquid douses the flames of glory. The thrill of the drift
is contrasted by the disappointment of spilled piss on my lap. I
temporarily forget this calamity as I spy the silver Lexus
ahead.

   I follow Alexandra, but not too close. We are almost
out of the Riviera and closing in on downtown. The residential
houses give way to offices, storefronts, and restaurants. She's
a creature of habit, so I know she'll be dining outside for
brunch, but at which establishment? She valets at a quaint
place on W. Victoria St., perpendicular to the main artery of
downtown State St. I illegally park approximately sixty yards
away and enhance my vision with the aid of binoculars.
Another lady greets her. I can't identify if it's Darcy. She's
wearing a ridiculously large sun hat and a long bulky jacket,
which is an odd choice of apparel for a seventy-degree day.
Darcy would not dress this way. My guess is they are
expecting more guests because there are four chairs and three
cups of tea and a Bloody Mary on the table. The waiter takes
their order, and Alexandra's gums flap away. My arms are
tired from holding the binoculars. I prop my feet on the seat
and position my knees as a platform to rest the binoculars. It's
a respite for my arms, but the waft of urine from my pants
punishes my nose.

   I can see Alexandra ordered the salmon quinoa, while
the mystery lady does a face first dive into a cheeseburger.
They must have ordered for their fashionably late friend. The
empty space at the table has a lonely platter of lamb and rice.
How delicious. I would have ordered the same. I've observed

enough from this distance and decide to move closer. In this new position, all is revealed. Changing the angle, I discover the identity of the mystery guest. The verification causes my hands to release their grasp on binoculars involuntarily. Fortunately, the straps around my neck prevent the binoculars from landing on the ground. Slightly in a daze, I move directly towards their table. Being hidden is no longer a priority. They spot me, laugh, and wave me over.

Alexandra says to me, "Your lamb is getting cold."

The mystery guest asks me, "Are you looking for this?" holding *The Stockpile* high in her hand.

Alexandra didn't steal it. Varla snatched *The Stockpile* when we moved the books inside the ranch.

"This is payback for stealing The Movement Letter," Varla says as she hands me the book, and then comments on my pants. "Did you have a little accident on your stakeout? Why didn't you piss in the empty container?"

I play it off. "Bad aim." And then jab back at Varla, "Nice disguise. Your hat and overcoat make you look like an upscale bag lady."

"You look like an incontinent bird watcher."

Alexandra intervenes. "Children, quit bickering. I'm trying to enjoy my beverage."

"I told you McGurski wouldn't swear when he found out I stole the book," says Varla.

Alexandra adds, "R. W., you lack refinement in countless ways, but I've always loved your avoidance of curse words. He's a role model for the rest of you riff raff."

Bingo, Alexandra said the word countless. It's clear she is responsible for polluting Ladders' head with the concept.

Varla continues her verbal assault, "McGurski's a great role model for the velvet jacket crowd."

"Cripes, frig, rats, and crap." The intent is the same, but the voracity is softened. There is an innocence in these words. As I've said before, words are a form of sorcery.

As we eat, Varla has fun sharing the details of her deception and how Alexandra turned into a willing accomplice.

"Varla tells me your favorite letter is five. Is that right?" Alexandra asks.

"My favorite letter is actually capital B, especially from a bird's-eye view, for obvious reasons."

They enjoy their opportunity to laugh at my expense, while I devour my lamb chops. The meat is tender enough to cut with a spoon. Chewing the savory meat and retrieving *The Stockpile* make all the calamities of the morning seem trivial.

While Alexandra is in a pleasant mood and a tinge tipsy from two Mimosas and a Bloody Mary, we push our new role in The Foundation. We expect her to be perturbed from being excluded from our discussion with Claude, but a slight frown is the only ire we draw. My guess is Claude already told her. She realizes the brilliance of our vision. She raises her Bloody Mary in a toast. We celebrate the destruction of normal behavior.

Our addendum to the mission statement includes rescuing abused pets and trouncing pet abusers. It earns a second toast. Varla believes clobbering pet abusers will surpass the rush from road rage. As a bonus, Alexandra agrees to violate her patients' confidentiality and share patient files that have a history of animal abuse.

***

I thank them for the comedy lunch hour and excuse myself. I'll stick Alexandra with the bill. For the entire lunch,

I've been sitting with my back to the rental car. My immediate concern is a parking ticket. Code enforcement is prolific in these parts. It's a short walk to the car, but the anticipation builds on whether a small rectangle sheet of paper will be fastened under my windshield wipers or not. I have the money to pay for the ticket, but the hassle of paying has turned into a phobia. Wearing pants with pee stains on them is enough indignity for one day. An extra bounce in my step is my physical reaction to relief. Today, I eluded the wrath of code enforcement. When I open the door of the rental car, it wreaks of urine and burned rubber. I forgot to toss the pee container out of the car. It's been marinating in the cup holder incrementally gaining in pungent strength. I dump the urine on a nearby bush and heave the plastic container into a trash can that is nine feet away. At this distance, I'm calling it a three pointer.

On the drive to the rental agency, I stick my head out the window like a dog. The fresh air opens the pores in my intellect to process this mini caper. I learned what it is like to have a valuable piece of literature missing and discovered the reason why Varla tried in vain to hold back her laughter when I explained my conspiracy theory regarding *The Stockpile*.

During the hours sitting in the cramped rental car and what transpired at brunch, the big picture is clearer. Revelations and inspiration occur outside the oxygen rich plant room pyramid too. In this case, ideas flowed into my brain while being cooped up in a compact economy rental car. Zen has no boundaries or confinements. I've concluded the letter Claude wrote to Varla and I is bogus. My past jobs exposed me to the rampant shams in the business world, and I'm realizing The Foundation fits in this dubious category as well.

The questions I ask myself are: Why does The Foundation pretend to be a cult and nurture people with disorders? Why would Claude and Alexandra rollover so easily without a fight? The answer is they didn't fight to protect their stake in The Foundation because The Foundation is a social construct. It's not real, it's not a building, or a person, it's an illusion backed by an idea based on psychology, books, and a bankroll. Claude alluded to it before that he and Alexandra believe they are the creators of a fantasy world. The only way they can feel alive is to surround themselves with ultra-aggressive, somewhat unpredictable people with disabilities. If they can control and predict our behaviors, it proves they are gods of their dimension. Their disdain for the general population proves my theory: the dull are too predictable. People with disorders and disabilities have an irresistible allure because of their originality and because they are conveniently prone to being gullible.

The Foundation library is a farce too. It played on our desires and naiveté. It's a gimmick Oscar created. It's cliché, but we fell for it. We invested in the lie. Oscar, the hermit, an avid reader, devised this fantasy of a library filled with ancient secrets from the past. I can picture Alexandra saying to him, "There are countless books playing to this tired troupe." Although, some techniques in *The Stockpile* are not mumbo jumbo and are based on wisdom from history.

Their tactic was to distract us with pretend duties while simultaneously sending us on alternative paths to heal. It's clear to Alexandra the office and couch modality for therapy are outdated. In the field is where significant growth is achieved. In order to document the field work, she needed spies and inscribers to document her findings. She used Varla, Darcy, and Ladders as spies and me to document the events. I bet they even predicted our mutiny. I wonder if Claude or Alexandra expected me to take the bait and become the leader.

Refreshingly, Claude and Alexandra's ambition is not based on a money grab. Claude barely blinked an eye when we told him we were collecting the money from Oscar's estate. They have the money to buy anything, so their goal has to be something that money can't buy. Their motivation came not from feeling good about helping people with disabilities either. They've proven that with what they've put us through. I realize what has driven Alexandra and Claude all these years. Individually, Alexandra's motivation was to look good. She had the Botox, the dresses, showed up at the events, and so forth. For Claude, his motivation has been to be in control. He demonstrated his power over The Good Time Boys, me, and Varla. But together, Claude and Alexandra's ultimate goal is to become pioneers. Their sole motive is to immortalize their names as accreditors in the next edition of the *DSM*, the most powerful book in America.

Another epiphany occurs to me. When Jeremiah said, "I guess we'll both be hanging it up," maybe he meant we'd both graduate from The Foundation after our duel. But me and Varla have flunked. In psychology circles, the term for our status is regression. Textbooks describe our relationship as codependent and toxic. We amplify each other's violence and weirdness. I clamor on about numbers, while Varla's rage is relentless instead of intermittent. If I want to stop, I can. I choose not to. I sound like an addict. Varla and I regressed as a deliberate choice; to test our compatibility, we must endure the potential worst in each other.

***

The guy driving in front of me turned without using his turn signal. In Varla's world, it's grounds for road rage. Bad driving snapped me out of my personal meditative orbit. Meditation happens in many forms, and on this occasion it happened while sticking my head out the window of a car to avoid the smell of piss. Back on earth, I gas the rental and hope they don't charge me for the smell of urine and burned rubber.

The attendant receives the tiny car and doesn't blink. He does a cursory check, and says, "Looks good." I'm sure he's pleased the car is devoid of fast food wrappers and I'm happy I don't have to pay extra for the pee smell. A few sprays of disinfectant and it'll be whisked off to the next temporary occupant. The decision to ride with the windows open paid off.

Running home from the rental agency is a mere eight miles. I attribute gratitude for the extra bounce in my step, but it's awkward running while carrying binoculars, a mating habits book, and *The Stockpile*. I am grateful to avoid a parking ticket and a cleaning fee. On my journey home, I stop at a horizontal tree limb approximately nine feet high. It represents an opportunity for pull-ups. I place the binoculars and books near the curb and elongate my stride until I leap to the branch, grasping it with both hands. Fifteen military style pull-ups. No kipping or half reps, complete pull-ups under full control. A friendly tip is to squeeze your abdominal and butt muscles while cranking them out. My brief communion with the tree provides me guidance for the rest of the day. Trees, plants, pyramids, water, and compact cars can generate clarity. I'm building my strength for our revitalized mission eating pure foods, climbing trees to connect with nature, and meditating.

At home, removal of the pee pants and a cleansing shower are first on the agenda. The bath tub is still full of water from last night. That's right, Varla didn't take her Epsom salt bath after being AMPed. No need to waste the water; I'm taking a bath today instead of a shower. In the tepid water, I formulate a plan. When Varla returns, we'll discuss nonviolent options on persuading Darcy to join our crew. We'll test our pitch on Darcy first and then tweak it if necessary for The Good Time Boys. I'm counting on The Good Time Boys to recruit huge numbers. With their social networks at the gym and bars, we'll be able to lap Oscar's measly recruiting figures.

## Chapter 30 Better Than Road Rage

*Pa-woosh, Pa-woosh, pa-woosh, pawoosh, ping.*

"What the hell is that noise?" Varla inquires.

"Is it the skunk hunter?" I guess. "His gun sounds different."

"Yes, I upped the stakes in my battle against the skunks and bought the kid an airsoft machine gun. The ping noise is when he hits his target," Darcy replies.

Varla and I look at each other, stunned she finally used the word "is".

"What a lousy job he's doing of killing skunks. It stinks out here," Varla states rudely.

Darcy clears her throat, clearly irritated by Varla's bold insensitive remark, but remains cool. "He needs more practice."

Varla peeks over Darcy's neighbor's fence. "His aim sucks. Who taught him how to shoot? I should mentor the kid to shoot straight. In the Army, I was an expert marksman. Wait … you see, the *DSM-5* was right about people suffering from IED. I am prone to hurting animals."

I try to ease her mind by contributing, "Skunks are not really animals; they're more of a pest."

Darcy adds, "They're like fluffy black and white avocado stealing rats."

"The skunk hunter is on his own. I'm not teaching him how to shoot. My conscience is clear." Varla rubs her hands together and walks away from the fence.

This is how our morning visit to Darcy's house started. We're here to activate phase two of our Foundation takeover. After small talk, we'll brief her on the new structure and her role. To prepare for this meeting and alleviate tension between the ladies, Varla assured me she'll employ a coping method The Specialist recommended. We cannot afford to let Varla's beef with Darcy jeopardize our plan. The consequences of not enlisting Darcy would weaken our team's infrastructure.

After squabbling about skunks, Darcy welcomes us both inside. My eyes are drawn to a picture of her in the ring wearing her championship Thai boxing belt. I point to the picture and ask, "Was that always here? Is that the night you won the belt?"

"After your last visit, I was looking through some of my old photos and found this one. It's my favorite. This was my first championship fight. I broke my hands and earned these scars. This picture is a reminder of what I can achieve with persistence."

I examine the picture closer and fixate on the gashes around her eyes and blood trickling off her face. Her hair is frayed out of the tightly weaved hairdo, sweat covers her entire body, and red welts are scattered across her thighs and shins. The average person can persist. This picture showed me she could persist while suffering, which is an entirely different realm of personal constitution. She's our number one draft pick for the role of enforcer.

Varla and I sit on her couch and she asks us if we would like a cup of Cha Yen (Thai iced tea). I've never had it before, but I've heard of it and enthusiastically say, "Yes."

While Darcy goes to the kitchen to prepare the Cha Yen, Varla leans into me and jokes, "Alexandra is clearly her mentor." She squeezes her stress relieving tennis ball. "Hooray, another tea party."

Before we discuss the purpose of our visit, we engage in small talk and sip on the Cha Yen. It's a tasty blend of cream, black tea, and syrup. It is full of vim.

I amuse myself and ask her, "Is this Sanka?"

Darcy replies, "You are such an idiot."

"We can both agree on that," says Varla.

Varla surprises me with her extension of the olive branch. Their mutual opinion of me being an idiot will segue nicely into my stab at a serious discussion.

"I've got some great news. Varla and I are overhauling The Foundation and would like you to—"

Before I can finish my sales pitch, Darcy interrupts. "I'm not taking orders from you two nut case jobs. She's too new and you're too wacky to even run a lemonade stand."

She has a point, but nut case job has me holding back my laughter. I don't tell her she should say either nut job or nut case.

Varla responds instead. "Let me ask you this, what kind of operations have you run since joining? Wait, I'll answer for you. So far you've been a gopher for Alexandra, and if you're not running errands, you're having tea parties. She's been squandering your talents. McGurski and I are both ex-military. We don't give or take orders anymore. Consider us planners. If you don't like a plan we design for you, reject the assignment. You won't be taking orders from us."

I nod to Varla. "Well put." Varla tags out, so it's my turn to close the deal. I perform a classic sales technique, The Takeaway. The High Fiving Awesomer sales force taught me a few things. "If you don't like the first job we have for you, then you're probably not suited to work with us, anyway."

Varla adds, "This assignment is so juicy I wanted it, but McGurski saved it for you."

Darcy bites. "What is it?"

She's hooked. We explain her first mission is to rehabilitate Fletcher. If she catches him tugging on his dog's leash, she is to persuade him to walk his dog properly and has the freedom to improvise as she determines. This implies we trust her decision making, and she is not merely taking orders from a dictatorship.

She smiles. "I like it. You two have the right mix of wacky and crazy."

Her smile widens as we inform her we rewrote the mission statement of the third position to include rescuing abused pets and battering pet abusers.

Varla says in excitement, "Smashing pet abusers could be better than road rage."

Darcy looks to me for sanity, but my crazy train left the station years ago.

Darcy asks, "How are we supposed to find these pet abusers?"

"Alexandra has agreed to share information on her patient's history. This is illegal, but she will alert us of potential pet abusers," I answer.

"Interesting."

"We have a joint mission tomorrow and we'd appreciate your support. Come with us to talk with The Good Time Boys," says Varla.

I realize Varla's strategy. Darcy has initially responded with apprehension about our takeover, and if The Good Time Boys feel threatened, it would be strategic to have a seasoned Thai boxer on our side and even the numbers out.

Darcy accepts it with a contingency. "Those guys are cool, but Eddy is a bit cocky. If he mouths off, he's mine."

I turn to Varla to gauge her reaction because I suspect she had aspirations of tangling with Eddy, too. Her knuckles turn white as she squeezes hard on the tennis ball as I say, "If The Good Time Boys get feisty and we brawl, you can bash Eddy."

We agree to meet at Hendry's beach tomorrow at noon for a beach barbeque and to discuss our new plans with The Good Time Boys. Before getting into the van, I ask Varla, "Are you feeling okay?"

"I'm fine, why?" Varla answers.

"I doubt Darcy poisoned us, but I haven't ruled it out yet. My heart is pumping full blast. I'm considering running at maximum speed to the grocery store."

"You had two cups of Cha Yen."

It's not unreasonable to conclude the caffeine from the Cha Yen is responsible. I throw her the van keys. "I'll race you to the grocery."

"We're eleven miles away."

"Go."

***

I'm off and running. A strange thing happens to me when I run—I'm nearly oblivious to my surroundings. I'm simply not there. My body glides and my mind is either blank or counting numbers. Grimaces from fellow runners baffle me. Are they in pain? I run with an open smile to increase oxygen intake and boost endorphin production. Running is primal.

Primal behavior and reflexes play a critical part in our development.

I factor my pace of approximately six minutes and thirty seconds a mile, and estimate it's one hour and eleven minutes to my destination. Periodically, I come out of my trance to survey the scenery. The town of Summerland marks the half-way mark to the grocery store. The caffeine is now wearing off, but the runner's high is kicking in. In thirty-five minutes and thirty seconds, the grocery doors will open for my entrance. I've chosen a fancy grocery for supplies because I'd like to make a statement to Darcy and The Good Time Boys. We shall woo them with a high end beach banquet of lobsters, scallops, and jumbo shrimp. I don't consider buying seafood and cooking it yourself too much of an indulgence. Treating the crew to a fancy restaurant would cross the line into a corrupt usage of The Foundation expense account.

Eleven miles later, as planned, the doors welcome my arrival. A direct line to the seafood department, twelve lobsters, three pounds of scallops, and six pounds of jumbo shrimp should be enough to feed the battle division of The Foundation. Each member will receive two lobsters, half a pound of scallops, and one pound of jumbo shrimp.

This mundane task of shopping is elevated by adopting Varla's POV. I imagine the aisles sprouting palm trees through the floor and the lobsters in the tank battling each other for aquarium supremacy. A disco ball descends to the chagrin of the checkout clerks who morph into busty go-go dancers. They shake it to the sounds of alternative rock music. The manifestation of Varla's world is complete with a battle royal food fight in the produce section. Battlelines are drawn. The seafood department chucks tightly backed ice balls, relentlessly pelting their sworn enemies, the dairy department, who counter with eggs. Team produce takes cover behind a stack of oranges and varies their attack with boomerang bananas, light artillery apples, and large caliber watermelons. The meat department is outmatched and can do nothing but beat their meat. Aprons serve as food proof vests. Produce and seafood form an alliance, pinning the dairy guys into a corner and lobbing bushels of apple exploding grenades. Dairy has no choice but to call in an airstrike of napalm milk. The shell-shocked baggers bite their fingernails, knowing they'll be summoned to clean up the squishy produce, and pools of milk. I tax my imagination by deciphering the sound, smell, and taste of a shattering watermelon. And then I snap out of Varla's POV. I leave the store with no sight of Varla or the tan van in the parking lot. I'll hoof it home.

I ran eleven miles and walked one mile with a bag of seafood, stalked by alley cats, and when I get home, Varla asks me, "Why did you buy seafood? I bought steaks."

Apparently, she won the race. I sense the disapproval in her tone.

"You are a walking contradiction. Tight with your money, but a gambler. You eat sardines, but splurge on seafood for Darcy and The Good Time Boys."

"You've never seen The Good Time Boys eat. This is great; it'll be a surf and turf bonanza. Besides, I'm not that tight."

"I've seen you pour water into salad dressing, ketchup, and shampoo containers to get the sticky remainders. You are the only person I know that cuts toothpaste tubes to retrieve the residual paste."

"I'm green with the natural resources. I have an issue with the general population's waste."

"But we're not a food pantry; these freeloaders will have to earn it."

"They will."

We spend the afternoon writing our sales pitch and reviewing our tactics for our beach barbeque. Our strategy of meeting The Good Time Boys at Hendry's beach is sixfold.

1.      The Good Time Boys lumbered around at Gaviota Beach, so if they have issues with our leadership, their lack of mobility will give us an advantage on the sand.

2.      Kicking is not in their repertoire, while Varla, Darcy, and I are adept kickers and could easily kick sand in their eyes.

3.      The beach is an unconfined area. This benefits the smaller agile combatant.

4.      It's a dog friendly beach. I doubt they'll be dog abuse here, but we'll keep our heads on a swivel.

5.      A surf and turf beach BBQ is the apex of picnics.

6.      It's where the ocean begins and ends.

Any one of these six reasons is sufficient to achieve a successful beach barbecue and with that checked off my list of things to do, I'll sleep easy.

## Chapter 31 Beach Meeting

The beach towels are spread across the sand, the folding table is unfolded, and the Coleman grill is ready to be lit. Darcy arrives with Fletcher's border terrier prancing head high and not pulling on his leash, but his fur is pink. Her loyalty is proven because she has completed her first assignment. I'm eager to hear the details of her adventure, but can wait until I receive my long awaited proper greeting from the border terrier.

"What's his name?" I ask.

"Gus."

"Hey, boy, hey, Gus. Do you miss dropping turds on Alexandra's yard?" I abruptly back away from petting him for good reason. "Oh, you are a stink pup."

"He's stinky, but for good reason. On the first night in the house, he crawled into the skunk den, and pulled them out one by one. Then he shook them, snapping their necks, and repeated it until all six were dead. Gus looked so proud of himself, but they must have sprayed him twenty times and not once did he whimper. My little guy has found his purpose."

"Did his coat turn pink from bathing in tomato juice?"

"Yes, and the tomato juice didn't even work that good."

"He killed six skunks, and you were paying the neighbor kid twenty bucks a pelt. Gus netted you a saving of a hundred and twenty dollars!"

"You sound like a math word problem," Varla teases.

Varla bends over to pet him too and my eyes readjust to zoom in on her chest.

"What is wrong with you? You act like you've never seen boobs before," Varla says as she mashes her chest aggressively into my face. "Had enough yet?"

I breach for air and say, "Two more servings please."

Darcy responds, "You two perverts are leading The Foundation. God help us."

The Good Time Boys roll in promptly at noon. Eddy asks if we brought furniture to smash and assures me they came prepared with sledgehammers in his jeep. As a collective group, we resemble the third stringers at a United Nations conference. Two representatives from the Isle of Samoa, one Haitian contingent, a curvaceous Lebanese delegate, a fiery emissary from Thailand, and me, from parts unknown but adopted by the descendant of a Polish guy and Irish woman.

It's an ordinary seventy-five degree sunny day in Santa Barbara with a perplexing amount of humans and dogs littering the beach on a Thursday afternoon. These beach humans who apparently are unemployed, are on vacation, or do shift work will be treated to an eyeful of beach judo. With our whole crew here, we have even numbers to spar or as the judoka players call it, randori. Instead of tea party chitchat, the McGurski way is to toss your training partner around in the sand. I'll get to the sales pitch takeover later.

The dogs on the beach express their uneasiness by barking at our antics. Frigging hypocrites. They romp around and scrap every day. Our beach judo leads to a refreshing dip in the Pacific. Although the air temperature is splendid year round, the water is always cold. I've adapted to it, but the rest complain about the cold and jump out immediately. I lecture them on how complaining is a voluntary weakness and they're acting like babies.

"I'm gonna act like a baby, I'm crying cause the water's cold and now I'm crying cause I'm hungry," Eddy says.

Appetites are primed, and the spotlight is on my basic culinary skills. It's incredible how much grub you can cook on two large cast iron skillets. I flash fry the scallops in a generous amount of butter and lemon juice. They brown quickly and in a few minutes I'm shoveling them out to the new Foundation members, which I renamed the *DSM-5* crew. I've also rebranded The Foundation to a more suitable fictitious name. There are all kinds of forces and force: The Special Forces, Air Force, Delta Force, Space Force, and more. In all these forces, they say the mind is the strongest force, so we shall become the force that penetrates the mind, The Mental Mind Force.

The smell of the seafood arouses the attention of a four-legged friend. A soaked golden retriever breaks from playing fetch in the ocean to introduce himself. He ditches his owner, races towards me, abruptly stops, sits on his hindquarters, and props both front paws on my thigh while melting me with his endearing eyes. I can't resist and slide him a few scallops before his owner scurries him away.

I steamed the lobsters at the ranch and wrapped them tight to maintain their heat. Reheating the lobsters is done in a snap. With the surf portion of the meal cooked and being consumed, the finale is the turf—ribeye steaks generously seasoned with garlic salt, and black pepper. I've come a long way from the days of sardines and noodles. I charge it to The Mental Mind Force expense account and although we dubbed this an official function, Claude and Alexandra are purposely left off the guest list. Our new ways eliminate formality and ceremony. Their presence is unnecessary.

While discussing our plans and their respective roles, Loto and Rangi ask for raises and mows through six pounds of jumbo shrimp and four lobsters.

"I haven't had lobsters in years. Thanks, man," says Loto.

"You're alright, McGurski, you're treating us like kings. These lobsters are tight," says Ragni.

"You're welcome." Their gratitude means I've done something right. I share with them the pay structure, bonuses, and how to fleece the rich recruits with cult style money propaganda. It's as simple as telling the suckers, "Money is evil and only the chosen few understand how to spend money without the temptation of misuse." It's a tried-and-true method that continues to separate the dumb from their money.

The *DSM-5* crew is moving in the right direction with the three branches in unison. We will clean the streets of Santa Barbara and plot a proactive invasion of LA. The days of underground research are done.

The meeting goes smoothly with no egos or resistance to our leadership, and then Varla says to Eddy, "You don't know how lucky you are, buddy. If this meeting went sideways, Darcy was going to punch your ticket."

She's stirring it up.

"What do you mean?" Eddy asks.

Rats, here it comes. Egos have been lit.

"Plan B was to convince you by force," Darcy states

Eddy laughs. "What kind of force can you generate? What are you, maybe 110 pounds?"

Loto and Ragni roll their eyes. They've endured this side of Eddy before.

Darcy's fluid movement is an obvious sign she's a professional. She's figured out Eddy is a lefty and is moving to his right, away from his power hand. Eddy conserves his energy, slightly pivoting to keep his eyes on Darcy. It's playful, but they could go full code red instantly.

My immediate concern is to ensure Gus doesn't tussle with them. I assume Gus has been through a fair amount of controversy in the last twenty-four hours, so I shield him from excessive drama, grab his leash, and comfort him with steak trimmings. We become instant pals.

The question Varla, Ragni, Loto, and I are contemplating is do we watch them scrap, break them up, or engage in a huge brawl? As the self-appointed new leader, I need to take the initiative and handle this skirmish. Varla loves to roughhouse and you don't dangle food in front of a hungry pit bull's mouth, so in this situation it's better to huddle with Varla before deciding. We step aside and game plan privately.

I ask Varla, "Any ideas for a diplomatic solution? Our takeover depends on The Good Time Boys and Darcy; we can't afford to have them busted up."

Even though Varla stirred up this trouble in the first place, it's therapeutic for her to resist her instincts. This is the kind of fieldwork Alexandra strived for. Therapy on a couch is for the crumbs.

Varla assumes command and announces to Loto and Ragni we will not be interfering with Darcy and Eddy. Maybe this is Varla's slick way of manipulating Eddy to handle her issues with Darcy. At ease, Loto and Ragni relax enough to lay on the blanket and continue to fill their faces with sea urchins. They appreciate our leadership and smile, or maybe it's the food they are saluting. Varla cracks open a lobster and the juice lands on her shirt. The top shelf fields its position well and catches crustacean splatter.

Out of spite, we consume most of the surf and turf, leaving scraps for Eddy and Darcy. They continue jarring and circling. It's my turn to be a leader and my devilish idea cannot fail. I casually walk between them and make eye contact with Eddy and then Darcy. An expectation hovers in the air. Will I lecture them, interfere, or sanction their beach brawl? My choice is diplomacy. I rip a loud fart and continue walking.

"Ah man, you're nasty, McGurski," Eddy says.

Darcy yells to Varla, "How do you live with that savage?"

Diplomacy through flatulence, although the diplomats at the embassy never tried the fart approach. Who knew farts could settle a dispute? Eddy and Darcy hug it out and demand steak and lobster. Their display of unprofessionalism warrants a handful of gristle, says the guy ripping farts.

With the tensions calmed, I carry Gus over to Darcy and inquire about her first assignment. Turns out Fletcher wasn't attached to the dog. Darcy waited and confronted him on the street. After scolding him for pulling too hard on the leash, he confessed to Darcy he intended to bring Gus to the pound because he hated taking him for walks. Darcy administered a well-placed debilitating kick to Fletcher's ankle and took Gus off his hands. A tip of the hat to irony, because Fletcher won't be able to walk for weeks. I ask her if this assignment matched the thrill of road rage. Darcy said Varla asked her the same question. She didn't have an answer, maybe because she's never road raged before. Unfathomable, but possible.

The distinct sound of flesh and bone mashing catches my ears. The other noise I hear is Loto and Ragni yelling "*Oooooooh*" and "*Aaaahhh*." I deliberately turn slowly to delay the carnage awaiting my consciousness. It can't be worse than Santos dying of cardiac arrest.

Varla and Eddy are playing bloody knuckles. A large contingent of beached humans gawk at my stunning middle-aged girlfriend and a muscular Haitian man punch knuckles to determine who will bleed or submit first. One look and you can tell Varla is in her element. She broadcasts a wide smile and radiates a glow similar to a pregnant woman. Organically, we found a good point to adjourn this meeting.

The crew leaves without offering to help Varla and I clean up. It's a missed opportunity for me to self-advocate. During our cleaning, Varla expresses to me that although she was itching for a fistfight, she values The Good Time Boys' role as our recruiters. It's a milestone in her growth. In hindsight, her compromise to play bloody knuckles on a populated beach is brilliant. She set a new standard for the crowd. A liberation exhibit of do whatever and don't act self-conscious. This random act of bloody knuckles meets the agenda of our mission. Next time, we'll hand out business cards.

Our team knows their roles, and they'll be called upon soon.

## Chapter 32 Recruitment

Friday morning at 11:00 a.m. my phone rings.

"McGurski, it's Sarrick."

"What's up, man?"

"We've got a game tomorrow, and two of my staff called out. I have to be at the laundromat. Can you coach the team?"

"What are you smirking about?" Varla asks.

"Sarrick wants me to coach his little league team tomorrow."

She thrusts her head back laughing, no doubt imagining me leading the little league follies and says, "Oh, this is going to be hilarious."

"You can count on me. What time?" I say to Sarrick.

"Warmups are at 9 a.m., and the game starts at 10 a.m."

"Who are we playing?"

"Big City Mattress."

"We'll knock the stuffing out of them," I say in a fake corny voice to imitate the humans.

"That's awful, McGurski, I owe you."

Varla and I scramble to the office, the only room in the ranch with a chair. Typing away on the computer, I prepare a promotional flyer. It reads, "Does your kid have ADHD, behavior problems, trouble focusing, or bad grades? Our non-drug treatment will get them flying high again. Contact us at www.mentalmindforce.com."

Varla hovers over me as I type out a marketing scheme. "While you're coaching, I'll stick the flyers on car windshields."Varla's excitement is contagious. She is bouncing around, and massaging my shoulders. "When we expand our recruitment, we'll buy farmland in Buellton and build dormitories," Varla exclaims.

"Each recruit will undergo extensive hypnotherapy sessions with The Specialist to convert them to the cause. The word awesome will be hard wired into their nervous system to trigger rage. Imagine a world when anytime a human uttered the word awesome, punches ensue."

"You'll reach your goal of eradicating the word awesome and dullness."

The phone rings again.

"Sarrick, is that you?" I answer.

"Coach McGurski, you've been benched. I got someone to cover for me at the laundromat."

"Oh, man. We were getting pumped."

"Thanks for being ready to step up."

"Good luck against Big City Mattress."

"Are you kidding me? It's off?" Varla asks.

"We'll flyer the cars, anyway."

Varla sticks her bottom lip out to imply a pout, and stomps to the kitchen.

\*\*\*

I'm sitting in the brown leather office chair, in front of the computer with a glass of water and comfortable. I should print the flyers, but I get sucked into a Craigslist rabbit hole—you can't blame everything on ADD.

"Varla, come here. Check this out, it's perfect." The Craigslist ad reads: "Martial arts instructor needed to teach children, no martial arts experience necessary, but experience preferred."

"Cooking up another scheme?" she teases.

"I'm applying."

This misadventure has to payout, not with money, but with either comedy, new recruits, or fisticuffs. The online application is brief, which is fine because giving these jackals pertinent personal information is a laundry chute to treachery.

An hour later, the call comes in. "Hi, we received your application and would like to interview you at 10:30 a.m. Is that good for you?"

"At 10:30 a.m., I'll be on a mission. Can we move it to 3:00 p.m.?"

The receptionist's response indicates her bewilderment. The word mission clouds her brain. She requires a long pause to regain her composure. "Ohhhhhhhhhh, okay," she stalls, and stretches her words to delay time and recalibrate. "I'll ask Sensei Ell if 3:00 p.m. will work and call you back."

In the meantime, I engage in my mission. If I'm infiltrating a martial arts studio, I'll have to submerge myself into the samurai culture. I skim through *The Art of War*, *The Book of Five Rings*, and *Hagakure*. From my research, it appears the samurai lived by a rigid code, pledged their allegiance and bowed to a shogun. Sounds like a cult.

My personality does not jibe with the samurai. To accommodate myself, I draft the concept of an energy samurai and customize it to fit my agenda. The morally flexible energy samurai is a ronin (a samurai without a master) that can be hired as a mercenary and rationally excuses himself from the antiquated feudal system. In my world, I recognize rigid things tend to break and honor does not come from blind allegiance.

At 12:03 p.m., the receptionist calls back. "R. W.?" she asks.

"Yes."

"I talked to you earlier. Can you come in for an interview at 3:30 p.m.?"

"Sure."

"At the interview, wear black pants, black shoes, and a white button-down shirt."

"Why?"

The receptionist, sensing my defiance, reexamines her statement. "Wait, are you applying for the security guard or the martial arts position?"

I reply laughing, "Martial arts; yeah that sounded like a waiter's outfit."

"No, it's not a waiter's outfit. Mr. Ell runs a security company and martial art studios. Hang on and I'll give you the address."

"Varla, they called back; my interview is at 3:30 p.m."

"Kick that guy's ass. If you don't, I will."

"You know what is hilarious? This Ell character runs a security company and a martial arts studio. The receptionist called him Mr. Ell while referencing security, and Sensei Ell when discussing martial arts. He's a hustler with a duel personality disorder." The possibility of his disorder piques my interest, but not enough to forget the line, "No martial arts experience necessary." What kind of scrub would swindle kids with an instructor with no skills?

"Can you imagine, class, today we punch and kick air. Sadly, this format has cheated millions," Varla laments.

"These franchised Mc-Dojos are terrible."

Mc-Dojos have what real estate agents call an open floor plan. Included within this space are extra-large glamor windows, padded floors, padded gloves, padded punching bags, padded headgear, and owners padding their wallets through grift.

At 3:15 p.m. I arrive at the business office of the Ell Corporation. It is pretty nice. They're on the sixth floor of a tall office building on upper State Street. I anticipate the possible outcomes. As I said before, a battle could break out between me and the Sensei shyster, or I could barrel laugh in his face. Out of the elevator, the hallway has rows of five chairs on each side. Nine of the chairs are occupied by individual cogs of the machine, wearing their tidy black and white outfits.

I approach the counter and announce my presence to the receptionist. "I'm R. W. McGurski, and I have an appointment with Ell at three-thirty."

I purposely left out the word Sensei and mister as he will have to earn his title. The receptionist, with her slathered on sleazy make up and extra-large gaudy jewelry, plays her role well and deserves her position as a shill. She's the type of human that chews gum like a cow and talks with her mouth full of food.

"Have a seat; he'll be with you in a moment."

Sixteen minutes later, at 3:31 p.m., I break my lobby meditation and kick off the fun. My personal constitution will no longer tolerate waiting for a charlatan, so I reproach the receptionist, "It is one minute past. The Count waits for no one." I see his ridiculous title of sensei and raise him one ... I too have a title, I'm The Count.

The receptionist answers with a dumbfounded, "What?"

I say again, "Tell him The Count waits for no one," then I lean in slightly as if sharing a secret. She leans in closer too and I say for dramatic effect, with one raised eyebrow and two tones quieter, "The Count waits for no one."

Her squinting eyes, scrunched up nose, and head tilted to the side reflect her perplexed state. She'll have to reboot her brain because in her world, my utterances to announce my departure are inexplicable. She responds with a predictable, "Okaaaaaaay." Unfortunately, the clever statement whizzes over her head. She completely misses the humor.

If this interaction got the press coverage it deserves, *Rolling Rock* magazine would herald the performance as a laugh riot. The Count is a tour de force, not to be denied his due diligence. The Count jumps off the screen to sidekick you in the chops and then welcomes you to his sequels while flipping you the double bird. A true champion of justice. The Count on Broadway is the must see show of the year.

I pity the poor slack jaw stiffs in the lobby donned in the black and white apparel of servitude as they wait motionless to apply for a dead end security job. They are left in a wake of turmoil and humor on the sixth floor.

The elevator opens and is flush with a colony of shy close quarter inhabitants. Securing a spot on the elevator, the facial expressions of my short-term travel companions remind me that in my haste to prepare for the interview, I forgot to apply deodorant to my armpits. My funk has invaded the elevator. In this moment, I choose to do something drastic.

I realize I have complete immunity from the mute spell of elevators and try to disassociate myself from my own smell by blaming it on a foreign country. "Hey is it me, or does it stink in here?" Obviously, it's me. "If it's body odor, it has to be the French. No Frenchies are allowed on crowded elevators. You may enter as long as you're not French. They're too lax with hygiene. Mix in a shower and scrub them pits Le Frenchies." I push the boundaries with my first proclamation; an over-the-top stereotypical discrimination social experiment. Actually, I love the France. It's an iconic landscape provided a habitat of inspiration for Henry Miller, Hemingway, and Jim Morrison. The country has incredible ski slopes and gambling too. Nobody bites. "You guys are Frenchist. Not one of you will stand up for the French; you failed the test." In my next outburst of words, I assume I'll have to supply my own questions and answers. "Has anyone ever popped the top of an elevator and climbed out Bruce Willis *Die Hard* style?" This stream of words is meant to comfort my audience. "I've climbed into an elevator shaft. You know why? Because I wanted to." An accurate account.

They pretend to be looking at their phones and turn towards the walls to avoid eye contact with the wild one. They are too domesticated. Fearful of strange words and unusual behavior in a confined space. There is no escape for them because, noting from my unofficial survey, none of them has climbed through an elevator shaft.

It's an uncharacteristic outburst. Normally, I rejoice in the quiet spaces amongst people and humans alike. The elevator is a sanctuary. I broke the unspoken vow of silence within the tight walls of the vertically ascending and descending temple. I think my lack of patience and loss of potential comedy with Ell discouraged me, and I lashed out. I consider my crude elevator behavior as a retaliation against the humans that have long polluted my air space with cluttered noise. Their music and foolish chatter in restaurants, streets, cars, talk, talk, talk; they never shut up, except in the elevator. This was my chance to unleash my un-silent rage back at them. In doing so, I intentionally violated the sanctity of a quiet place. As my own judge and jury, I found myself guilty and self-imposed a punishment for my noise crime by sentencing myself to three years of stairwells. It's a light sentence, but I'm a first-time noise offender. As a full-time optimist, I see the benefits of my imposed sentence. The stairs are quiet too and a great cardio workout.

The elevator humans are too boorish for games, so I reflect on the nonexistent interview. Fists do not fly, but my candor slices the Ell organization open with style.

My whole morning is shot. All the research for nothing. In the interview, I had planned on ranting to Ell about my idea for an item by item recall of ineffective martial arts moves. If automakers can recall defective parts on their cars, then I demand a reevaluation on tainted Kung Fu parts. First inspection is on Tiger style. Tigers attack with their claws and teeth, but the system never addresses biting or scratching. Dragon style is off the table because they are fictional creatures. Crane style is a joke because cranes are flimsy. If I'm fighting bird style, I'll choose a two-headed bald eagle. Praying mantis? They target insects below their weight class. Be the goods and fight like a man. Vicious to the core, get in, get out, and appreciate the scrum later at a distant location.

I climb in the van and call Varla.

"I failed my mission. I didn't have the patience to wait any longer. My ego couldn't wait for this crumb."

"I'm coming over there, to finish the job," Varla states.

"You'll kill this guy. I'm sending Darcy."

"The hell you are."

"I've got a plan. If it doesn't work, you can do your thing."

"What's your big plan?"

"Darcy goes deep undercover, infiltrates the school, actually teaches Muay Thai and indoctrinates the kids to reject high fives and awesomes."

"If it doesn't work, I'm smashing." *Click.*

Varla took the news better than expected, or maybe I misread her tone. I'll call Darcy and run this scheme by her.

"Darcy, how's Gus doing?"

"He sucks at Muay Thai. But his English is pretty good."

She didn't waste any time trying to teach her dog to punch, kick, elbow, and knee. "Maybe he's more of Jiu Jitsu kind of dog. Doberman pinchers have a good physique for Thai boxing."

"Cut to the chase. Why did you call?"

"I've got a hot lead. It's a sweet mission; Varla wanted it, but you are more suited for it."

"No more pets, Gus is a handful."

"This one's not about pets. There's a guy pretending to be a sensei and hiring people with no experience to teach Kung Fu to kids. We want you to check it out."

"What kind of shrub would rip off kids with a no-skills instructor?"

"That's what I said." Except I said scrub instead of shrub. Calling him a shrub is hilarious, but I hold back my laughter. Darcy and I are always on the same page, and maybe that's why Varla is jealous.

"You want me to beat him up?"

"Whatever you think is necessary. You could even go deep undercover, take the job, teach the kids Muay Thai, and recruit kids from within his studio."

"That sounds like the movies. I'll try that and then beat him up."

"I'll send you the details."

Instead of filling the van with recyclables, I'm a big shot making business calls out of the mobile headquarters. I flipped the script, and my failed mission turned into the ideal situation for Darcy and provided comedy. She'll teach the kids real martial arts, teach Ell a brutal lesson, and then we'll teach the kids to reject high fives and awesomes.

"What the … ? Why is my knee bouncing?" I punch it three times and release its tension. I'll be at the ranch in a few minutes, and I'm not sure how Varla will react in person to me giving the martial arts assignment to Darcy.

## Chapter 33 Motorcycle Laundromat

Varla is rummaging through her dirty clothes. In the last couple of days, Varla has spilled lobster juice, blood, and water on her blouses and my once white sheets used for Ladders' hydrotherapy are a light rust color. For whatever misdirected rationale, Varla is wearing her blood stained tight white t-shirt again.

I look to soften her mood with a compliment and say, "Wow, you look dynamite in that t-shirt."

"Did you just get in, or have you been sneaking around for a while?"

There it is, a slight jab, but nothing too harsh. I ignore her remark. "If you'd like, Sarrick can bleach those blood stains out."

"I'm deliberating whether I want the stains out or to make more blood stains."

"Another warpath? Whose blood are you spilling?"

"Yours," she firmly says, while staring me down. She's not joking.

"What did I do?" I'm aware of my misdeeds but stall.

"You let Darcy square off against Eddy instead of me, and gave her the assignments for the dog abuser and the martial arts guy. Since everyone here is big on nicknames, I'm calling her Getz, because Darcy Getz what Darcy wants." After spitting all those words out, she squeezes her tennis ball rapidly and with considerable force.

I spin it. "We're leadership now, and we don't do OPs. Aren't we supposed to send our crew for the assignments?"

"I guess, but how come you went to the martial arts studio?" she yells, while staring at me without blinking.

"I had to do some recon and then decide who the best fit was for the OP."

And just like that, she's calmed down considerably; her volume is lower, her breathing has slowed, and she is blinking again. "I'm dealing with the next pet abuser," she states, and then drops the tennis ball.

"Deal." Sighs of relief are a real thing. "So, what about those blood stains?" I ask.

"I'm torn between keeping the stains or washing them."

"Sentimental for a blood stains, that's my girl. I'm taking a load of laundry to The Motorcycle Laundromat, so are you interested in riding over there?"

"Yeah, let's bother Sarrick."

Varla removes her bloody shirt and tosses it in the dirty clothes pile. Her new attire is an homage to Tura Satana, who played the role of Varla in the movie *Faster Pussycat Kill Kill*. To match the femme fatale character, she dons a black deep u-neck shirt, black leather driving gloves, skintight black jeans, and black boots. The outfit captures her essence and is a middle finger to society. She, too, is a villain.

We fill my tattered Air Force backpack with the soiled sheets and our sandy workout clothes, and hop on my Suzuki

Intruder. It doesn't start. Varla suggests driving her car. No way, this is officially a declaration of war on the motorcycle. I will not relent until I hear the rumble. Coughing is an intolerable noise from humans and motorcycles. I kick start it Fonzie style, and of course it turns over. She slings the backpack over her shoulder, straddles the bike, and presses her chest hard against my back. What a delicious sensation. Riding with Varla, it occurs to me I have health, wealth, positive relationships, a cool place to live, and time to do things I love … this is top of the pyramid self-actualization.

***

We arrive at The Motorcycle Laundromat on an actual motorcycle. Sarrick heard the rumble of my bike and meets us at the door. On my mental checklist, I list drop off the laundry and I'll wing the rest.

"Welcome, my friends. It was good to see you at the game last week," says Sarrick.

"Sorry, we had to (fake cough) leave early. How d'you do?" I ask.

"We lost nine to three."

"On the bright side, those are great numbers."

"I don't even know what that means."

"Nobody does, only McGurski and Tesla," says Varla.

"Did either of you see what happened to the Muffler Man?" he asks.

We play coy.

"Who?" I ask.

"You've seen his commercials, The Muffler Man, the owner of The Surfside Auto Muffler team. Somebody decked him. It was kind of funny; when he regained consciousness, he ran around crying because somehow he got hot sauce in his eyes."

"Somebody should have told him to pour whole milk in his eyes. I feel his pain, I got to tell you, as hot sauce and pepper spray rank low on my thrill-seeking achievement charts."

Varla and Sarrick both turn their heads at me. I'm unsure if their reaction is to my history with pepper spray or that I have a thrill-seeking achievement chart.

"It was a weird day. After the game, I noticed all the cars had flyers on them, something to do with ADHD and troubled kids."

"I put those flyers on the cars," asserts Varla.

"The flyers are very savvy. Guerrilla style low cost marketing to a target rich environment. Tell me more about your program," Sarrick says.

"Varla and I formed an LLC called Mental Mind Force. We're a mentorship program for adults and youth."

"Oh, very good. I think my whole team needs Mental Mind Force for better focus. Did you see my right fielder picking daisies?"

"Yeah, we did."

"And my third baseman stares at clouds half the game, I don't pretend to know what's going on inside his skull."

"We'll have those pipsqueaks focused in one session," Varla boasts.

"If you were to coach the kids tomorrow, what changes would you make?"

"First, I'd teach them how to swing a bat properly, then I'd ban high fives and the word awesome from the dugout."

"I'm not about to bail on the cricket swing yet. Banning high fives and awesome sounds reasonable."

I dump out the sheets and clothes on the counter. Sarrick nimbly sorts through them.

"Hey, McGurski, what's this? No linen shirts or velvet jackets? What's on these sheets?"

"Oh, those stains aren't from us. A teenage boy McGurski is mentoring made those stains," says Varla, jumping into the comedy.

He raises Varla's blood stained t-shirt. "Can you explain this one?"

"Aunt Flow paid a visit," Varla jokes. "I changed my mind, give it back to me. It's my trophy." Varla then asks, "Would you send a flower bouquet for a dead horse?"

He doesn't flinch and moves on with his gripes. "What's with the sand, and why do your clothes smell like smoke?"

"We had a daytime bonfire on the beach while we practiced judo throws."

"What about this shirt with the three holes in it? Do you want me to mend them?" asks Sarrick.

"No, it's my latest invention, the three-holed shirt," I proudly state.

"I'll bite. What's the story behind the three holed shirt?" asks Sarrick.

"While training for a duel, my friend Darcy blasted me in the solar plexus and ripped a hole in my shirt. I liked the look and made two more holes."

"I feel like I'm being setup every time I ask you a question. But literally this is the most you've ever shared with me, so I got to ask, what's the purpose of the holes?"

"I didn't say because I thought it was obvious. The holes ventilate my sacral, solar plexus, and heart chakras. The middle hole also shows off my two-headed eagle medallion."

"Whoa, slow down, there's a lot to unpack. Is the two-headed eagle a religious thing?"

"I bought it years ago. I think it has to do with Scottish Masons or the Byzantine Empire. I thought it was cool. It symbolizes the unity of my speed and Varla's strength. My wisdom and Varla's ferocity. Together we are an invincible combination."

"You two are a regular Bonnie and Clyde. We need to ride more often."

Out of the corner of my eye, I see Varla digging through Sarrick's trash can and she's wearing the bloody t-shirt around her head like a headband. I accidentally blow her cover, laughing at her indifference and makeshift bloody headband.

"What are you doing?" I ask.

"Intel for Alexandra. She lost her dry cleaning receipt for her green, sparkly dress. I promised her I'd pick up her dress, if she would agree to prank you at the restaurant."

"That makes little sense; why would she take a receipt from Sarrick and then throw it away?"

"She probably threw away the new receipt and mistakenly kept the old one."

"Oh, the old switch-a-roo. It happens quite a bit," Sarrick says. He turns around, unfazed by Varla rooting through his trash. "She's a wild one."

"She's the best."

"Varla, don't worry about the receipt. I'll find Alexandra's dress," says Sarrick.

"Are you sure?" she asks.

"Twice a year, Alexandra brings in the same green dress to be cleaned. She wears it for St. Patrick's Day and the

Avocado Festival. I've personally dry cleaned it at least fifteen times."

"This case is closed. Great investigative work, Varla," I say.

"Shut up. You're the one that told me to rifle through the trash, smartass."

"Sarrick, I'll call you and we'll go for a ride soon, unless the Enfield is in the shop again."

"That's Royal Enfield to you. Hey, Varla do you ride?"

"Yeah, but I'm more of a Harley woman. It might hurt my image if I'm seen riding with someone on an English bike."

"Ouch that stings, she got you good, Sarrick."

"I'll bring an extra can of oil for your Harley, young lady."

"It's been a pleasure to pick through your trash, Sarrick."

"The pleasure is mine. See you tomorrow at the game?"

"Oh yeah," we say in unison.

"I think we got a chance against Big City Mattress."

\*\*\*

When we leave the Motorcycle Laundromat, a young man wearing a fedora and holding a late evening coffee strolls toward us, "Nice jacket," he says with the snottiest, sarcastic, condescending voice.

I respond, "Thanks, man," and raise my right hand, offering him a platform to high five.

It's too irresistible for him to pass and his autonomic high five reflex kicks in, as his eyes zero in on my wide open palm. He has high fiving tunnel vision. I interrupt his programmed distractive high fiving trance state by cracking him—*whap!*—with a left hook to his jaw. It corkscrews him into the ground sideways. He's out. I can tell he's unconscious because his face went pale and he's not moving. In the cartoons, the indication for a concussion is the letter X over his eyes. The letter X is a fine letter because it moonlights as the symbol for multiplication. Since there are no letter Xs over his eyes, I kick at his legs to make sure. "What a shrub." I liked the sound of it when Darcy mistakenly called the sensei shyster a shrub instead of scrub.

"Did you call him a shrub?" Varla asks.

"Yeah, shrub is my new nickname for humans." The verdict has been out for a while … I'm diabolical. "I call that punch the Razzle-Dazzle."

Varla grabs the shrub's fedora and deposits it on her head.

The random act of violence is a statement. I'm optimistic this will close a chapter in our lives. We know this lifestyle isn't sustainable. You can't live to fight and fight to live your entire life. We have to adjust our lifestyle. A new day, a new way. I'll express this to Varla in a manner directed at her sensibilities by singing part of the theme song from *Faster Pussycat Kill Kill* by The Bostweeds.

"If you want wild living FAST!

And if you want to end up giving your all

That's … because

Pussycat is living reckless

Pussycat is riding high

If you think that you can tame her,

Well, just you try!"

That's all I can remember from the song. Varla acknowledges my pathetic effort to sing with a slight nod and grin. I believe this is our Golden Age. We'll reminisce about our bloodbaths and file these endeavors into pretty compartments in our memories. We cast our self-weaved net of violence over ourselves, but at some point will need to evolve. She understands I'm not trying to tame her. It's her choice.

Varla smiles again before saying, "I see where you're going. One last ride."

It's the equivalent of an alcoholic saying one more drink.

She catches the keys and kick starts the bike. If it didn't turnover, Sarrick would tease me for months. We ride fast and hard.

"Hold on to your cocker spaniel," she chirps.

It's her colorful way to warn me of an impending sharp turn. I brace myself, grabbing her waist tight as she deftly maneuvers the turn. The sweet rumble carries us closer to our dimension.

At the stoplight, Varla turns to me and says, "I didn't find Alexandra's receipt, but I learned Sarrick's customers have high cholesterol from eating too much fast food."

"They need three-holed shirts to ventilate their heart chakras."

"Santos, Oscar, and the horse all bit it from heart attacks, so maybe you're on to something."

"Things happen in threes."

We cruise at deluxe speed causing the fedora to fly off. She doesn't care. At the next stoplight, Varla asks me to teach her the quick step technique. Her incentive couldn't be better. She says it will be cool to bust out the quick step while training with The Good Time Boys. She jokes that she'll have to wear three sports bras before attempting it. Can you imagine Varla with her triple D breasts running at 25 mph? I can and it is delightful. Santos and Oscar's hearts blew up from the doing the quick step too many times, so I'll be certain not to let Varla get overzealous with the move.

We cruise the night, raging on the road.

The other thing on my mind is, it's time to recruit.


THE END

Thank you for reading! Please add a review on Amazon and share your thoughts. Your Amazon review is helpful to find out what you loved and what can be improved. Spread the word about *The High Fiving Awesomers* to friends, family, and strangers. Otherwise, McGurski will throw you through three sheets of drywall! To read the contents of The Mental Mind Force manuscript (given to Jacob) and get free sensory training drills to help treat ADHD, behavioral issues, and more go to www.mentalmindforce.com.


Sincerely,


Matthew P. Barkevich

Made in United States
North Haven, CT
07 December 2021

12143792R00152